The Bride's Song by Linda
Dora Grant isn't cut out t͟ͅ
homesteader's existence. She is content with her nursing
job in a small Canadian town. But when a cowboy with
bold dreams of heading west becomes her patient, Dora
is forced to reevaluate her clutch on comforts and security. Is love worth the risks?

The Barefoot Bride by Linda Goodnight
The widow Emma Russell is crazy, according to the
people of Goodhope. But the talk doesn't scare off
Matt Tolivar, who answers the widow's intriguing ad for
a husband. Perhaps on a secluded Kansas homestead he
can finally escape the past that torments him.

A Homesteader, a Bride, and a Baby by JoAnn A. Grote
Diphtheria has robbed Lorette Taber of her only sister and
left her to care for her infant nephew. The homestead the
child inherited isn't profitable, even if Lorette could manage to run it alone. How can a single woman earn a living
and raise a child? And how can she avoid ugly rumors that
plague her friendship with a helpful homesteader?

A Vow Unbroken by Amy Rognlie
Pregnant and recently widowed, Abby Cantrell has
vowed never to love again. Yet when she leaves her past
behind and travels west, she finds herself becoming a
bride again—but this time in name only. Can she learn to
love again, or will her vow remain forever unbroken?

Prairie BRIDES

Four New Inspirational
Love Stories from the North American Prairie

BARBOUR
PUBLISHING, INC.
Uhrichsville, Ohio

Cover Art by Randy Hamblin
Illustrations by Mari Goering

ISBN 1-57748-712-5

Published by Barbour Publishing, Inc., P.O. Box 719, Uhrichsville, Ohio 44683 http://www.barbourbooks.com

 Member of the
Evangelical Christian
Publishers Association

Printed in the United States of America.

Prairie
BRIDES

The Bride's Song

by Linda Ford

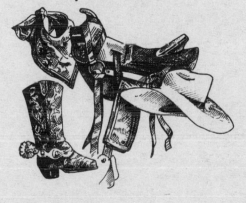

Chapter 1

1898—Freebank, western Canada

A gust of wind swept shiny strands of black hair across Dora Grant's cheek as she hastened across the pleasant, tree-lined street. Lifting her face into the wind, she laughed. At twenty-two she had found the ideal place and she was supremely happy.

The prosperous town of Freebank was the perfect place for a determined young woman to carve out a life for herself. Situated alongside the Canadian Pacific rail line, which headed west to free land, opportunity, and prosperity, the thriving community boasted of schools, over twenty stores, six churches, a theater, and an abundant social life.

Climbing the three stairs to Doc Mackenzie's office, Dora stepped inside. She smiled at her reflection as she paused at the hall table to brush her hair back from her face. Her hazel eyes sparkled, revealing her happy state of mind. With deft movements, she tied a crisp white apron over her skirt and blouse. She had changed her mind about wearing her new white lawn blouse this morning, deciding to do the wise thing and save it for a social occasion. Her plain, oft-worn apparel was more appropriate for work.

Her footsteps kept pace with the happy tune she hummed as she completed her routine morning chores. Placing freshly boiled instruments on a tray, she covered them with a clean towel.

If Doc Mackenzie doesn't get back soon, he won't have time for his noon meal, she thought when she glanced at the clock over the bookcase. Perhaps she should go into the living quarters and sit with Mrs. Mac until the doctor returned. But before she could cross the room, a buggy rattled into the yard followed almost immediately by Doc's heavy footfall on the stoop.

Instantly, her anxious wonderings eased. Doc would get a chance to eat the simple meal she'd left for Mrs. Mac to serve. Now, Dora could relax until their afternoon office hours began.

But the racket of a fast-approaching wagon sent tickling fingers of apprehension up her spine.

"Whoa," a deep voice called out, followed by a frantic inquiry. "Doc. Doc Mackenzie. Are you home?"

Dora hurried to the window, pushing aside the lace curtain. Two heaving and sweating horses stood harnessed to a wagon that still shuddered from its sudden halt. Her gaze followed two men as they jumped down from their seats and reached back into the wagon's bed to lift out a blanket-wrapped body.

The driver gave the reins a quick twist as he leapt

to the ground. "Doc," he hollered again. "Injured man here." He hurried to assist the other two.

Dora's heart dipped for an instant before she sprang to the door. Poor Doc would be missing his meal again.

"Bring him in," she instructed the trio of men as they staggered up the steps with their burden. "Doc will be here right away." Dora half extended her hand but quickly pulled it back and stepped out of the way when she saw the extent of the injuries.

"You're sure he's still alive?" At the sound of Doc's familiar voice, her head spun toward the door leading to the living quarters. Doc wiped his mouth on his hanky as he entered the office. Had he grabbed a mouthful of food or only managed a hurried drink? But there was no time to think about Doc's eating requirements.

"He ain't kicking much but he's still breathing," one man grunted.

"Right here." Dora led the men to an examining table.

Doc flipped aside the blanket and bent over the patient. "A bit battered up, are we?" With deft fingers he lifted the eyelids then bent closer to examine the cut on the forehead. "Dora, give me a hand."

Immediately, she was at the doctor's side. Her breath caught for one fleeting second, but she had worked with Doc long enough to know how to closely observe blood, injuries, pain, and death while still maintaining her composure.

There were a number of bruises on the injured

man's face. A head wound oozed over crackled patches of dried blood. The left side of the man's shirt was stained dark red. He was deathly still and pasty-white.

The dark spot on his shirt grew.

She shook her head. No telling how much damage was hidden under the torn garment, yet his chest fell and rose with assuring regularity.

"You boys going to tell me what happened?" Doc flashed the trio a glance as Dora unbuttoned the shirt and slipped it from the man's shoulders. Doc probed the kidney area and across the abdomen then pushed the edges of the wound together.

"We found him," the driver answered.

"Thought he was dead," mumbled the younger man as he removed his hat and shuffled his fingers along the rim.

Doc snorted. "Where did you find him?"

"Across the river. About ten miles away." Again it was the driver who supplied the information.

"He was passed out, sittin' in his saddle."

"Just like he was dead." The hat went round and round.

"Shut up, Jack." The third man straightened. "He gonna be okay, Doc?"

"You boys get the sheriff and tell him everything, you hear?" Doc said, casting a glare in their direction. "Now run along so we can take care of him."

Dora smiled. Doc might be getting a little round in the middle and his hair might be gray and thinning but, on occasion, he looked and sounded like an army major and received the same instant obedience. She didn't wait for their noisy exit before she filled a basin with warm water. Pulling the tray of instruments close, she began dabbing at the blood.

She worked quietly. Doc didn't care for idle conversation. Her movements coordinated with his as he cleaned and stitched the wounds.

Before the men returned, the patient had been washed and eased into a clean gown. Twice he had moaned and tried to say something before fading back into unconsciousness.

At the sound of shuffling boots, Doc straightened. "They're just in time to help get this young man into bed." He washed and dried his hands before he opened the door to the outer office.

"Come in, Constable." The local Mountie entered, closing the door on the others.

Constable Andrews yanked his hat off as he stared down at the injured man. "He say anything?"

"No. He's a lucky young man to even be alive." Doc lifted the patient's eyelids again. "Can't tell how serious this head wound is." Straightening, he faced the RCMP officer. "There's not much more I can do."

The Mountie nodded. "They brought in his horse and tack." He sighed. "I hoped he'd be able to tell me what happened."

"In good time, my man. In good time." Doc hustled to the door. "Now if you and these gentlemen could give me a wee bit of help, we'll see this lad settled into bed."

Minutes later the patient rested in the sickroom off the office, and the room was cleared of nervous men. Doc and Dora stood side by side staring down at the man.

"He's a bonnie young man." Doc lapsed into his Scottish brogue. "He'll be turning heads on many a young lass."

Dora blinked then looked intently at the patient. Dark curls lay flattened across his head. Despite his paleness and bruises, he *was* handsome—in a rugged sort of way.

But his clothing had revealed his occupation. A cowboy. Decisively, Dora shook her head. "Not this lass."

Doc chuckled. "No, my bonnie lassie. You're knowing what you want and how to get it."

She laughed too. "No wandering cowboy for me."

❧

Office hours over, Dora shooed Doc away for a meal and some much needed rest before dragging a chair to the bedside of her patient. She prepared to keep watch for a few hours.

The injured man tossed and moaned.

In response to his pain, Dora murmured soft, soothing assurances.

His eyes flew open, and she stared into brown eyes so velvety that her breath caught in her throat. The flicker of pain and confusion in those dark orbs quickly reminded her of her duties. "You're at Doc Mackenzie's. You have a cut on your head and another in your side, but you're safe now. If you lay quiet and rest, you'll soon be right as rain."

He flinched.

She offered her most encouraging smile. He could use something for pain, but she didn't dare leave him to fetch Doc. Besides, she knew Doc would be in shortly to check on his patient.

"Can you tell me your name?"

He groaned and his lips moved.

She leaned closer. It sounded like he said "Rivers." Was he trying to tell her what had happened?

But before she could formulate another question, his eyes closed. She leaned back in her chair, thankful that he hadn't grown more restless. A few minutes later, Doc entered the room.

"Any change?" He bent over the patient as he spoke.

"He opened his eyes for a moment."

Doc nodded, lifting a corner of the dressing on the man's side. "I'm not happy with the looks of this. Could you please get me a clean dressing, Dora?"

She hurried to do as he had asked and quickly returned to his side. Handing him a basin for the soaked bandage, Dora noticed the inflamed edges of the wound.

"Did he say anything?"

"Rivers."

"What does that mean?" Doc stared at her.

She shrugged. "Suppose he was trying to tell us something about where he got hurt."

Dora sat with the patient until late in the evening. The uninterrupted quiet gave her plenty of time to study his features. Doc was right. Many a young woman would throw this man a second look—and a third—while hoping for more. An unsettled feeling surfaced. A familiar feeling. Although she loved her work and where she lived, every once in awhile she wished she weren't so alone.

Doc came in. "Dora, you go get your rest now."

"But what about you?" she protested. Doc never got enough rest. When he wasn't caring for patients, he was tending to Mrs. Mac, who had grown weaker with each passing winter month. When hoped-for improvement did not materialize with the arrival of spring, Dora could no longer deny the truth; Mrs. Mac was not going to get stronger. This strange ailment, which had literally eaten the flesh from her frame and left her barely able to function, was not going away.

No wonder Doc looked tired most of the time. She wished she could do more to help this couple who had become as dear as any parents.

But, despite Dora's objections, Doc gently pushed her from the room.

"I plan on dozing in the big chair. The laudanum will take effect in a few minutes and our patient should sleep soundly."

With no other option but to follow the doctor's orders, Dora let herself out and hurried across the street to the little house she called her own. A sense of peace and satisfaction swept over her as she lit the kerosene lamp in the room that served as parlor, kitchen, and dining room. Tacked onto the back of the house was an equally small bedroom.

Would she ever enter this house or cross the street to the doctor's office without experiencing a swell of gratitude for God's wonderful provisions? Knowing she would not, her weariness lifted. A smile played on her lips as she murmured, "Thank you, God."

Her prayer of thanksgiving shifted to one of petition as she quietly spoke to the Lord. ". . .And, dear Father, please bless Doc and Mrs. Mac—and that poor injured man." Breathing a quick "Amen," Dora began to hum while she bustled about the kitchen, preparing tea and a plate of boiled egg sandwiches.

When Dora arrived for work early the next morning, she found Doc asleep in the chair. Noiselessly, she pulled the patient's door closed and headed for the office to prepare for the day's work. A bit later, upon hearing the murmur of voices, she returned to the sickroom.

Doc glanced up from his examination of the patient's abdominal wound. "Another dressing please."

As she passed a clean bandage to him, she saw how the lesion oozed.

Doc finished and straightened. "He's conscious now but I've just given him another laudanum." He handed the instruments to Dora and dipped his hands in the basin of water. "His name is Josh Rivers."

She smiled at her misunderstanding of the night before.

"He was set upon by two men who robbed him and beat him up, leaving him to die." Doc dried his hands on a fresh, white towel. "But he refused to die." He handed the towel to Dora and stood over the patient, his expression serious. "He's got a fight ahead of him yet, I fear. I'll leave him in your care for now. I have house calls to make. Do your best to keep him quiet. I'll leave another dosage of laudanum, should he need it."

Before she could do more than nod her head in agreement, the doctor had gone.

The morning passed slowly. Mr. Rivers stirred several times but settled quickly when she touched him and spoke softly.

Doc returned prior to the afternoon office hours. "I'll manage without you in the office this afternoon." He touched Josh's brow. "I want you stay by our patient and keep a close eye on him."

Within an hour, Josh was burning with fever.

Dora poured rubbing alcohol into tepid water and sponged him. His life depended on her fighting the fever and keeping him as quiet as possible. She determined to do her very best. As always, she felt a fierce defiance at the illnesses and injuries that attacked her patients.

Doc came in later that afternoon to check the dressing. "Nasty injury," he exclaimed as he pulled the bandage away from the wound. "Let's apply a bread poultice and see if that draws out the infection."

Dora and Doc labored over Josh, his moans tearing

at her as they fought the raging fever. Toward morning it abated and the patient fell into a deep sleep.

Dora sank into the chair and let her breath out in a whoosh, tired to the marrow of her bones.

"You run on home and catch some sleep," Doc commanded. She started to argue but he shooed her from the chair.

"Sleep as long as you need then come and take over —though, I'm hoping the worst is over. If we can keep him quiet a few days I believe he'll mend."

Dora still hesitated but Doc had already sunk into the chair, tucking a pillow under his head and stretching out his legs. He waved her away. She stole one more glance at Josh in order to assure herself that he was really and truly better. But she stilled the protective urge to feel his brow one more time before hurrying from the room.

Three hours later she awoke refreshed and, as always, anxious to check on her patient. If she felt a bit more urgency this time, she refused to admit it.

Doc slept in the chair, his head tilted to one side. "Doc," she whispered, "I'll take over." He moaned as he jerked to his feet and wearily plodded from the room.

Josh rested peacefully. She pressed her fingers to his brow and nodded. His fever had not returned. Dora lightly pushed at one brown curl that stubbornly hung over his forehead. The quiet of the house settled around her, and she relaxed into the cushiony softness of the big armchair.

"So you *are* real."

The voice shocked her bolt upright. Dora gaped at her patient, his warm brown eyes on her face, a smile tipping his lips.

"I thought I'd dreamed you." His voice was deep and slow as a lazy river. She found herself wondering if he always sounded like that or if it was the result of pain and drugs. Then she forced her attentions back to their proper place.

"Welcome back. How are you feeling?" *Certainly his color is improved*, she thought.

In response, he grimaced. "A little like I was run over by a stampede of longhorns."

She smiled. Awake and more alert, his eyes took on a life of their own, darkening with warmth then flashing with pain. She leaned over his bedside. "Can I get you something for the pain? Doc Mackenzie left a powder for you."

He closed his eyes. "The medicine will make me sleep, won't it?"

"Yes."

"But I don't want to sleep." Jaw tightening, eyes flashing, he shot her a determined look. "I have things to do." Dora gasped as he tried to sit up. Instantly, he fell back against the pillow, his face chalk-white.

"You must lie still. You have a deep wound in your side that needs time to heal."

He grunted. "Time's one thing I ain't got. Where's my horse?"

"I heard the Mountie say he has your horse and gear."

"What about them rattlers that robbed me?" She shivered at the hard note in his voice.

"They were long gone."

"I gotta get going." He twisted his head from side to side.

"First, you must get better." Dora's lips tightened. If he kept this up, he would start to bleed again. Maybe she should give him the laudanum. What would Doc want?

As if in answer to her question, Doc strode in. "Well, what do we have here? Glad to see you looking alive, young man."

"Doc, I gotta get moving." Again, Josh attempted to sit up.

Doc pressed Josh's shoulders to the bed. "Now you look here, young fella. You're mighty lucky to be alive. And I intend to see you well. Either you lie quiet until I say otherwise or I'll keep you so doped up you won't have any choice." He glared at Josh.

Josh met Doc's gaze. Neither spoke. Neither flinched.

Dora held her breath. Doc meant every word and he would not relent. She hoped Josh would see this and save himself a pack of trouble.

Josh suddenly relaxed and smiled. "You're the doctor," he announced, almost cheerfully.

Dora grinned. Not only did he have spirit, this man had brains. He would be a good patient.

Doc relaxed. "There's a good man." He patted Josh's shoulder. "Now let's have a wee look at that wound."

Dora hurried to get fresh bandages as Doc rolled

back the dressing. Peering over his shoulder, she saw the edges of the wound were inflamed but not oozing, an improvement since yesterday.

Doc applied a new dressing. "You must keep still until this heals," he said as he washed his hands. "Dora, get the young man something to eat. Liquids for now." Scowling at Josh, he ordered, "You, young man, are to let Dora feed you. I want you absolutely still. Do you hear?"

Josh grinned. "I hear ya, Doc."

Doc snorted.

Josh's quick flash of humor was a pleasant treat after the many complaining patients she'd had over the winter, and Dora smiled as she headed toward the kitchen.

Mrs. Mac sat at the table, toying with her empty teacup.

"How are you today, Mrs. Mac?"

"I'm managing." Her hand shook as she brushed a strand of white hair back. "But I worry about Ian when he works such long hours."

Dora nodded. Doc's hours were long and doing nursing duty added to them. But there was no other doctor. And Doc would not ignore someone needing medical attention. She tried to put in some time every day helping Mrs. Mac with housework and meals, but Doc had made it clear that her duties as his nurse came first and she understood it had to be so.

"I'll clean the kitchen while I wait for the water to boil." She quickly put away the food then gathered and washed the dishes. Mixing a spoonful of beef concentrate with hot water in a bowl, she wrinkled her nose at the smell. She'd make some real chicken broth later, but for now this would have to do.

"Thank you, dear," Mrs. Mac said as Dora put away the last dish and prepared the tray.

"You're welcome. I wish I had time to do more, but Doc has ordered me to feed our patient." She checked the tray. Tea, sugar, if he desired, and weak bouillon. Not much for a young man. Imagining how he would feel about his liquid meals, she grimaced.

Yet her lips changed to a smile as she entered the sickroom.

"Good, you're back." Doc stood, pulling his jacket straight. "Keep him on clear fluids today and keep him still. I don't care how. Give him laudanum if necessary."

He made it sound near impossible but she would not disappoint him. "I understand."

Doc fixed his glare on Josh. "I expect your full cooperation, young man."

"Doc, relax. I'll be a good boy. I promise I won't move a muscle until you say it's safe." He sighed. "I'm sure hoping you don't mean not moving my mouth though. I'd have a hard time keeping it shut for very long."

Doc snorted. "Flap your jaws all you want, sonny. Won't do you any harm." He dipped his head toward Dora. "Might drive your nurse crazy, though."

Dora lifted her chin. " 'Spect he can't be any worse than some of the people I've put up with."

Doc chortled at Josh's groan. He was still chuckling as he left the room.

Ignoring him, she asked Josh, "How about some nourishment?" Then, she pushed another pillow behind Josh's head before she pulled the tray close.

He eyed the cup and bowl suspiciously.

She hesitated. "Which would you like first, tea or broth?"

His gaze darted to her face in disbelief. "Does it make a difference?"

"Not to me," she answered cheerily, and lifting the bowl to his chin, she gave him a spoonful of bouillon.

He grimaced. "I've tossed better stuff than that in the fire."

Before he could say more, she fed him another spoonful. "Who says it's supposed to be good? All that matters is it's full of nutrition."

His eyes narrowed. "If it's awful, it must be good for me; is that what you're saying?"

She laughed. "I suppose I am."

He shook his head. "What a dreadful idea." He got a faraway look in his eyes. "Thank goodness life isn't like that. God has given us so much to enjoy. Like nature, friends, and. . ." He darted a look at the tray. "Good food."

She blinked. He had put into words a sentiment that had been flickering in the back of her mind for a long time. With all her heart she believed life was not *all* pain and disappointment. There was so much good to be enjoyed—gifts from a good and loving God. Like her home, her job, her life here in town. So many of life's un-pleasantries were self-inflicted. She clenched her teeth, vowing, once again, not to make any of the same unwise and devastating choices that her parents had made.

"Ah sweet Dora, you should not look so sad."

She stifled a gasp. Heat raced up her neck. Such brashness. But she'd heard about wild cowboys.

He held both palms toward her. "Don't get all flustered. I'm not meaning to be bold."

She kept her head bent, unwilling to meet his gaze.

"Some of that tea would be good."

With a guilty start, she realized she had forgotten about feeding him. He downed the last of the broth and drank his tea, then nestled back into his pillow. Filled with an uncomfortable restlessness, she gathered up the utensils and tray and hurried to the kitchen. It was empty, and the house quiet. Doc had undoubtedly gone on his rounds and Mrs. Mac would be resting.

Dora quickly washed the dishes. Josh's remark about enjoying good things triggered her interest. Obviously, he was a God-fearing man. It might be amusing to get to know him. She bit her bottom lip. Too bad he was a cowboy.

When she returned to the sickroom, Josh lay with his eyes closed. Dora hesitated, but Josh sensed her presence and slowly opened his eyes. "Glad to see you back," he said with a smile. "I thought I might have scared you off and would have to spend the rest of the day staring at the walls." His eyes darkened. "I was thinking about going to find you."

Remembering Doc's orders, she shook her head. "Doc would have my skin if you did."

"I guess that means you have to entertain me then." The smug look on his face made her laugh.

"I'm not sure that's what he meant."

He sighed deep and long. "I feel like I've been hogtied. All the while, my insides are yearning to move."

Dora made a cluck of sympathy. He had capitulated so completely to Doc's orders that she had failed to realize how much it cost him. Now her heart reached out to ease his restlessness. "What are you so anxious to be doing?"

His eyes brightened. "I'm headed west."

She closed her eyes for a heartbeat. Another fool after land and riches. Chasing an empty bubble. And just when she had decided that he thought the same as she.

"Why are you heading west?" As if she didn't know the answer. The lonely feeling that had surfaced earlier now returned, and she struggled to submerge the emotion. Life was good and pleasant. She would allow nothing to mar her happiness. Not after God had so generously provided.

"I'm going to find me the nicest piece of land ever and start my own little farm." His gaze drifted away and she knew he was seeing his own dream world.

She shook her head. How often she'd seen that look and heard that tone. Yet, even more often, she had seen the helpless desperation in a child's gaunt face. Her insides coiled and she pushed away the memories, forcing herself to concentrate on making conversation with her patient—this dreamer headed into the unknown with nothing by a headful of second-hand lies.

"Have you any idea what you're headed for?" She managed to keep her voice smooth and tried to ignore the unreasonable twinge in her heart.

"I've seen it. A few years ago I was trailing a herd to Cochrane Ranch. Prettiest country I ever saw. The air is so pure you can taste yesterday's rain. The moon was so big and golden I was sure it was snagged on a pine tree." He took a deep breath. "I never saw a sky so blue. Seemed like you could reach out and touch it." He turned to Dora with an eager look in his eyes. "You should have seen the flowers. Wild roses so sweet that I dreamed of them at night. Harebells like fine china." He grinned at Dora. "Why I bet you could hear them ringing if you sat real still."

Not certain what he meant, she stared at him. Then, seeing the twinkle in his eye, she laughed low in her throat. "Indeed?" she replied. "I don't believe I've ever heard the sound of harebells ringing."

He chuckled, beaming at her. "Me neither, but who knows. The country is dandy. So purdy—the land nearly sings." He lay back and stared at the ceiling. "I already knew that I didn't want to be trailing doggies the rest of my life. I made up my mind the minute I saw that little spot of heaven. I would work and save until I had enough to set me up in a nice little place of my own." He heaved a chest-raising sigh. "And just when I figured that the right time had come, I find myself laid up here."

She didn't answer. He made the west country sound like paradise on earth. She could almost hear the music and the bells he described. But she had seen another version of paradise, one with dark corners.

"Perhaps you've been given a warning. . ." At the sudden change in his expression she clamped her lips together.

"There you go again. Figuring bad things are good for you."

She wanted to argue. That was not what she had said, nor meant. But he drew his brows together and continued.

"Don't you think I've had plenty of time to think and pray about this?" The fierceness in his expression disappeared as quickly as it had come. "This is a delay. For what purpose, I have no notion. However, my aim is still the same."

Stung by his words, and even more by his judgment, she faced him squarely. "I suppose you know all about farming?"

"I've been keeping my eyes open, and I know enough to run myself a few cows and grow them some feed." He paused. "Besides, I learn quick."

Her annoyance fled as fast as it came. "I'm sorry," Dora offered, shrugging her shoulders. "It's none of my business. Perhaps I've seen too many people lose all they had in the trying."

He chuckled. "Maybe I'm a fool but I don't see I have much to lose."

Just then, Doc appeared to check on his patient and

repeat his order for quiet and rest. A few minutes later Constable Andrews arrived to ask Josh a few questions and get his description of the two men who had attacked and robbed him. Before the Mountie left, he brought in a pair of saddlebags from the waiting room.

"I have no way of knowing what's missing, but I thought you might like to have your things at hand." He tossed the leather bags on the foot of the bed. "The rest of your tack is at the livery barn. You can pick it up there when you are able to be up and about."

Josh received his liquid meal with a wrinkled nose. When he had finished drinking his dinner, Dora insisted that her patient rest for a few hours. While he slept, she made a quick trip to the butcher shop and bought a stewing hen, which she put on the stove to simmer. After preparing a meal and dining with the Mackenzies, she helped Doc with his office patients. Despite her busyness, her mind kept returning to the sickroom and her patient. She hoped he was resting quietly and his wounds were healing.

Doc glanced at the door several times as well. "Hope the lad is obeying orders," he graveled under his breath between patients. But another rush of patients prevented either of them from checking on Josh.

"We're done now, Lass," Doc said as he closed the door on their last patient. "Go see how our cowboy is getting along."

Doc sat behind his desk and drew his heavy green ledger close. She hurried toward the sickroom, knowing that the doctor would be preoccupied for some time.

Chapter 2

S he brushed a tendril of hair from her face and reached for the knob, then pulled back, not wanting to waken him if he were asleep. Turning the glass knob slowly, she eased the door open and tiptoed into the room.

The afternoon sun filtered through the lace curtains shooting bright light across the room and making it difficult to distinguish details. Before her eyes adjusted, Josh called out.

"Dora. Thank goodness. I thought no one was coming back." His voice rang with desperation. "Tell me, please. What is that gut-wrenching smell?"

She chuckled. "That would be Lister's spray. A disinfectant that keeps disease from spreading."

"I can believe that. No disease would want to get near such a stench!"

Her eyes had adjusted to the light and she gasped. "How did you get that stuff?" Items lay scattered across his bedside.

"From my saddlebag." He sounded apprehensive. "I was so bored." He grew defensive. "I barely had to move. Knew exactly where they were. Just had to reach out my toe and drag it close."

She shook her head. It would be a miracle if he hadn't started the wound bleeding again.

"You won't tell Doc will you? I promise I was very careful and didn't pull anything loose. Please, Dora, be a pal."

She looked away from his begging eyes. She knew she shouldn't agree to such a scheme, but she also knew that she would. For the life of her, she couldn't explain why.

"We'd better tidy up." She gathered up the items, surprised when she examined them more closely. Besides several rolled up pairs of socks and a new pair of leather gloves, there was a well-worn leather Bible, its cover as soft as velvet. He retrieved an equally worn book, *The Great Lone Land*, and a picture before she could pack them away.

He watched her, smiling gently. "Thanks a heap."

She straightened and smoothed the crazy-patch quilt, carefully avoiding his gaze—a gaze that somehow compelled her to do things she wouldn't normally agree to do.

Again, his voice softly pleaded. "Could I ask one more favor?" His words made her feel that to refuse him would be mean.

She steeled herself. "You can ask."

He chuckled. "All I want is for you to open those curtains so I can enjoy the sunshine."

His request was so mundane that she had to laugh

at her defensiveness as she crossed the floor to do his bidding. Light flooded the room when she pulled back the curtains. Turning back toward Josh, she observed a look of pure pleasure on his face as he lay with his eyes closed. She quickly turned away, for she felt as though she were intruding on someone in the midst of private prayer.

"Does the window open?"

"Certainly." She pushed the sash upward. A refreshing breeze, full of spring warmth and laden with the musky smell of recent winter snow, lifted the lace curtains to brush against her arms. Dora filled her lungs with fresh air.

The room was quiet. A child's voice sounded somewhere in the distance, and a horse clip-clopped down the street. Dora turned to look at Josh. In the bright light, his skin was even more tanned, a stark contrast to the bandage on his forehead. Gold streaks played through his brown curls.

As she studied him, his eyes opened. His expression warm, he said, "Now I can breathe." He smiled. "I've been looking at the picture of my family. See, here they are." He motioned for her to come to his side.

She looked down at the picture, still feeling the lure of the spring breeze.

Then she bent closer. "How many brothers and sisters do you have?" She hadn't meant to sound so startled.

"I'm the oldest of ten." There was no disguising his pride.

"These three," he explained, pointing to the smaller

ones, "Ruthie, Tessa, and Mark were born after I left home. Ruthie's nine years old, Tessa's seven, and Mark just turned five."

Dora bent closer. "You're the eldest?" There seemed to be several adults in the photo.

"Firstborn. That's me. This. . ." With his index finger he pointed to a young man who bore a resemblance to Josh. "This is Andy. He's twenty-four. As soon as I saw he was keen on running the mill, unlike myself, I declared I was going to follow my dream. Ten years now I've been working, mostly as a ranch hand or trailing cows." He ran his finger back and forth across the picture. "Good work. Good experience. But I'm ready to settle down and build something for myself. And someday, God willing, for my family."

Dora kept her head bent over the picture. These faces stirred an all-too-familiar feeling within her. The same old dream. The same empty hope she'd seen before. The lure of owning land and creating something for future generations to have and hold. So much hope. So much disappointment and despair. Such a waste. Finally she lifted her gaze to Josh. "Don't your parents need you at home?"

"There was barely enough of everything to go around. As we grew into adulthood it seemed there was less."

She narrowed her eyes, amazed that he seemed to feel no bitterness at such a lean existence.

"I go and visit whenever I can." He let his hands drop to his chest. The photo pointed toward the ceiling.

"I spent a fortnight with them before I started west. Saying good-bye this time was harder than lassoing a racing bronc, knowing it might be a long while before I see them again." His thumb rubbed the photo. "The little ones will hardly remember me."

She clenched her hands into fists. Her insides screamed to tell him to give up this foolish chase. Instead, she took a deep breath and said, "I put a chicken on the stove to simmer several hours ago. Perhaps you'd like some homemade chicken broth."

He pressed his hands to his chest. "Dora, now I'm certain you're an angel of mercy. Sure you can't add some noodles or potatoes?"

She shook her head. "Not 'til Doc says so." She hesitated at the door. "I'll be back in a few minutes."

In the kitchen, Mrs. Mac stood at the table cutting meat from the chicken carcass.

Dora came up beside her. "Why thank you, Mrs. Mac." She reached out for the knife. "Here, let me finish."

Mrs. Mac nodded and relinquished the knife. "I'm feeling a little better this afternoon."

Dora pulled Mrs. Mac's arm through her own, leading her gently to a chair. "I'm glad."

"I think I'll get stronger with the warmer weather." She leaned heavily on the table as she sat down.

Dora poured tea for her and waited until she grasped the cup and took a sip before she turned back to the counter. She finished the deboning, then peeled potatoes and carrots for a stew for Doc and Mrs. Mac.

Straining some broth for Josh's supper, she set aside the remainder and some diced meat. Doc would probably order soft food tomorrow. She would prepare some chicken noodle soup.

As she diced potatoes into the stew, Mrs. Mac asked, "How is your patient this afternoon?"

Dora glanced up and smiled. "He's on the mend but I think he finds being bedridden difficult." She shook her head. "But he must remain still if he wants that gash in his side to heal."

"Aye, this being idle is not a task to be envied."

Dora dropped the knife and hurried to the older lady's side, bending over to hug her. "Oh Mrs. Mac, you're not idle. You do what you can and that's all any of us can do."

Mrs. Mac patted Dora's hands and leaned against her shoulder. "Thank you, dearie. You're such a sweet lass. Makes me ashamed of me grumbling."

Before Dora could think of how to respond, Mrs. Mac tipped her face up and flashed blue eyes at her. "My dear, Ian says that your patient is a curly-headed young man handsome enough to melt any woman's heart."

Dora laughed. "Now don't you go getting any ideas. He's much too young for you. Besides, what would Doc say?"

Mrs. Mac smacked Dora's hands gently. "Ach, 'Tis for you I'm thinking of him. And don't you go pretending you haven't noticed."

Dora grinned as she returned to dicing the vegetables.

"Noticed what? That the edges of the abdominal wound are less reddened? The bruises on his face already fading? And the poor man is starving as we talk." She covered the stew and prepared a tray for the sickroom.

"Aye, that of course." Mrs. Mac turned so she could watch Dora's reactions. "And a whole lot more."

"The dumplings are ready to drop in. Wait about fifteen minutes," she called over her shoulder as she left the room balancing the tray.

Mrs. Mac called, "You got eyes in your head, girl. I know you do." The door clicked, shutting out anything more the older woman would have added.

Dora's grin faded. Certainly she'd noticed some of Josh's more appealing features. But she was no fool. She'd not be letting pretty curls or a handsome face cause her to make choices she'd regret.

Outside the sickroom, she paused to take a deep breath before she shoved open the door.

"That took awhile."

She nodded. "I made stew for Doc and his wife."

"Stew?" He perked up.

"And broth for you."

He groaned.

She pushed another pillow behind him and straightened the covers before setting a bed table across his chest to hold the tray.

He sniffed. "At least it smells like food." And he leaned forward eagerly as she fed him. He had just drained his cup of tea when Doc entered the room. Dora hurried to get a fresh dressing.

Doc lifted the bandage on Josh's forehead first. "Very good," he murmured then turned his attention to the lower wound. "Your injuries are healing well, young man."

"Does that mean I can get up soon?" Josh half pleaded.

"Now don't go undoing everything. You must wait awhile longer yet." Doc patted his shoulders. "You just lay still and enjoy the attention of a pretty young lass."

"I've been doing that, Doc."

Josh's gaze met Dora's. At his teasing grin, heat flooded up her neck and she turned away.

Doc stood. "Josh, Dora's going home to get a good night's sleep, but I'll leave you with a cord that rings a bell in my living quarters. Should you have need of anything, just give it a yank." He turned to Dora. "I'll take the tray to the kitchen. You go on home now, lass."

Dora hesitated.

"Aw, Doc," Josh fussed. "You tell me to enjoy her company and then you send her home."

"I know, laddie. But she needs her rest." He shot a stern look in Dora's direction, but his voice was gentle as he said again, "You go on home. We'll see you in the morning."

She bid them both good night and left the office. As she stepped into her house, she knew Doc had been wise in sending her home. She was bone weary. She made a pot of tea, then sank into a big armchair and let her head fall back. Had only two days passed since Josh had been carried into the clinic half-alive? It seemed like she'd known him so much longer. Pushing to her feet, she decided she was more tired than hungry. She headed for bed, blaming her weariness for these thoughts that strayed down useless rabbit trails.

Doc was downing a cup of coffee when she hurried in the side door the next morning.

"Mrs. Mac is still sleeping. Josh is restless and bored. Do your best to keep him quiet." He took another swig of coffee. "He can have soft foods today." He was quiet for a moment. "And let him feed himself. All of his moving around yesterday appears to have done him no harm."

Dora met his flashing gaze. She should have known that they hadn't fooled him.

He set the cup down and grabbed his bag. "I'm off to visit Mrs. Smith. Have a good day." With no further ado, he was gone.

Humming, Dora quickly cleaned up Doc's breakfast and cooked some soft porridge for Josh. She set a place for Mrs. Mac, covering it with a clean towel. Still humming, she pushed open the sickroom door.

"I thought you'd never come back."

She smiled. "I've got your breakfast."

"I'm starving."

"Doc said you could have some real food today." She set up the bed table.

Josh looked at her suspiciously. "I'll bet."

"Really." She glanced at the tray as she set it before him. "Well almost. And Doc says you can feed yourself.

Says you didn't do any damage yesterday with your moving about."

He grinned. "Wily old coyote." Without waiting for a response, he grabbed his spoon and, within minutes, polished off everything she'd prepared.

After she removed the tray, she set a basin of water before him. "Why don't you wash up a bit?"

Giving him some privacy, she took the dishes to the kitchen and plunged them into hot water. Her hands idly swirled the suds as she stared out the window, humming.

He was done when she returned and she tidied the room.

"How long before Doc lets me up?"

She could feel his barely-contained restlessness and hated to answer. "Probably ten days."

"Ten days." He closed his eyes.

"Perhaps he'll let you sit up in bed in two or three days."

He turned his tortured gaze toward her and whispered hoarsely, "I had hoped to be at my destination by now. Ten days! How can I delay that long?"

She bit her bottom lip. It was going to take a great deal of patience on his part to remain immobile as long as Doc wanted. She would do her best to help. Perhaps she could turn his attention to other things. "What made you take up the life of a cowboy?"

He took a deep breath and she knew he was trying valiantly to deal with his disappointment. "Horses, I guess. I wanted to be outside riding horses, not bent over machinery, never seeing the sun except on the way to and from the mill." He smiled and the tautness in her nerves unwound. "I wanted to see the sun cross the sky, breathe air off the damp soil, feel the wind in my face. I wanted the birds to be the song I heard while I worked, not the grind of millstones. I wanted to see the flowers as God created them, not the flour ground by man."

She laughed.

He continued. "Never mind God's goodness in providing the grain." He locked his fingers together under his head, his elbows wide, and grinned at her. "Guess that tells you more than you wanted to know."

Dora had stopped to watch the play of wonder and awe in his expression. Now she quickly bent her head and gave the basin another swipe with the towel. "Not at all." The way he talked made her yearn to see and feel things like he did, with open eagerness. He had accused her of thinking bad was good, which she did not. But neither did she embrace the beauties of life with such trust. She couldn't. She'd learned the hard way to plan her path, testing each step before she took it. She wanted to see where life was leading. She needed some control over the direction. Trusting God meant following carefully the way marked before her, not throwing oneself into riotous enjoyment without any regard for the future. No. That wasn't the way for her. She couldn't imagine it being the sensible way for anyone.

She was suddenly aware of his scrutiny and realized she had been quiet for several minutes. Gathering up her thoughts and containing them, she asked,

"Didn't your folks mind?"

He nodded. "They minded me going. They didn't mind what I was doing."

"Tell me more about your family."

"We're big and noisy but I think we're a nice family. How about yours?"

Rather than answer, Dora asked, "You said something about a mill?"

"Yes. My dad and Uncle James own the mill at Morgan's Creek. It's a steady business but there's not enough income to support us all, even though Uncle James and Aunt Martha have no children." He shrugged. "That's why I was glad when Andy made it plain that he liked working in the mill. I didn't."

"I remember." She grinned. "You wanted to see the sky and taste the dust and smell the ground after a herd of cows had passed."

He laughed, then groaned and pressed his hands to his side. "You knew that would hurt, didn't you?"

She tightened her lips. "I didn't know you'd laugh." But she knew her eyes gave her away.

"Right. And I don't know what side of a horse to mount."

She could no longer hide the mirth bubbling inside her, so she turned away.

"Think it's funny, do you?"

She sobered and turned to face him. "Of course not." Laughing at someone's pain would be cruel. She would never do such a thing. But there was no stopping her wide smile.

An answering gleam shone from his eyes—eyes that held her own in a steady gaze. Her heart danced to a song in her head.

"You never did tell me about your family."

She blinked and pulled back, shaken by how quickly her thoughts had spun out of control. "No, I didn't." Pursing her lips, she turned away. Hands wringing, she sought some task to disguise her discomfort. The first thing she saw was the window. Three quick steps took her to stare out at the quiet street, her hands pleating and unpleating the curtains.

"Well?" Although quiet, his voice prodded her. She crushed the pleats in her hands then shrugged and turned.

"There's not much to tell." At least, not much she cared to tell. "There are four children. Two boys and two girls. I'm the oldest girl. My folks have a homestead twenty miles from town."

At the word homestead, Josh practically jerked upright. "What's it like? The homestead? How long has your father been there?"

Dora took a deep breath as the questions tumbled out of Josh's mouth. She had no desire to talk about it, but she guessed Josh would plague her now that he knew that much.

"They have a tough life." Dora intended to say no more. "I can't talk now. Doc will have my hide if I don't have the office and waiting room cleaned in time for his patients."

She crossed to the door then paused. She had

briefly forgotten that Josh was also her patient. His care came before her own needs and desires. "Is there anything I can do for you before I go?"

Josh groaned behind her and Dora jerked around. Had he pulled something? But he stared up at the ceiling, his arms crossed over his chest. "I need to be out of here." He raised one hand in protest and grinned. "Don't say it. I already know. Lie quiet. Be patient." He groaned again. "I never realized how hard it is to do nothing." He made a shooing motion with his hand. "Go. I'll be all right."

Her duties called, but Dora hesitated to leave. She wanted to ease Josh's suffering during his stay. "Are you sure?" *I would love to talk with him all day—if only he wouldn't ask me any more questions about my family.*

He nodded.

She didn't hum as she tidied the rooms and prepared them for office hours. Instead, her thoughts circled round and round. It had been four years since she had escaped the homestead. Surely long enough to be able to think about the past without her insides getting brittle. Yet, just an innocent question or two turned her into a quivering mess. She pressed the heels of her hands into her eyes and moaned.

Grabbing the wet cloth, she scrubbed the examining table. Her pounding thoughts kept time with her frantic efforts. There had to be a way of putting aside her memories.

Prayer. That was the answer. She had prayed to be rescued from that situation, and God had wonderfully provided her with this chance. She would never cease to thank Him for it. Her thoughts slowed and she smiled. When Josh asked again about the homestead—and she was certain he would—she would tell him about life in town.

She glanced at the clock and gasped. *Lunch!* Rushing to the kitchen, she barely had time to prepare the chicken noodle soup that she had planned yesterday and take Josh a bowlful before Doc was calling her to the office. His first patients had arrived early.

They were rushed all afternoon. Then she hurried to make supper.

"You've had a busy day," Josh said as she carried in his tray. He waited as she set his meal on the table. "I heard an awful commotion one time."

"That was probably when Mrs. Baker came in with her brood of kids." Besides his Bible and the book he had yesterday, a child's storybook lay on the bed. Little Sam had left the book behind last winter after his recovery from pneumonia. She had planned to return it when she saw his family again. She laughed. "Found some good reading, did you?"

Josh grimaced. "It was the best I could do." He shook his head. "I'm so bored."

"And this helped?" She opened the pages. " 'See Dick run. Run, Dick, run.' " He cradled one arm under his head and looked down his nose at her.

"It made a very interesting study."

"I'll bet." She chortled. "And exactly what did you learn from this 'interesting study'?"

He turned to face her, his eyes dark and unreadable. The laughter died in her throat. Her chest tightened. "I learned how boring recovery can be." His sigh lifted the bedcovers momentarily. Something ticked inside Dora's head, making it impossible for her to speak.

"Boring, boring, boring." Then he grinned. "But now that you're here I feel much better."

She blinked. It was nice to be appreciated. Josh made it seem even more special by his acknowledgment. "I'll find you some more mature books," she promised. "Unless you prefer this age level."

He grinned. "It's better than nothing. Almost."

"Doc has a collection of books and I have some as well. You are certainly welcome to borrow them."

Just then Doc entered and stared at the books on the bed. "I trust that you've been obeying orders, young man."

Josh held up his hands. "Best I can, Doc."

Doc waited until Josh finished his meal and Dora removed the tray before he checked the wounds. "You're doing fine." He stood. "Dora, ye go on home and remember tomorrow's the Sabbath. This young man will manage without nursing care tomorrow. If he needs anything, I'll see to it."

Dora had forgotten what day it was. She turned a startled gaze to Josh and caught the same protesting thought in his eyes. "But—"

"I mean it, Dora. Go home and enjoy a day of rest."

There was no arguing with Doc when he got that stubborn look on his face so she nodded. "I'll just get him a few of your books to read, if that's all right."

Doc nodded. "Aye. That will help him rest."

She ducked into the office and, skipping the medical texts, chose four adventure books. Doc had a fondness for tales of the north. She had skimmed through several and knew they were full of encounters with wild animals and accounts of fighting the elements, as well as equally unkind residents. These were not the kind of stories she enjoyed, but perhaps Josh would. She delivered the books to his room.

Doc was still there, glowering. She hid a grin. Doc was determined to make sure that his orders were obeyed to the letter.

As she handed the books to Josh, he crooked his finger, indicating she should bend close. When she did, he barely whispered loud enough for her to hear. "Better hurry home. Doc looks like he'd as soon fry an egg on my forehead as have you miss your day of rest."

She choked back a chuckle and straightened slowly, giving herself time to compose her expression.

"I'll be going home now, Doc," she said in her sweetest, most compliant voice. "Say good night to Mrs. Mac for me."

Josh's chuckles followed Dora out of the room. Just before the door closed, she heard Doc growl, "Young whippersnapper." But she didn't know if his words were aimed at her or Josh.

❦

Dora remained in the pew for several minutes following the service, her thoughts mulling over the points of the sermon. Pastor Luke Daley's favorite topics were faith, love, and forgiveness, and today he had chosen to preach about faith. As usual, his sermon was rich with illustrations and his message clear. Today, he had shown how one's choices in daily life revealed the depths of personal faith.

"It takes faith in God's provision," he had said, "to venture into the unknown."

Dora had agreed with him until he used home-steaders as an example of that type of faith. Perhaps, she conceded, for some folks, homesteading was a step of faith. Yet, others were drawn, not by faith, but by an illusion. Of this she was certain.

Dismissing her lingering thoughts, she joined the others as they filed out. Mary, Pastor Luke's wife and Dora's best friend, waited for her at the bottom of the steps.

"Stay until I've spoken to the rest, then we'll talk," Mary whispered as they hugged.

Dora nodded and stepped aside as Mary greeted each of the departing parishioners.

"You'll come for lunch, I hope," Mary said as she joined Dora.

"I was hoping you'd ask." It was a Sunday tradition for them. Even if Mary had invited others, as she often did, Dora was always included.

But today Dora was the only guest. They had barely sat down when Mary leaned toward Dora. "I hear you have a patient."

Dora nodded. "A cowboy who was hurt on the trail."

Mary lifted one eyebrow. "A young cowboy?"

Dora kept her face expressionless, knowing that Mary would read a hundred meanings into anything she imagined she saw. "A handsome, young man." Let her guess what that meant.

Mary's mouth made a perfect *O*.

Luke laughed. "She's setting you up, dearest," he warned.

Mary wrinkled her nose at him. "I know that. But I don't care." She turned back to Dora. "How young? How handsome?"

Dora pretended to give her questions a lot of thought. "Let's see." She pressed her finger to her lips. "He said he left home ten years ago. I guess that would make him at least twenty-six. Maybe a few years older."

Mary sighed and leaned back. "Just right for you."

"Why, I'm only twenty-two." Dora did her best to sound shocked.

Mary tsked. "Much too old to be without a husband. Or at least a beau."

"Indeed? Well, I have news for you. I'm quite happy without a man in my life. And much too busy to need one."

"Of course." But Dora knew Mary wasn't agreeing. "And you admit he's handsome?"

"Oh yes." Dora closed her eyes, pretending to be overcome. "Dark curly hair and eyes as warm as—" She sighed rather than finish her sentence.

"Why I declare. I believe you're already half in love with him." Mary practically gloated.

Dora instantly grew serious. "Sorry to disappoint you, but he's headed west to get himself a homestead. Not my kind of man." And she took a mouthful of roast beef.

Luke laughed. "Told you, Mary."

"Some day she'll fall," Mary promised.

"I believe you're right, dearest," he said, turning to speak to Dora. "Someday I expect you'll make the astonishing discovery that some things are worth the risk-taking. Remember, security is not found in a place, or a position, or possessions, or even in security itself, but in God."

Stung by his assessment of her, Dora stared at him. "Do you really think I'm trusting in something other than God?"

Mary rushed to her defense. "I'm sure he didn't mean that, did you dear?"

"No, of course I didn't. I've seen your faith. But I believe God stretches us all lest we grow complacent." He pushed his chair back. "Now if you girls will excuse me, I am going to my office."

After he left, the two young women were quiet a moment.

"I'm sure he didn't mean to criticize you, Dora." Mary kept her face toward her plate.

Dora touched her friend's arm. "I don't feel like he was." But a shiver flickered across her neck. He had warned of change and she didn't welcome the thought.

Determined to lighten the mood, she asked, "Are you looking forward to the concert?" She spoke of the traveling singing group scheduled to appear next week.

Mary wriggled in her seat. "With great expectation. I can hardly wait. I hear that this is the best group we've had yet."

"You've managed to get some good entertainment." Mary belonged to a committee that arranged a special concert three or four times a year. "After that there's the church picnic, then the debating team."

"Don't forget the ball tournament."

Dora nodded. She enjoyed the crowd and visiting much more than the sport, but Luke was an ardent ball player so Mary counted ball tournaments high on the list of activities.

Later, at home in her tiny rooms, Dora thought about the day. Let Pastor Luke make his dire predictions; she knew better. It wasn't lack of faith that made her determined to enjoy what God had provided. After all, hadn't she proven her faith when she left home with nothing more than a worn satchel containing a second dress? She had prayed fervently for God to help her find a place to stay, and He had miraculously provided. He made it possible for her to finish her schooling by working after classes in return for her board. And, incredibly, a job in the hotel had opened up for her right after graduation. The job was not one she liked, but again she had prayed and trusted God. Now He had given her this job with Doc Mackenzie. And she loved her job. Perhaps, someday, she would enter formal nurse's training and improve her skills.

All the talk of Josh had triggered Luke's comments.

He and Mary were always nagging her about finding a fellow and getting married.

But, she vowed, she would never allow herself to fall in love with someone like Josh.

She prepared for bed early, anxious for the morrow when she could return to work.

❦

The checkerboard lay across Josh's bed. Dora put the checker pieces in place. "I'm going to beat you this time for sure."

Josh lay back, his arms under his head. "You probably could if you paid attention."

"Paid attention, indeed."

"I'll even let you go first."

She narrowed her eyes and studied him. Did letting her go first give him an advantage? Ducking her head to study the board, she admitted she didn't understand strategy. What difference did it make which checker she moved first? Oh, she hated to see him win so easily. Finally she moved a checker.

"Did I ever tell you about the time a grizzly bear licked my boots?" His attention was riveted on the game board, so she couldn't see his eyes. "Your turn."

She hesitated then moved again. "Is this another of your tall tales?"

His hand to his chest, he drew back. "I swear I didn't make up any of them. Though I couldn't guarantee the same for my friend, Twister. He insisted that he got his name from riding a corkscrew mustang. But I always kinda figgered it was because of the way he twisted the truth. Your turn."

Dora's hand hovered over the game pieces then she jumped one of his checkers and set it on the edge of the board.

"Anyway, we were taking a break from branding and I wandered down by the river. The day was nice and sunny, so I sat down by a log and closed my eyes. Your turn.

"All of a sudden, I felt this bump against my foot. I opened my eyes and there was a grizzly licking my boots. It's your turn again."

Dora squinted at the board. How did he make his plays so fast? She hadn't even followed what he'd done. She reached for one checker but caught herself before she touched it. Moving that one would set up a chain of jumps. She chose a different one.

"It was just a cub, maybe two or three hundred pounds.

"Well, you can bet I figured I was bear breakfast. I gave a quick look around for the momma and saw her about two hundred yards away with a second cub. They were rooting at an old tree stump. Probably eating bugs." He jumped his man across the board and set three of her game buttons on the side. "Your turn.

"I eased away from the cub and, slow as I could, got to my feet. You understand, now I was in a big hurry to leave, but I didn't want to set the cub to crying. All the same, the cub woofed. Old momma bear rose up on her hind feet. Your turn."

His checkers were all over the board, but if she

moved one of hers against the edge. . .

"I high-tailed it out of there. I could hear that momma bear thudding at my heels. I raced toward the camp." He paused. "Your turn again."

"Josh. For goodness' sake, tell me what happened." She gave the board a quick glance and saw an opening.

"I got ate up."

"Yeah. And came out the other end almost normal."

His smirk changed to a frown, then he laughed. "I guess not. No, I ran and ran. As soon as I saw the men gathered around the fire, I started hollering, 'Bear. Bear.' They just stood there gaping at me. I skidded around the cook wagon, wheezing fit to kill. As soon as I could, I looked behind me. And there was nothing." He shrugged. "Guess what I thought was the bear chasing me was really my own heart thudding." He jumped three more of her checkers. "Crown me."

She was staring at Josh, caught in his bear story. She closed her mouth and gave Josh his crowning checker, then moved one of her own men.

"I never did quite live it down. Every so often, when things got boring, one of the men would get all big-eyed and flap his arms in my face and yell, 'Bear.' " He shrugged. "It was kind of funny."

Dora began to chuckle. "I can just see you." She nodded—"Bear. Bear."—and laughed harder. "Wish I could have been there."

"Yeah, well, it might not have turned out so good." He crossed his arms over his chest. "By the way, I beat you again."

Sobering instantly, she studied the board and saw he was right. "It's not fair. You distracted me."

He shrugged. "Wasn't much of a challenge."

"Why you!" She flung a handful of checkers at him.

He flipped them away, except for one that he flicked back at her.

She ducked, laughing. "Stop now. You're supposed to be resting."

His deep chuckles made her laugh harder and just about the time she had it under control, their eyes met and she started again. She couldn't remember when she'd had this much fun.

Chapter 3

Over the next few days Dora and Josh spent a great deal of time together as she tried to help him while away the hours. They talked about books they'd read, things they enjoyed, and Josh told her more about his family.

She did what she could to make his convalescence pleasant and, in so doing, grew to enjoy his company more and more. He was a good patient, striving to be cheerful and cooperative even when she knew he ached to head west.

Five days later Doc bent over Josh's dressing. "Young man, you have done very well." He wiped his hands on a towel. "How would ye feel about getting up for a wee while this morning?"

Josh's eyes grew wide, then narrowed suspiciously. "You wouldn't be pulling my leg now, would you, Doc?"

Doc beckoned to Dora. "You take one side, lass, and I'll be holding the other." He flipped the covers back and eased Josh's legs over the side of the bed. Dora helped him to sit and steadied him as he swayed.

"Not to worry, son. You'll be a bit shaky at first." Doc kept his fingers on Josh's wrist, checking his pulse. "Sit until the dizziness passes and then we'll try standing."

Josh hung his head and groaned.

"Take a deep breath and let it out slowly," Dora instructed.

"Ready?" Doc asked after a moment.

Josh nodded and together they stood. He swayed, his weight pressing against Dora. She watched his face, saw the color slip away and return as he gritted his teeth and steadied himself.

"I'm all right," he grunted.

Dora glanced at Doc. He nodded slightly.

"Let's try a step or two." They shuffled forward as a unit and stopped. "Turn now, lad," Doc said.

With Doc and Dora on each side, he turned and shuffled back to the bed where he collapsed, sweat beading his brow.

"That was fine, laddie. Just fine." Doc checked Josh's pulse and lifted his legs to the bed. "Now you rest a bit and we'll get you up again later. Dora, get the boy some lunch."

By suppertime, Doc announced that Josh could join them in the kitchen if he felt well enough.

"I'll do it," he eagerly replied. He had insisted on donning his clothes earlier in the afternoon and now he jerked to his feet.

Dora tightened her lips as Josh, holding himself stiff and upright, walked down the hall to the kitchen.

The next day Doc suggested that Josh might like

to sit outside on the verandah and enjoy the warm sunshine. "You'll soon be well enough to be on your way, lad."

Doc's words thumped into the pit of Dora's stomach. Her hands froze in mid-air.

"I'm glad to hear that." Josh sounded a great distance away.

She took a steadying breath. Had she caught a hesitant note in his voice? She darted a glance at him. A mix of emotions flashed through his expression. She was sure his eagerness was tainted by something sad. Well, what should she expect? He'd never faltered in wishing he could be on his way.

Nevertheless, Dora would be sorry to see him go. He had been a good patient and she enjoyed his company.

Before Doc could scold her for dilly-dallying, she hurried outside and moved the wicker rocker into the sun. Josh came out with Doc at his heels. Dora waited until Josh settled into a comfortable position, then she followed Doc inside.

"There's a lad who's through and through nice," Doc said as he folded his stethoscope into his bag and prepared to leave. "You'd do well to have a closer look at him, lassie."

"I—" But not waiting for her reply, Doc grabbed his hat and headed for the door.

Dora stared after him. What a strange comment from Doc. He knew better than anyone how hard she had worked to be where she was.

Pausing on the threshold, Doc glanced over his

shoulder at her. "Be sure, lassie, that you don't overlook a prize when you find it." Then, before she could answer, he was gone.

She put the instruments to boil, tidied Doc's desk, and swept the waiting room floor. All the while, her thoughts circled round Doc's comments like a buzzard after a bone.

She would miss Josh something fierce. He had proven himself amusing and entertaining. But his plans hadn't changed. He was headed west to try his hand at farming.

Dora's plans had not altered either. She intended to enjoy what God had provided right here in Freebank.

Her chores done, she checked out the window. Josh sat with his feet up on the rail and a book in his lap, but his gaze on some distant spot.

A pair of girls passed—Jenny, the storekeeper's daughter, and another she didn't recognize. Jenny's eyes widened as she spied Josh and she nudged her friend. The two giggled, then Jenny called, "Hello, sir. I trust you are enjoying the sunshine."

Josh slowly lowered his gaze and smiled at the passing pair. "Good morning, ladies. It's a fine day." He seemed oblivious to their adoration and returned to his contemplation of the far horizon.

They hesitated then sauntered past, preening and smiling.

Dora smiled. If they thought to engage him in a flirtation, they had failed. Feeling rather pleased, she headed to the kitchen to make coffee and start lunch.

That done, she prepared a tray for Josh and marched down the hall toward the verandah.

At the sound of her footsteps, he looked up, his eyes dark with welcome.

A shock shot through her as her heart responded to his look.

She almost dropped the tray. The rope handles ground into her palm. The coffee scent stung her nose. The bright air was filled with birds' song and the happy sound of children at play. Her heart leapt for the dazzling sky and she nearly stumbled.

He attempted to rise as she stepped outside.

"Stay where you are," she ordered, her insides wobbling as she set the tray on the railing. "I thought you might like some coffee."

"You read my mind."

Keeping her face averted, she poured him a cup and offered him a cookie, all the while trying to ignore her tempestuous emotions.

"Aren't you going to join me?"

His words jolted across her nerves and she jerked to attention. "I have work to do," she muttered. Without so much as a backward glance, Dora raced inside.

Pressing her palms to her tight chest, she leaned against the door waiting for her panic to subside.

She'd promised herself that she would not let this happen. Josh was set on heading west, and she could not—would not—venture into the way of life he had chosen.

She would not allow herself to love such a man. Yet

her pulse throbbed at the mere thought of him.

How could she have fallen in love with him? She wanted to cry and shake her hands in his face. Instead, she moaned.

I do not love him. I will not love him. We are headed in opposite directions. All I have to do is keep my distance for a few more days. Doc will surely discharge him and I can forget I ever met him. Nodding briskly in agreement with her renewed resolve, she hurried off to the kitchen to prepare the evening meal.

Josh came in a short time later and looked around the kitchen.

"Where's Mrs. Mac? I thought I'd keep her company until supper is ready."

She must have heard his voice, for Mrs. Mac scurried in from the front room, her cheeks flushed like she'd been dozing.

"Ah, Mrs. Mac, I was hoping to see you." He plucked two cups from the cupboard and poured coffee. "I want to hear all about your trip from the Old Country." He ushered her into the front room. Dora heard a chair being moved and knew he was making sure Mrs. Mac was comfortable.

Dora smiled. It hadn't taken him long to discover that the doctor's wife loved to talk about the Old Country and her family back there. Their voices rocked back and forth, one deep and strong, the other soft and reedy.

She tried not to feel annoyance at Josh's preference for Mrs. Mac's company over her own. She gave her head a flick. Things were better this way. The less time she spent with him, the easier it would be to forget him when he left.

Doc returned and the four of them sat down for their evening meal. Dora jumped up every few minutes to get something from the stove or pantry. If Mrs. Mac wondered why Dora felt an urgency to have jam on the table during supper, she didn't mention it. However, Doc raised his eyebrows when Dora got a second gravy boat and transferred the gravy from one container to the other.

The minute Doc set his fork down, Dora scooped up his plate and started washing dishes.

"Seems we aren't going to linger tonight," Doc commented, his voice dry. "Dora seems anxious to get the place cleaned up."

She felt three pairs of questioning eyes on her but kept her back turned and her hands immersed in soapy water. She hadn't meant to rush them. But she felt a sudden, desperate need to get to her own rooms where she could sort out her thoughts.

"I think I'll run along." She swiped the table. "That is, if I'm not needed for anything more." She hung the towel and wet rag over the towel bar.

"I expect we can manage without you." At Doc's teasing tone, she glanced up and caught him winking at his wife.

A small frown furrowed Mrs. Mac's brow before she turned and smiled at Dora. "Yes, dear, you go on home. You've worked hard all week."

Josh tipped his chair back. "I can certainly take care of myself. Have for years."

Dora lowered her head. She knew she was behaving strangely, but she couldn't stop her insides from twisting and turning. Even so, she knew she had no excuse. She took a steadying breath and looked up. "I'm sorry. I didn't mean to be impolite. I just suddenly realized how much I have to do at home." She let her gaze touch each of them then turned and prepared to leave.

Doc harumphed.

"It's quite all right, dear," Mrs. Mac said. "We do understand."

"You have a good night, Dora." Josh's voice, so filled with kindness, was almost her undoing. Nodding, she hurried out.

By the time she closed the door of her house she was gasping for breath. She leaned against the wall of the dark room and waited for the pounding in her head to ease. Slowly she relaxed and gained control of her thoughts.

She had gone and done what she promised herself she would *not* do. She had fallen in love with Josh. How foolish to let this bother her so! Josh need never know how he had affected her. He would leave town in a few days, and she would soon forget all about him. In the meantime, she must still serve as his nurse—though there was little she needed to do anymore. She simply had to act normal.

Having thus consoled herself, she prepared for bed.

She overslept the next morning and had to hurry to get ready for church. She was about ready to walk out the door when a knock sounded on the other side. Dora drew her hand to her chest in alarm. Her heart thudding, she pulled open the door.

"Hi," Josh greeted her, his face swathed in a smile. "Doc said it would do me good to go to church. He seemed pretty sure you'd be willing to show me the way."

Dora snorted. The old codger was determined to get the two of them interested in each other. She wondered what he would say if he knew that he didn't have to try on her behalf.

"Certainly," she said to Josh. "You're more than welcome to come with me." Her insides as unsteady as a newborn calf, she faced the room, foolishly relishing every minute spent with him. How could she bear the bittersweet moments of his company while still keeping her secret? And what on earth was Mary going to say?

Filling her lungs and ordering her insides to be quiet, she demurely announced, "I'm ready."

He stepped aside to let her pass, then fell into step beside her as they walked the four blocks to church.

"It's a fine morning, is it not?"

Dora's stomach fluttered at the sound of his voice.

"Why, I can hear a half-dozen different birds singing in the trees as we pass. Listen. Can you catch the robin's song?"

She cocked her head as though to listen, then nodded in agreement. But she hadn't heard the robin's song. The music she heard was the music of her own heart. Dora let the sweet melody swirl through her until she thought she could contain it no longer. Closing her eyes, she took a deep breath.

I must stop. My heart is running away from my head. He'll soon be gone.

She blinked, struggling to settle her emotions. Then a wayward thought surfaced. *All the more reason to enjoy every precious moment we have left to share.*

They'd come to the corner and he grasped her elbow, gently guiding her across the street.

Her nerves tightened until she feared her heart would burst. She forced herself to stare straight ahead. Surely his behavior was as always, and it was her heightened awareness of him that now made his every word and every touch reverberate with shock waves.

"I hope you don't think I'm presumptuous." He let her arm go as they reached the other side of the street. Suddenly, her legs went weak. To cover her confusion, she paused to smooth her skirt.

"I ordered a picnic lunch," he said. "I was hoping you'd share it with me in the park after the service."

"Why I'd like that very much." Her throat tightened so that her words squeaked. Thankfully they met several others on their way to church and a round of greetings and introductions gave Dora's breathing a chance to slow.

Her senses remained razor-sharp throughout the service. The singing seemed richer and fuller than she remembered as Josh's deep voice blended with hers. The light coming through the windows seemed to have a white quality about it, cleansing those in its path.

Luke spoke of love and every word dripped honey into Dora's heart.

Afterwards, wrapped in a glow, Dora filed down the aisle until she stood before Mary and Luke.

"I'd like you to meet Josh Rivers." She tried to ignore Mary's pleased expression as she made the introductions.

When Mary hugged her, Dora whispered in her ear, "I've agreed to have lunch with Josh. I hope you don't mind."

Mary snorted. "Mind. I guess not. I'm glad you've decided to open your eyes."

"It's not that way." But she knew her protests were wasted as Mary patted her cheek and nodded.

"Dora, I've got eyes, too, and I know what I see."

Dora gave up and said good-bye.

*

They walked to the hotel where Josh picked up the picnic lunch he had ordered. Then, they sauntered to the center of town to the park burgeoning with spring.

"The young preacher delivered a good sermon." Josh spread a blanket on the grass and opened the basket.

"He's a good man." She helped set out the jug of lemonade and glasses. "We're blessed to have him."

Josh passed the plate of sandwiches to her and she chose egg salad. He chose one with roast beef and leaned his back against a tree. "This seems a real nice little town."

"I think it is. We have all the essentials—school,

church, stores—plus lots of nice extras." She went on to tell about the social activities.

"This park is really beautiful." She followed his glance from the little footbridge to the gazebo nestled in the trees and to the winding path along the lake.

"It began as someone's yard. A lady from England. She loved flowers and gardens. Many of the flower gardens were made by her." She pointed out the ones she was certain had been original. "Her husband built the footbridge. When she died, she left the land to the town with the stipulation that it be used as a park." Josh nodded, his eyes warm with interest.

Her tongue grew thick at the look on his face and she ducked her head to finish her story. "That was Mrs. Free. The town was built on a piece of her husband's land. Hence the name, Freebank."

"Gives the town a right nice feel. I can see why you like this place so much."

He didn't know the half of it. And she couldn't tell him.

Neither of them spoke. Around them filtered the sounds of other people in the park, accompanied by the swelling songs of birds rejoicing in spring and love and building new nests.

Josh cleared his throat and Dora jerked her gaze to him.

He watched her with a keenness that sent her heart into flight.

"Doc says I'll be able to go in a few more days."

She nodded, her mouth suddenly dry. She knew this

moment would come. Perhaps it was best to come sooner rather than later—before her heart led her where she could not go. Nevertheless, her insides plummeted like a rock.

"I need to get going."

Again she nodded, well aware of how much work faced him.

He pushed away from his backrest and leaned toward her. He was so close, she could have touched his face with her trembling fingertips. She squeezed her hands into a tight ball and buried them in her lap.

"Dora." His voice was low and intense. "I haven't known you very long but it's long enough for me to realize that—er." Josh stumbled on his words. "I–I . . . well, I can't imagine never seeing you again."

Her heart pounded in her throat as, dumbstruck, she stared at him.

"Dora, I've fallen madly and completely in love with you. Just seeing your face and hearing your voice makes my heart sing like these spring-crazed birds around us."

Every word dropped like gentle rain into her heart, adding to the emotion that she had been collecting there—emotion that now threatened to overflow the barriers she had erected.

"Dora, I'm asking you to marry me and go with me to the foothills. We'll find the prettiest spot in all the world and build our own little home, filled with love and laughter."

His words were a song of love—the sweetest sound she'd ever heard. And she almost succumbed. Almost.

Then she forced herself to remember the years she'd spent on the farm with her parents. Homesteading held no allure for her. She knew all too well what it meant.

She would never again make herself endure such suffering and hardship.

"Josh, I'm flattered." She avoided his gaze. "But I can't."

She heard him sharply inhale a breath and hated herself for hurting him.

"I guess I read you wrong." His voice sounded strained. "I thought you might care about me."

Her heart shredded. "You weren't wrong," she whispered. "I do care about you." She swallowed hard. "I love you."

His smile flashed and he leaned forward eagerly.

But she turned away. "But I would never go homesteading."

He jerked back like she'd slapped him. "Why not?"

Stung by his reaction, she faced him. "I spent two years of sheer torture living without enough of anything and never having one bit of luxury or enjoyment. Homesteading meant nothing but work and depravation, and I vowed I would never do it again."

The light fled from his eyes and for a moment she wished she could change her mind. But remembering those years, she stiffened.

"I literally thought I would die." Every nerve in her body ached just remembering. "My dad knew nothing of farming. He made every mistake in the book. We ran out of food the first winter and had to accept charity from some neighbors. My dad and brother built a house, but there wasn't enough money for more than the shell. Snow came through the cracks. I woke up more than once with my toes numb from cold." She choked back tears. "I didn't get warm all winter." Suddenly she couldn't stop. "I outgrew my clothes and had to wear some of my grandmother's old dresses, which made me feel dirt-ugly. Day in and day out, we did nothing but work. There was no church, no school, no nothing." She caught her breath. "I didn't know if we'd starve to death or freeze or simply die of exhaustion." Her voice dropped to a whisper. "I'll never go through such torture again."

Josh stared at her, his eyes round. She turned away not wanting his pity.

"Oh, Dora, it sounds all horns and rattles. I'm sorry it was so bad." He paused. "But homesteading isn't always that way. I've talked to many—"

"I've heard plenty of lies, too," she hissed. "But I've been there. I know."

He nodded. "How are your folks now?"

"They were fine when I saw them at Christmas." She found it impossible to understand how the rest of her family could now be so content. She wouldn't attempt to offer Josh an explanation.

"Are things any better for them?"

"I suppose." The inside of the house had been finished, the oilcloth placed on the floors, and Mother had been given a new dress. Father talked about spring like it held all the diamonds in the world.

She felt, rather than saw, Josh nod. "They believed the dream and set out to realize it."

She flung around to face him. "What dream? More like a nightmare, if you ask me." She swept her gaze over the park. "A dream would be beautiful like this—full of pleasure and enjoyment. Not pinched, barely-alive torture."

He shrugged and held out his hands in surrender. "I can see you aren't prepared to look at this any other way."

"What other way is there?"

"There's sacrifice in order to achieve a goal. You said your father wasn't a farmer, yet many people have learned because they're willing to learn. That's what I meant when I asked how things are now. Did your father learn how to farm? Did your family have faith? Do they still?"

"Faith?" She fairly spit the word out. "Faith is believing in what God promises, not what the government promises. Faith is using the good sense God gives us, not jumping in front of a train and expecting God to rescue us."

"You're right as far as you go—but faith also includes venturing into the unknown and believing, even when we can't see the end result."

She shook her head. "I guess you can use words any way you want, but it all boils down to one thing. It's madness to try and build something out of nothing."

"Ah, but there's where you're wrong. It isn't, as you say, 'nothing.' God has provided the best land in the world, practically free. And I know about cattle and farming. I know how to make something out of the bounty God has offered."

She frowned. "What about grasshoppers, hail, frost? What about sickness? What about all the things over which you have no control?"

He smiled sadly. "None of us can control the future whether we live in town or on a homestead. That's where faith comes in. If you think you can guarantee a safe and predictable future by living in town and refusing to accept love or take risks, then I fear you are in for a dry-bones existence or a very harsh disappointment. Trusting God means leaving the future in His hands."

Rather than answer, Dora gathered up the leftover sandwiches and the untouched cake and returned them to the basket. Josh flung the blanket over his shoulder and scooped up the basket, waiting for Dora to draw abreast. Silently, they headed home, their steps quicker and more determined than they had been earlier. As they crossed Main Street, Josh drew in a sharp breath and ducked down a lane.

Dora stared after him. He hurried to the shadow of a wood shed and pulled close to the building.

"Josh?" She squinted, trying to see his face in the gloom.

"Shush."

Hesitating, she tried to decide if she should follow or wait. Finally deciding it would be best to join him, she turned into the alley. At the same time, he reappeared from the building's shadows and stepped into the sunlight, his eyes searching behind her. "I'm dead certain that was Slim and Chester."

She wrinkled her brow. "Who?"

"The varmints who stole my money and left me half-dead." His eyes darkened and he frowned. "Bet they'd be surprised to see me."

Dora gaped at him.

"In fact, I might just jump out of the shadows and scare the dickens out of them."

Her heart did a strange little flip-flop and her throat seemed suddenly too tight. "Do you suppose they're looking for you?" She had visions of them hunting Josh down and finishing what they'd begun almost two weeks ago.

"I'm guessing they think I'm dead."

A shudder raced up her spine. Josh's steps halted and she was surprised to see that they were in front of her house. Her glance jerked from her front door to Josh's face and then past his shoulder. When she saw no approaching figures, she turned her concentration to Josh and what he was saying.

"I wish you'd give my offer more thought. The future is not as frightening as you think—especially when you share it with someone you love."

She shook her head. The present was suddenly frightening enough. Never mind the future. But her anger had disappeared and she regretted saying all those things. "Josh, I really do love you. But I cannot possibly become a homesteader's wife. I'm sorry." Unable to bear the pain in his eyes, she fled indoors.

Chapter 4

Dora peered out from her bedcovers into the darkness and prayed for strength.

She knew what was right for her, but as she reflected on her conversation with Josh, her choices seemed childish and fearful. Hadn't God given her this place and this job? She wasn't about to toss these blessings back in His face.

In time Josh would forget her.

She tossed about seeking a comfortable position, trying desperately to avoid the truth.

She would never forget him. Not if she lived to be a hundred years old. She tried in vain to ignore the ache in her heart.

Abandoning the hope of sleep, she waited for morning and the moment that she could hurry across the street. Even as her pulse raced at the thought, she wondered how she would face him.

The next morning, she hesitated before she opened the door and entered Doc's house. Doc greeted Dora by saying, "Our young man is out."

"Josh?"

"Aye, Josh. He was dressed and waiting when I got up. Said he was going for a ride. Time to test his strength, he said." Doc shook his head. "Seemed mighty troubled about something in my opinion." He studied Dora with questioning eyes.

In no mood to match wits with Doc, she turned and hastened across the room to fling open the door to the bedroom. The bed was tossed, but Josh and his clothes were missing. She swallowed hard.

Perhaps it was for the best. Then she saw his saddlebags hooked on the post, his books, and the picture of his family lying on the shelf. Relief flooded her.

Doc had followed her and she said to him, "He must have gone for a ride like you said. See, he's left his things."

"Well, I didn't think he'd leave without saying good-bye," Doc gruffly replied. "I must be on my way."

She nodded. "And I have much to do."

But all the time she cleaned and dusted and prepared meals and helped Doc with patients, her ears were tuned to catch the sound of a horse riding into the yard or boots crossing the verandah.

The day ended without hearing the sounds she strained to catch and she returned home without seeing him.

Her nerves tight as fence wire under a heavy frost, she paced her rooms for an hour then, unable to endure the strain any longer, she grabbed a sweater and hurried out the door. Perhaps a visit to Mary would ease her mind.

At the parsonage, Mary drew Dora quickly inside. "I've been longing for some company. Luke's at the church."

Dora hid her relief at the news. Sometimes Luke seemed to see through her with startling clarity. He was often right, a fact which, she admitted wryly, did nothing to make her more comfortable. Smiling at Mary's eagerness, she allowed herself to be led into the kitchen. She could always talk freely with Mary.

"What brings you here so early in the week? I thought you'd be taking a stroll in the park with that handsome young man of yours."

"He's not mine."

"Girl, you must be blind. I saw the way his eyes followed you. If that young man isn't head over heels in love, than I'm–I'm an old fat hen."

Dora grinned, and putting her hands in her armpits, she strutted around the room. "Cluck, cluck," she said, flapping her elbows.

Mary scowled. "You don't fool me. I saw the two of you together." She waited for Dora to return to her chair. "So what's the problem?"

Tossing her head, Dora asked, "Who says there's a problem?"

"Fine. Pretend you didn't come to see me because something's troubling you. We'll simply have ourselves a nice cup of tea." She filled the pot as she spoke. "And we'll talk about something else." She brought the pot to the table and set out two cups. "Did you see the new outfit Mrs. Mellon had on? Where does she get her clothes? There's nothing like that in town, and I certainly didn't see anything that special in the Eaton's catalogue. I think it was real fur on the collar of her dress." Mary closed her eyes for a moment. "Don't you think I'd look lovely in such a nice outfit?"

She poured the tea and hurried on. "And where was Abigail? She hasn't been to church for three weeks now. Have you heard if she's ill or away?" She hesitated barely long enough to catch her breath. "No? Well, I was just wondering. And how's Mrs. Mac? She's such a nice lady. I hope she gets stronger now that spring is here. I shudder to think of Doc taking her away. What would we do without him?"

Dora scowled at her friend, annoyed at her silly chatter. She'd come to tell her problems, not listen to a recital of what everyone else said or wore. Mary should know better.

Then, again, Mary had offered to listen, but she had refused. As Mary's incessant prattle continued, Dora felt a chuckle rising from within. Finally, she could contain her laughter no longer. "Enough. Of course I came here to talk. You don't have to make a production out of it."

Mary grinned and leaned back. "So what's the problem?"

"Josh."

"No." Mary pretended shock, covering her mouth with her hand.

Dora shook her head sadly. "I'm afraid so." Suddenly all the silliness was gone. "I love him."

Mary nodded.

"He says he loves me."

Mary clapped her hands. "Lovely."

Dora shook her head again. "Not lovely. He wants me to marry him and go with him to stake out a homestead in the Wild West."

"Yes?" Mary waved her hands impatiently.

"That's just it. I can't go west with him."

"Why ever not?"

"I'm as far west as I plan to go."

Mary shook her head. "I don't understand."

Dora stared at her. "He's a cowboy with a head full of dreams and pockets full of dust. And a gilded tongue to boot. But you, of all people, should know why I can't go."

Her eyes narrowing, Mary studied Dora. "Are you referring to the life you lived out on the farm before you came to town?"

Dora's lips tightened. "I could never live like that again. I won't have people feeling sorry for me."

Mary jerked back. "Sorry? Who feels sorry for you? Or your family? As far as I know, your father is a respected man. He's worked hard and has every right to be proud. What makes you say that?"

Dora shrugged. "It's just that life is so uncertain. Sometimes you get a crop and have money. Other times you don't know how you'll survive. And life is so barren."

Mary smiled. "Enjoyment is a state of mind."

"What's that supposed to mean?"

"Don't you realize that even the most mundane things become events if your heart is happy and whole?"

"It's hard to be happy when life is so uncertain." Dora shook her head unable to fathom how Mary could be so obtuse when she was generally so agreeable.

Mary continued. "I don't understand. A preacher's life is uncertain. We'll never have much. Some days we don't have enough for the next week. Some would say we depend on other people for our survival. Of course, we don't. We depend on God." She drew herself up stiffly. "Do you feel sorry for us?"

Dora sighed. "Of course not. But you're so happy, why would anyone feel sorry for you?"

Mary nodded. "That's it exactly. We're happy anyway. Our circumstances don't dictate how we feel."

Miserable, Dora studied her fingernails. How could she explain how she felt when her emotions were a tangle of fear and reluctance and resolve? She had vowed never to make the kind of mistakes her parents had made—risking everything for a bit of land; facing disaster, failure, and hunger for the right to own one miserable quarter section.

As Dora prepared to leave, Mary looked troubled. "I fear you are clutching too hard to a security that is an illusion. Who can say that life in town will always be so pleasant? Besides, it is always a meaningless sacrifice to forego love and cling to shallow substitutes."

Dora frowned. It was easy for Mary to talk. From the time she'd seen Luke she'd known what she wanted.

Mary, having read her expression, hugged her arm. "I don't mean to give you pat answers. I'll pray God will guide your steps."

Dora hurried home. As she rounded the last corner, she strained to catch a glimpse of light coming from the window of Josh's room. Only blackness greeted her. Dora's steps faltered. Even though she had refused his offer, she hadn't expected him to simply disappear.

With heavy feet, she climbed the steps to her house.

The next morning she entered Doc's house as he rushed out. "Our young man has not returned." Doc shook his head. "I don't understand these modern young people."

Dora watched him hurry down the steps, then turned her attention to the day's work. She spent a few minutes in Josh's room straightening the bed and rearranging the articles. She barely had time to clean the office before there was a burst of activity. The day was busy with a rash of broken bones and some minor injuries from children recklessly enjoying the freedom of spring.

But despite the busyness, the tightness around Dora's heart intensified with each passing hour. She hurried from the last patient to the kitchen and began supper, cooking a large pot of potatoes and frying an extra steak all the while refusing to admit that she expected Josh to walk in at any moment.

Mrs. Mac came into the kitchen. "Where is Josh? I haven't seen him all day."

Her voice echoed the impatience of Dora's heart. Poor Mrs. Mac. Josh had brought a ray of sunshine to her life. Now he was gone. Disguising her own disappointment and concern, she answered gently, "He told

Doc he was going for a ride. I expect he'll be back soon."

"That was yesterday. He should have been back long ago." She perched on the edge of her chair. "Something must have happened to the poor boy. I know it."

Dora grabbed the back of a chair as pain shot through her. Could he be injured? "Not again," she whispered, remembering his condition such a short while ago.

"Did you say something, lassie?"

"I was only thinking aloud."

"Care to share your thoughts with an old lady?" Mrs. Mac waggled her eyebrows.

Dora smiled. "I don't think you would want to hear my muddled thoughts."

Mrs. Mac snorted, and Dora knew she was waiting for her to say more, but she turned the steaks again and checked the pots without adding to her comment.

Doc came into the room and pulled out a chair. They were all waiting for Josh's appearance.

Finally, Doc sighed loudly. "I expect we might as well go ahead without him."

The three of them had little to say as Dora dished up the food.

"Perhaps he's decided he feels well enough to continue his journey," Doc said. "Though I would have thought he would say farewell." He paused then added, "I suppose he will write when he settles and have us send his things."

*

Doc's words echoed as Dora returned to her house to

prepare for choir practice. Josh had left without saying good-bye. It hurt, even though she realized it was for the best.

Choir was one of her greatest pleasures. She loved music and she found tremendous enjoyment in blending her voice with the others. At least she had until tonight, she thought after she missed another note.

One of the young married women asked the group to her home for refreshments following practice, and Dora agreed despite the ache inside. After all, she reasoned, wasn't social activity one of the reasons she insisted she had to live in town? But the chatter and noise made her head ache, and she slipped away early, pleading tiredness. She returning to her home to spend another troubled night.

The next morning, she stepped into Doc's kitchen and blinked. Mrs. Mac was up and dressed, eating toast with her husband.

"Did you notice the Mayday tree?" she asked happily. "It's in blossom."

Dora stopped in her tracks. It had become a tradition to measure the seasons by the trees and flowers. The Mayday tree was their spring marker. When the tree blossomed with its fragrant white flowers, they all agreed, spring had officially arrived. Dora had watched for days, hoping to be the first to spot the blooms. She thought she had an advantage, for she passed the tree each morning. But she had walked by this morning without seeing the tree or even noticing the scent. She shook her head. She must have been half-asleep.

The day, although busy, passed slowly. Dora tried to tell herself that she had accepted Josh's leaving. But as she rubbed her aching brow she wished she could convince her heart.

By evening she wanted nothing but to crawl into bed and cover up her head. Still, her thoughts kept sleep at bay.

Since she moved to town, life had been full of enjoyment and peace. Then Josh arrived. Now everything seemed hollow.

She should never have allowed herself to fall in love with him, and she vowed she would dismiss him from her thoughts. But try as she might, she was unable to erase thoughts of him from her mind. Words circled inside her head. *Security. Trust. Risk. Faith.*

What did she want? A safe place free of fear? Fear had been ever present on the farm. Yet, deep down, she knew that, among her family, only she had felt that gut-wrenching worry about what they'd eat and how they'd live. More than once Mother had assured her, "We don't have a lot but we'll get by. And things will get better."

But she hadn't stopped agonizing until she got her job with Doc and found this house.

Security is not found in a place, position, or possession— but in God.

The words bolted into her mind. Where had she heard them? Luke, of course. What else had he said? Something about faith being revealed by one's choices. But did taking risks prove one's faith?

She was certain it did not. Still, she was forced to admit that refusing to take risks didn't reveal faith either. God had provided this situation for her in answer to her prayers. And it was warm and cozy. Like a cocoon.

She bolted upright in bed.

It was true. She was trusting her situation for security. No longer did she cry out to God to meet her needs. She shivered, feeling suddenly lost.

But God hadn't changed. She had. She took a deep breath and lay back down. She was glad of this reminder of what she truly believed. Security was found in God alone.

God, I don't know what's right anymore. I thought I was right to appreciate what You have provided. But I fear that I am finding it too comfortable and not as enjoyable as I once thought. I love Josh and miss him already. Are You leading me into a new adventure? Is my lack of faith keeping me from considering the life of a pioneer wife? God, please bring him back.

She lay quietly for a moment and let her anxiety ease away. A new resolve grew within her. Wherever God led her, she would contentedly go. Even if it meant leaving town, this house, and the job she had come to love.

Her heartbeat quickened and she pressed her palms to her chest as she admitted that which she had been pushing away: to share a new life with Josh would not require one ounce of sacrifice.

Still, it was too late to think of such a thing. She'd thrown away her chance with Josh. If only she hadn't been so blind. She'd learned her lesson too late. An aching hollowness echoed through her thoughts.

❦

With the dawn of a new day, she crossed the street and headed up the path to Doc's house. A white petal on the ground riveted her attention and she tipped her head to see the Mayday tree in a garment of white, heavy-scented blossoms. But the scent triggered no answering song in her heart. The branches were full of birds exulting in spring, but there was no response in her heart. Spring had lost her song, when only a few days ago creation had rung with music and happiness.

She moaned. Without Josh, life lay before her muted and bland. Turning away, she slowly climbed the steps, her head dipped close to her chest.

Dora entered the sickroom and she crossed to the bedpost where Josh's saddlebags hung. With trembling fingers she caressed the smooth leather, hungrily breathing in the scent.

Perhaps he would return for his belongings.

❦

The next day, when afternoon office hours were almost over, a young boy clamored in from outside and ran to where his mother sat, waiting to see the doctor. "Mom, guess what? A man just rode up to the sheriff's with two men tied up in ropes. They sure looked mad, too."

Dora smiled at his enthusiasm, knowing that the activity of town was new and exciting for the boy.

Shortly, Dora announced to Doc, "That's the last of today's patients." But, before she finished speaking, she heard the clatter of boots on the steps.

Doc groaned. "Not quite, lassie."

The door flung open and Dora gasped. Josh stood facing them, breathing hard.

Dora knew her mouth hung open but she couldn't stop staring. Nor could she find her voice.

Josh's gaze held Dora's until she thought she was drowning in something unfamiliar—yet comforting. Doc broke the spell as he spoke. "We thought you had headed west, my boy."

Josh blinked and turned to face the older man. "Sorry about that, Doc. I hadn't planned to ride away without so much as a good-bye."

Dora couldn't stop looking at Josh. She noted the smudge of dirt along one cheek, the white sun-squint creases that radiated from his eyes, and the way the sun had frosted his eyelashes. And then she was looking into his warm brown gaze again, lost in a thousand sensations that sent her heart rocketing from height to depth. Seeking equilibrium, she tried to tear her gaze away but found she could not. She knew this unsettled state would last until she could explain how she'd changed her mind.

What if Josh has changed his mind as well? The painful thought caused her chest to tighten until she could barely breathe.

"I went out to ride and think, but I soon discovered that I wasn't alone on the road. I caught sight of the two men who had robbed me." Josh continued to watch Dora. "I was near certain that they weren't following me, but I decided to round up the varmints and bring them to justice." He shrugged. "It took longer than I expected to circle round and get the drop on them." At his crooked grin, a tremble raced across Dora's shoulders.

Doc harumphed. "I best go see how Mrs. Mac is doing. She'll be glad to know you're back." He turned on his heel and left the room.

Dora took a deep breath. God had blessed her with another opportunity and she wasn't going to waste it. But before she could speak, Josh stepped closer.

"I had plenty of time to think while I was gone," he began. Josh's eyes darkened as he studied her face with a hunger that made her cheeks warm. She swallowed hard, hopelessly trying to corral her thoughts. The power of his nearness turned her emotions into a tumult. She held her breath for a moment trying to slow the quivering of her insides long enough to say the words she'd practiced half the night.

Josh looked down at his hands. The sudden loss of his gaze gave her a rash of goose bumps. Then he looked once more into her eyes, his expression so serious she could feel her pulse under her tongue.

"I don't want to go anywhere without you. Doesn't matter how pretty the country is—without you it is nothing." He paused and the silence thundered in her ears. "I've decided to get a job in town and live here." His Adam's apple bobbed. "That is if you meant it when you said you loved me."

He would give up his dream for her! He was willing to live in town!

She caressed the idea for a moment and found that it gave her no pleasure. God had surely done a work in her heart. A glow began somewhere behind her heart and radiated to her toes, her fingers, her face. It made her want to laugh and cry and shout all at the same time.

"I meant it when I said I love you, Josh." Her voice shook. "But I don't care where we live or what you do." She grinned as his eyes grew round.

"I don't understand."

Her smile widened. "I've had plenty of time to think as well. And I prayed that God would give me another chance to tell you—I will go with you to the farthest mountains if you still want me. . . ."

He didn't wait for her to finish but wrapped her in a hug and swung her off the floor, yelling, "Yahoo." She was gasping when he set her on her feet, his arms still circling her. He dipped his head in order to look into her face. "Are you sure about this?"

"As sure as can be. I realized life in town was a life of quiet desperation if it meant giving up the love of a lifetime." She had learned so much more and someday she'd tell him. Someday, but not now.

He nodded, still serious. "Even so, I'm willing to live in town. I don't want you to be unhappy."

She shook her head. "That is not necessary." She realized she had turned a corner in her thinking and was no longer afraid to face change or even uncertainty. Excitement replaced her fear.

"I don't want to miss the adventure of a lifetime."

His arms tightened, pressing her to his chest. She rested her face against his dusty shirt, listening to the steady beat of his heart. With warm fingers he tipped her head back.

"Dora Grant, I love you with all my heart. Will you marry me and make my life complete?"

She smiled up at him, listening to the song in her heart. "Josh Rivers, I love you more than anything, and I will marry you and follow you to the ends of the earth. Your love is my song."

He laughed low in his throat. "We'll only go as far as the foothills." Sobering quickly, he added. "I will sing you a love song every day."

She sighed and placed her ear against his chest again so that she could hear his heart. "This is my love song. . . ," she whispered. As was his smile, his voice, his touch. Each new day with Josh would bring a fresh love song.

He caught her chin in his palm and turned her face upward. "I love you so much, Dora." His lips, warm and possessive, found hers. She tangled her fingers in the curls at the back of his neck, letting her kiss say what her heart felt.

He lifted his head. "Ah, my sweet, sweet Dora. I can't imagine life without you." Their gazes sought and held each other for many long moments before he stepped away, catching her hand. "I've something to show you." He drew her to the sickroom and snagged his saddlebags from the end of the bed. Flipping them onto the quilt, he dug into his trousers' pocket for a knife. He flicked open the blade and jabbed it into the side of a saddlebag, ripping open the seam.

Dora gasped as a false back opened up and paper money spilled forth.

Josh stood back and grinned, his hands on his hips. "This is what those men were after. There's more in the other bag. More than enough to build a house and start a herd of the best English cows." He sobered, studying her closely. "I thought about what you said—how some people risk everything and sometimes lose it. And you're right. So I propose to put half of this in a bank account as our nest egg. That way, should disaster strike, we'll have enough to start over."

She wanted to say that such a plan wasn't necessary; they could depend on God, but she knew he was right. Her heart was ready to burst. Barely able to speak, she whispered, "You are a very wise man. No wonder I love you."

His lips warm and gentle, he kissed her again. Then he pulled away and grabbed her hand. "Let's go tell Doc and Mrs. Mac."

She laughed, a breathless sound of pure joy. Somehow she didn't think the good doctor and his wife would be surprised to hear how things had turned out.

LINDA FORD

Linda draws on her own experiences living in the Canadian prairie and Rockies to paint wonderful adventures of romance and faith. She lives in Alberta, Canada, with her family, writing as much as her full-time job of taking care of a paraplegic and four kids who are still at home will allow. Linda says, "I thank God that he has given me a full, productive life and that I'm not bored. I thank Him for placing a little bit of the creative energy revealed in His creation into me, and I pray I might use my writing for His honor and glory." She has had three novels published with **Heartsong Presents.**

The Barefoot Bride

by Linda Goodnight

Chapter 1

Goodhope, Kansas, 1883

H*usband wanted. Must be God-fearing, hardworking and clean.*

Dr. Matthew Tolivar frowned as he read the carefully lettered sign hanging inside the door of O'Dell's General Store. Removing his battered hat, he swiped a hand through his dark hair, a shaggy reminder of the weeks spent on the road. A second swipe, this one over his square jaw, grated against several days' growth of whiskers.

"What kind of woman would advertise for a husband?" he muttered, half to himself.

"A crazy one."

Matthew turned slowly toward the speaker. The little man stood behind a long, rough-hewn counter, surrounded by an odd assortment of horse tack, yard goods, and canned foods. *Crazy.* His crude answer echoed in Matt's head. *Yes,* he thought, *or desperate.* And Matt Tolivar knew about desperate.

"Name's O'Dell. Jimmy O'Dell. I'm the proprietor

here." The storekeeper's woolly tufts of red hair circled his balding head like a fuzzy horseshoe. "You'd be new in town, I'm guessing. Most folks from these parts know all about Emma Russell and her crazy ways."

"So this quest for a husband is just part of her dementia?" Matt let his hat dangle in one hand as he surveyed the store. It reminded him of a hundred other stores he'd visited in his wanderings.

He stifled a weary sigh. He was tired of running. Tired of always being a stranger. Tired of being alone. A situation like his made even a crazy woman's offer sound good.

"No. No," O' Dell answered, "Emma's after a man, all right. That big old farm won't run itself, and she's just a little bit of a woman. Can't do it alone. But her sign's hung there for a year or more, and only the new folks pay it any mind. I just leave it up for conversation. Once in awhile some fella takes a notion to head out that direction. Six sections of prime grazing land is a mighty big temptation, you know?"

"Why doesn't she just hire someone?"

"She's touched, I tell you. Young Dan Barton worked for her a bit, and she nearly scared the poor boy to death. 'Possessed,' he said. She was dancing with brooms and talking to the air." He shook his head, foreboding in his expression. "I saw Dan myself, come running into town one day, white as St. Patty's ghost. Since then, the townsfolk keep their distance. No telling what that woman might do."

"Dancing and talking never hurt anyone. Is she

dangerous?" Matt was curious. In his days as a physician, the insane had stirred his heart to compassion. Though the common practice was to put them away, Matt had remembered the compassion of Jesus toward the sick in soul and mind. How could a physician do less than try to help them? Sometimes treatments worked; sometimes they didn't. But Matt had always tried.

"You wouldn't be thinking of going out there, would you?"

Was he? Matt didn't know for certain. While he considered the question, a curtain behind the counter parted and a copper-haired woman stepped out, sea green eyes flashing. "Da, are you talking about Emma again?"

"Now, Maureen. . ." O'Dell grinned at Matt. "This avenging angel is my daughter, Maureen. Always she's fighting for those she pities."

Maureen laughed. "An angel, he's calling me. And the two of us always quarreling over something." She came around the counter, pink skirts swaying. "And who might you be, Mr. . . ?"

"Tolivar," he said. "Matthew Tolivar."

Maureen snitched a peppermint stick from a jar on the counter and aimed it at him. "Well, Mr. Tolivar, don't you go listening to this da of mine. Emma Russell is a gentle woman who's had more suffering than the Lord should allow, and this town has turned its back on her instead of helping out."

"Maureen." Her father scowled at her from behind the cash register. "Don't be getting none of your funny notions. That woman never belonged here in the first place. Old Jeremiah Russell had no business sending off for a mail-order bride. We all told him no good would come of it. Only the demented or desperate would consider such an offer." O'Dell shifted his gaze to Matt. "She was an orphan, you see. And old Jeremiah needed someone to help him care for that big old place of his. Orphans got bad blood, we told him. And we was right." He pursed his lips and gave a knowing jerk of his head. "Now that Jeremiah's dead, we folks in Goodhope have to keep our eyes and ears open lest that crazy widow steal our children or murder us in our sleep."

"Emma would never hurt a soul, Da." Maureen tossed her head, and a red curl bounced down upon one shoulder.

"You're the only one who believes that, girlie. Now, you mind what I've told you and stay clear of her, or I'll be tearing a strip off ya."

The harsh warning brought a flush to Maureen's pretty face. Rebellion burned in her eyes, but she gnawed silently on the candy stick.

A tiny seed of compassion sprouted in Matt's chest, both for Maureen and the Widow Russell. No one knew better than he did about being an outcast, about suffering the sly, speculative glances of his neighbors.

"Where does this widow live?" Matt asked, more curious than ever about the woman. "I could use a day or two of work."

"Just like the sign says." Maureen spoke quickly, casting a defiant glance at her glaring father. "Take the road north out of town about three miles and follow the creek to a stand of cottonwoods. 'Tis the only house for miles."

"Maureen, this young feller can find work somewheres besides there. Now, hush your jabbering and go help your ma with the little 'uns. She's feeling poorly this morning."

From the attached rooms in the back came the noise of playing children. Maureen slanted a glance in that direction, then gave a saucy shrug and disappeared around the curtain.

Shaking his head, O'Dell said, "That girl has a heart of gold but doesn't know what's good for her. I 'spect she sneaks off to that crazy woman's house, though I can't catch her at it. Thank the good Lord she's devoted to her mama, or there's no telling what kind of nonsense she'd get into."

"I'm sorry your wife's feeling poorly. I hope her ailment isn't serious." He clamped his teeth together to keep from asking if the woman needed his services. Thankfully, the storekeeper didn't notice.

"Nah, same as always when she's expecting. Sick in the mornings, sleepy all day. After ten of the darlin's, though, she's an old hand at it. Be right as rain in a few months."

A sick ache, worse than the grippe, pulled at Matthew's belly. Visions of Martha rose to haunt him, her body round with his child. Martha, his own wife, the one patient his skilled medical hands couldn't save. He gulped back the wave of guilt and sorrow that was never far away.

"I hope Mrs. O'Dell feels better soon, sir," he said,

shifting to safer ground. "Now, if you don't mind, I'd like a tin of sardines and a few crackers to take along for my dinner."

The Irishman scuttled around, his boots scraping on the wooden floor, as he gathered up the items and pushed them across the counter.

"Plan on staying in town long, Mr. Tolivar? 'Tis a nice little settlement. Folks are friendly. Plenty of opportunity for a hard worker." He took the coin Matt handed him, testing it between his teeth. Satisfied, he poked at the cash register until the drawer chinged open. "I suppose that Russell woman is the only blight on the whole county, and she knows better than to show her face in town too often. Stay clear of her, and you'll get along fine around here."

Matt didn't appreciate the not-so-subtle warning. He was a man who took care of himself and made his own decisions. Whoever this Russell woman was, she led a hard, solitary life—an existence as lonely and empty as his. That fact alone won her his sympathy.

Matt looked over his shoulder at the faded paper. Suddenly, it took on new meaning. The Widow Russell needed a husband and a ranch hand. Matt Tolivar needed a place to hide and a purpose in life. Maybe they could work out a deal.

With his lunch in one hand, he clapped on his hat and headed for his horse.

❦

The people of Goodhope were right. Emma Russell was crazy.

Barefoot, she danced in circles around the early stalks of green corn standing tall in her garden. Her laughter bubbled up and echoed over the vast grasslands surrounding her ranch.

"Thank you!" she called, voice loud and joyous, though Matt knew for certain she wasn't talking to him. "How can I ever thank you enough?"

Whirling wildly, her plain calico skirts flapped against the cornstalks and made a *whap, whap, whapping* noise. "I do declare that's the prettiest sound in all the world. Don't you think so?"

She was turned sideways, talking to the corn or some unseen visitor.

Matt tied his horse to the rough-barked rail running along the front porch of her cabin and waited for her to notice him.

Watching her now, he wondered why he'd bothered to come out here. He'd been warned. But after six years of roaming the frontier, he was too weary to travel on. Besides, he'd long since discovered that a man couldn't outrun his own conscience.

"Ah, would you look at that?" she said to the warm May breeze. "He's back, the little rascal."

For a moment, Matt thought she spoke of him. Then he saw the rabbit hopping toward the garden. To his surprise, instead of flapping her skirts to chase the varmint out of her corn, she pulled a young green stalk and laid it on the ground in the animal's path.

"Now, maybe you'll leave the rest alone."

With a smile as pretty as Maureen O'Dell's, the

crazy widow hefted the hoe and started toward the cabin, singing and chattering all the way. Halfway there she looked up, spotted him waiting in the cool shade, and stopped to appraise him.

"Lovely day, isn't it?" she asked simply, as though the sight of him standing in her shade was a common one.

"Yes, ma'am," Matt answered in the same matter-of-fact manner, then he stepped forward, removing his hat. He had expected her to be old and ugly as a witch, but she was neither.

"Did you see Noah, then? He's gathering in the animals, two by two."

Her words brought Matt to a halt. He blinked in confusion. Didn't seem to be anyone around but him and her. She *was* crazy. He had to be careful until he knew the extent of her dementia.

"Oh, you have to see him," she insisted. "Come on. I'll show you."

As she crossed the yard, a beatific smile greeted Matthew from beneath honey-colored eyes that matched her hair. Back home in Virginia, women had creamy pale skin, carefully protected from the sun, and their hair was neatly groomed on top of their heads. Emma Russell's skin was as golden brown as freshly baked bread, and she wore no bonnet on the wild, windblown hair that flowed freely over her shoulders and down her back. Her arms and neck were as bare as her feet. She was oddly beautiful in a wild, earthy manner that reminded him of the untamed mustangs he'd seen in his journey across the plains.

As she reached his side, bringing with her the fresh green scent of growing things, she took his hand as easily as if they'd grown up together. Too surprised to pull away, Matt let her lift his arm and point it toward a huge, fluffy configuration of white fair-weather clouds.

"Right there. See?" she said. "It's Noah, I'm certain. See his staff? And that long, flowing beard?"

A chuckle worked its way up inside Matt's chest, but he repressed it. Like a child, the Widow Russell was forming pictures in the clouds. Her insanity was most likely harmless, a return to childlike ways.

"Maybe it's Moses, striking the rock," Matt said, responding to her game. How many years had passed since he'd done such a silly, lighthearted thing?

"You could be right." She dropped his arm and turned to face him with those pale gold eyes. "Are you a God-fearing man, then?"

"Yes, ma'am." The remnants of his faith were all that kept him going, though he'd long since stopped bothering God with his day-to-day worries.

"Good. Good. He wouldn't send any other kind, now would He?"

Matt blinked at her, baffled. "Who?"

"Why, the Lord, of course."

"Oh. I suppose not." *What is she talking about?*

"He told me you were coming. I just didn't know when." She leaned the hoe against the side of the porch. "Come on in."

"Who told you I was coming?" He followed her

across the porch ducking his head to miss the dangling onions hung in bunches from the rafters. "The Lord?"

Emma turned back, her gaze moving over him as softly as the breeze, which lifted the tendrils of hair from her forehead.

"I've waited two years for you to get here, and now that you've arrived, I can tell you're the right one. God wouldn't send anyone but the best."

She talked crazy, and her behavior was unusual, but her calm, amber eyes looked as sane as any he'd ever held in his gaze.

"Come in. I'll fix us a nice lemonade while we talk."

Matt asked himself again why he didn't just get back on his horse and ride away. But for some strange reason—most likely his medical curiosity—this woman fascinated him.

Or could it actually be the Lord's doing, him being here? Could Emma be right? Did God work that way?

Somewhere from the past he remembered the saying, "God works in mysterious ways, His wonders to perform."

Well, Emma Russell and this bizarre situation were certainly wonders.

He followed her inside, noting how large the cabin was compared to most he'd seen. She led him through a small parlor. A rocking chair and a cradle sat beside the fireplace and colorful rag rugs covered the plank floor. The place was homey. Pleasant and cozy. The kind of home where a man could put up his feet and relax after a hard day's work. The kind of home that

Matt hadn't had in a very long time. As he considered the cleanliness, he thought it unlikely that an insane mind could bring such order. Could the people of Goodhope be wrong about the Widow Russell?

Graceful as a deer, Emma moved about the kitchen, her hair catching the sunlight now streaking in between the yellow curtains. Matt settled at the round oak table to watch and found the experience much more pleasant than he could have imagined. She emanated a gentleness, a peace that stirred him in ways he'd long since forgotten. What was it about her?

"I'm Matthew Tolivar," he said, breaking the silence and his own wayward thoughts. "I saw your sign at the store in town."

"And?" She handed him a cool glass, then took one for herself before sitting across from him, as calm and rational as he.

"Why do you want a husband?"

She sighed, a breathy sound that raised the hair on Matt's arm and made him even more aware of Emma Russell's peculiar loveliness. When she began to speak in a low, sweet voice, he set his glass aside and leaned forward, suddenly eager to be convinced, not only of her sanity, but of her need for a husband.

"Two years ago, a blizzard hit this part of Kansas and lasted for weeks."

"The blizzard of '81." Everyone knew about that terrible time when men froze in their saddles and cattle froze in the fields.

"We thought we were safe and snug here in the

cabin—my husband Jeremiah, Lily, our little girl, and me. Jeremiah wasn't a young man, but day after day, he stumbled from the house to the barn, taking care of the stock, bringing in wood. He was so good, so kind. He'd never let me go out there." Absently, Emma drew circles on the table with her glass. "I wasn't surprised when the fever struck him, just scared. Then, soon after, Lily took sick. The wind kept blowing and the snow piled higher. I couldn't go for help." She glanced up. "Goodhope has no doctor, even if I could have gotten out. There was nothing I could do but pray and wait."

A lump formed in Matt's throat. He didn't want to hear this; didn't want to be reminded of his own lost family. He sipped at the tart drink, washing down bitter memories. He'd asked. Now he had to listen.

"Lily was so small, she couldn't fight the sickness. Her little chest closed up so tight that all the mustard plasters in the world couldn't open it up again."

"Pneumonia?" Matt asked quietly, recognizing the strangling symptoms.

Emma nodded, her voice small and distant. "One night, I sat beside her bed, listening to the howling wind and counting every breath my baby took. Soon, there was only the wind, blowing, blowing, blowing."

The tortured story pulled at Matt. He knew just how hard the loss of a child could hit a parent.

"I'm sorry, Mrs. Russell." As he'd done many times with his patients, Matt reached out and lay his hand over hers. She didn't pull away and a warmth crept from her small, weathered hand upward to his icy heart.

"I know," she ventured a sad smile. "So am I. Jeremiah died the next day, and there I was, all alone in a cabin with my dead family while the blizzard raged on."

"How long before help came?"

"I don't rightly know, Mr. Tolivar." She shook her head and looked away. "You see, for a while, I lost myself. I know how that sounds. That's why the townsfolk still think I'm crazy to this day. It's hard to explain, and I don't expect you to understand. But my whole world caved in when Jeremiah and Lily died."

Yet, Matt did understand. He knew how grief could tear away at the inner man until he was so lost he couldn't find his way back. Hadn't the same thing happened to him in a different way? Hadn't he roamed the plains, searching for something, and all the while that something was within him?

"Grief does strange things," he said kindly.

"In those dark, terrible days after Jeremiah and Lily died, I prayed to die with them. Why should I, with nothing and no reason to live, remain here, when they, who were so good and perfect, were gone? But finally, as I lay on my empty bed one night, the sweetest presence filled that room." She smiled softly, an inner radiance lighting her eyes. "It was Jesus."

Jesus? Matt stiffened, struggling to keep his expression bland. "What did He say?"

"Say?" Emma seemed to come back from a distant place. She tilted her head to the side and shrugged one thin shoulder. "Oh, He didn't say anything. He just stood there, watching me with His wonderful, kind eyes and letting His peace flow around me like a great cleansing river of light. When I woke up the next morning He was gone, but He'd left behind such a strength and joy that I could no longer lie in bed feeling sorry for myself. God had given me life and Jeremiah had given me this place. I had to do right by both of them."

A dream. That was all. In her grief, she confused a dream with reality. Matt breathed a quiet sigh of relief.

Emma slipped her hand from beneath his and inhaled deeply. "That, Mr. Tolivar, is why I need a husband. Jeremiah left me a fine ranch, but I cannot run it alone. Hired men are either dishonest or afraid of me. They think I'm crazy, you see. Maureen says that some folks in town believe I should be put away and my land sold. A husband can keep that from happening."

Matt set his glass on the table and scooted his chair back, meeting her gaze. "According to the law, Mrs. Russell, a woman's property belongs to her husband. Had you considered that?"

She twisted her hands nervously in her lap. "Yes. I know. That's why I have to find the right person. An honest man who'll do right by me. I've prayed a very long time. And now you've come."

Matt wanted to promise her, then and there, that he'd always take care of her. He didn't know why. The idea didn't make a lick of sense to him. Perhaps her sad story struck a tender chord in his own sick soul. Whatever the reason, he knew he would stay. And he knew he would marry the crazy Widow Russell.

Chapter 2

Matthew awoke to the sound of voices. No, not voices. One voice. A sweet, feminine voice somewhere below.

"Daisy dear," the voice said. "What would I do without you?"

From his prickly bed in the hayloft Matt opened one eye and peeked through the missing planks in the barn roof at the first pink-gray hint of morning. Slowly, memory returned to his sleep-fogged mind as he recalled where he was and what he'd agreed to do. Last night, over the best home-cooked meal he'd had in months, he'd consented to marry a woman who, this very moment, was somewhere below him, babbling to herself like a lunatic.

"The Anderson children will appreciate this so much. There are four of them, you know, and children are always hungry." She laughed softly. "But you're taking care of that, aren't you, dear heart?"

Quietly, Matt edged toward the sound until he was lying on his belly peering down at the top of Emma Russell's head. Now he saw what he couldn't see from his bed of hay. She was talking to a sleek, docile Guernsey cow while her small hands rhythmically squirted milk into a gleaming bucket.

"Thank you, Lord, for Daisy." The conversation suddenly switched to prayer, an unsettling habit Matthew had encountered more than once the previous day. "And thank You for sending Matthew Tolivar my way. He's the right one, I know. Though I never expected him to be quite so handsome."

Matthew held his breath, listening. Handsome, was he?

"But I don't mind a bit, Lord, that looking at him is pleasant. Especially since he's sturdy built with shoulders strong enough to do the things around here that I'm too small to do."

A curl of pleasure rose in Matt's belly, warming him like smoke rising from a chimney on a chilly day. She thought he was strong and handsome. For the life of him, he didn't know why her opinion mattered. But it did.

"And his blue eyes, Jesus, as pretty as a summer day, but so full of sadness. You know his secrets. You know what's hurt him. Help him find the peace he needs."

A familiar heaviness descended upon Matthew, erasing all pleasure in Emma's rambling over his good looks. He had come here to hide, to bury himself in hard, mind-numbing work; hoping to blot out all memory of who he was and what he'd once considered his calling in life. By helping the poor widow, he could make amends for his own failure and never have to think of medicine again. That alone was reason enough to marry her. It didn't matter if she thought him as plain as a stick.

Wearily, he rose and thumped back to his bedroll, making enough noise to warn Emma that he was awake. The black medical bag he'd used as a pillow more times than he could remember now mocked him as he rolled it tightly inside the woolen blankets. He stopped, unrolled the bedding, and stashed the bag in the far corner of the loft beneath a pile of hay. He wouldn't need the bag or its contents ever again. He didn't know why he'd kept it so long, except that his selling it might raise questions he didn't want to answer. Someday, a traveling peddler would come along, and he'd be rid of the bag for good. For now, he didn't need the reminder of all he'd lost. Today, he'd start a new life and leave the old one behind forever.

There was plenty here to keep his body busy and his mind preoccupied. The Widow Russell had done her best to keep things going. He could see that. Even the barn was neatly kept, the hay raked to one side, fresh straw in the stalls. The animals were healthy and well fed, the garden planted and sprouting. But everywhere he'd noticed signs that the job was too big for her to tackle all alone. The barn door sagged to one side. A half-finished row of fence trailed from the barn to nowhere. And the woodpile was woefully low. No doubt, a further inspection would reveal more, and he was glad for that. Glad for the opportunity to hang up his hat and exhaust himself at something worthwhile.

Buttoning his shirt, he descended the ladder. The widow heard him coming and looked over one shoulder.

"Are you ready for some flapjacks?" Emma asked as she spread a clean white cloth over the brimming milk bucket.

"Sounds good." Matt took the pail from her hands. "I'll wash up a bit first, if you don't mind. You did specify clean in your advertisement, didn't you?"

"Did you hear that, Jesus?" With a merry laugh, Emma reclaimed the milk bucket and led them out of the barn, her yellow dress a bright spot in the early morning.

Matt followed behind, shaking his head. Just when he'd decided that only a logical, rational woman could have kept the farm going so long, she talked to a cow or a rabbit or the Lord Himself, raising fresh questions and doubts in his mind.

"How long have you been up?" He stopped to scrub himself at the well where Emma had placed a rag and sliver of soap in anticipation of his needs.

"Awhile. I love the hours before sunrise when the stars are still out and the rest of world is sleeping. You can see things in the darkness that are never around in the daylight." She set the milk on the wooden ledge of the well and drew the water bucket to the top. Pouring a bit of the liquid on a rag, she rinsed her hands and swiped her grass-covered feet. The hem of her gingham dress was dew-drenched, letting him know that she'd been farther than the barn this morning. He couldn't help but wonder where she had gone in the darkness. Did she roam the woods baying at the moon or communing with the devil?

Matt shoved the damp hair back from his forehead and dismissed the ridiculous notions. The conversation with the storekeeper had filled his head with nonsense. He was a man of science, not an ignorant country bumpkin who believed the insane were all devil-possessed. Emma Russell was a Christian woman. Of that he was certain. And with each minute spent in her company, he became more convinced that the town of Goodhope was wrong about her mental state.

Tossing the towel over one shoulder, he hefted the two buckets and followed her to the house. A half-dozen red chickens clucked around the front porch, running full speed toward Emma when they saw her coming.

"Not yet, girls. But give me six eggs today, and there will be corn for everyone this evening." To Matt she said, "Just set the milk on the sideboard, please, and sit down. I'll have breakfast ready in no time."

Ignoring her command, Matt strained the milk, set it to cool, and rinsed the bucket, hanging it upside down on a nail by the back door. If he was going to live here, he might as well let her know he wasn't lazy.

Emma opened the cookstove and poked at the fire, then she rubbed an iron skillet with lard before clapping it onto the stovetop. Pancake batter sizzled against the hot skillet and the smell of sausage set Matt's belly to rumbling. He'd missed this. Missed the familiar warmth and smell of a kitchen and a pretty woman bustling around, preparing a meal.

"Mrs. Russell."

"Might as well call me Emma."

"All right, Emma." He sipped at the coffee she handed him and wondered when he'd last drunk from anything but a tin cup. "I reckon I'll go into town later and fetch the preacher."

Her hands stilled. "You're still agreeable, then?"

"If you'll have me."

"I will." Drawing in a deep breath, she turned toward him, twisting her hands in her apron. "I got no false notions about this, Matthew. You're marrying me for my land. I'm marrying you to hang on to Jeremiah's dreams and the only home I've ever had. A business agreement, pure and simple. That's all I'm asking. I'll look after you and you look after me."

He heard the relief in her voice when she'd gotten the words out, and he understood her meaning. In Virginia, men and women courted, fell in love, and married, though a few still agreed to arranged marriages. Things were different out here. Men ordered wives through the mail or bartered for them when a farmer had more girls than he could feed. Emma was trying to make it clear to him that she wasn't looking for a love match, just a husband to work her farm. That was fine with him. Absolutely fine. There was nothing left inside him to love.

"People marry for worse reasons," he said, half to convince himself. "We'll do all right, if we set our minds to it."

"Thank you." She piled the flapjacks onto a plate and circled them with sausages. "You're a good man."

"How could you possibly know that?"

"I know." She set the steaming breakfast in front of him. "And Jesus knows."

Matt sighed. There she went again. "And I suppose He told you?"

Innocent amber eyes widened. "How else would I find out?"

How else indeed? But was such a thing possible? Was God the reason that marrying the Widow Russell and resurrecting this farm appealed to him more with each passing moment? Or was it because he could hide here on a farm that other people avoided?

Emma refilled his coffee and placed a jar of molasses next to his elbow. Then she settled into her own chair and plunged into her meal as though she married a stranger every day of the week.

Matthew lifted his fork and looked down at the butter pats on his flapjacks. They were shaped like daisies.

A chink of ice melted in one corner of Matthew's frozen heart. Emma Russell was fanciful, childlike, utterly fascinating, and certainly in need of a man's protection, but he didn't think she was crazy. The more he knew about her, the more she beguiled him, and the more he wanted to stay.

❧

Later that morning, Matt rode away from Goodhope Church, madder than he'd been in years. All the way back to Emma's place he rehashed the conversation with Reverend Jeffers, trying to come up with a winning argument.

"It's against the laws of God and common sense for the insane to marry, Mr. Tolivar," the parson had said as they stood in the sunlight just outside the church where Matt had found him pounding nails in a rickety step.

"I tell you, Reverend, Mrs. Russell is not insane." Matt leaned against the railing and gazed in frustration at the kneeling man. "Unusual and childlike, yes, but as rational and sound as either you or me."

Laying his hammer aside, Reverend Jeffers stood and dusted his hands down the side of his trousers. An angular man with hollow cheeks and burning eyes, he pierced Matt with a look. "Mr. Tolivar, how long have you known Mrs. Russell?"

"Long enough," Matt hedged, hesitant to admit he'd agreed to marry a woman less than a day after meeting her. "And, in my opinion, Mrs. Russell is perfectly sane."

"I see. And by what authority do you judge her mental state?"

"I. . ." Matt stopped and ground his teeth in frustration. As a doctor, he carried the knowledge and authority to make that judgment, but his profession was part of the past, buried when Martha died. He had no intention of resurrecting it. "I've observed her closely," he finished, lamely.

The reverend narrowed his eyes. "Begging your pardon, Mr. Tolivar, but you're a stranger in this town. As the only clergyman for miles around, it's my duty to protect poor Emma from unscrupulous souls who might take advantage of her to gain her land." He held up a bony hand as Matt's expression darkened. "Not that I'm saying you're that kind of man. I don't know you, but I do know Emma. And she has no business making a decision as important as marriage."

"And I'm begging your pardon, Reverend, but this is between Emma and me. All we're asking of you is to perform the ceremony."

"I'm sorry, sir. I cannot, in good conscience, do that. Now, if you'll excuse me," the preacher turned away, "I need to finish this step and get over to the Anderson place."

The dismissal was clear. And so was the message. The Reverend Jeffers would not marry them. Matt crammed his hat onto his head and mounted his horse. The only other preacher was a train ride away, and Matt had no money. He could ask Emma, but most likely all she had was property. Cash was hard to come by.

He stewed over his dilemma the entire three miles back to Emma's place. He thought about praying. Certainly Emma would have. She prayed about everything, talking to God aloud without a bit of embarrassment, then listening with head tilted and expression rapt until Matt was almost sure he could see the Lord whispering in her ear. But that was Emma's way. He was a man, and any man worth his breakfast could find a way without bothering God.

As he rode into the yard, Emma came rushing out the door, amber eyes alight with expectation. When he dismounted and faced her, some of the light faded.

"Parson Jeffers wouldn't come," she said, matter-of-factly.

"No." Resisting the urge to ride back into town and drag the minister to the farm, he tethered his horse to the porch. How did he explain that the preacher thought her too unbalanced to marry? "He didn't think it would be right."

"Well." Emma's delicate face registered only momentary disappointment. "We can't blame the parson. He's only following his conscience."

Matt gave her a solemn appraisal. "Are you saying he's right?"

"To his way of thinking, he is." She pushed a tangle of hair behind one ear and tilted her head, looking up at him. "What about you, Matthew? Do you think I'm crazy? Are you certain you want to be married to a woman like me? Shunned by the town, unable to attend church. Is six sections of land worth that much trouble?"

"Is that what you think? That I'm marrying you just for the land?" Anger, all out of proportion to the question, sizzled inside him.

"Why else then?"

He couldn't honestly answer that question, not if he was to keep his secret, and that bothered him. Even when he'd had little else, he'd kept his honesty. "There are things about me you don't know, Emma. Things that might make you change your mind."

"The Lord sent you. That's all I need to know."

Matt shook his head. Maybe he was the crazy one for considering matrimony with this woman. She talked out loud to Jesus. She accepted a husband she didn't know, and she wouldn't stand up for herself against a town that had badly misjudged her. But then, wasn't that what brought him here in the first place? The crazy widow needed help, and he needed a reason to keep putting one foot in front of the other.

"Then, we'll have to go somewhere else to wed."

With a smile she extended a hand and touched his arm. "Don't fret, Matthew. God will provide a way."

Glancing down at her weathered little hand lying against his sleeve, a new determination overtook him. Instantly, he knew how he would get the money. He'd show the town of Goodhope just how little he cared for their opinion. "There's a preacher up in Dodge who can do the job. Though from what I hear, he does more burying than marrying."

Emma laughed. "Then he needs the practice. And I'd love a train ride to the city."

Just like that she accepted the town's rejection and set her sights in a different direction. Without animosity. Without complaint. If that was crazy, Matt wished the whole world would lose its mind.

❦

As Matt guided the team down Goodhope's narrow Main Street, past playing children, chatting ladies, and the occasional horse and rider, he noticed a strange occurrence. Activity stopped each time one of the townspeople caught sight of him and his companion. Not a single person spoke a word of greeting, but all turned to follow their wagon's progress.

A glance at Emma told him that she noticed too. Head held high, a sweet smile on her lips, she stared straight ahead, but her hands were tightly clenched against her yellow cotton skirt.

Anger surged up in him again. Word must have gotten around that he'd asked the parson to marry them. He yanked the team to a halt in front of the livery and leaped to the ground.

"Emma?" he said, reaching up to her. After a moment's hesitation, she stood and let him swing her down. A woman coming out of the livery gasped, jerked her child against her long skirts and rushed back inside, voice raised.

"Lucas, hurry. That crazy woman is out here."

A young man, tall, lank, with hands the size of shovels appeared at the door. "Now, Mama," he said to the woman. "Why don't you and Patsy go on to the house? I'll see to Mrs. Russell. And thank you kindly for the dumplings. They was mighty tasty."

The woman cast another worried look toward Emma, then hurried away.

"I'm Luke Winchester." The man wiped his hand down the side of his trousers before offering it to Matthew. "And you must be Matthew Tolivar."

Grimly, Matt inclined his head. "News travels fast."

"Yes, sir, it does. Especially when it concerns Emma."

Matt bristled. "She's not deranged."

The stable owner nodded, his expression sympathetic. "I never said she was. But some folks in this town would disagree."

"So I noticed." Matt scowled at the departing woman and child.

"What can I help you with today, Mr. Tolivar?"

With reluctance, Matt reined in his angry thoughts. No use adding to Emma's embarrassment. "I'll be leaving the team here for a day, maybe a night."

"The bay, too?" Luke asked, indicating Matt's horse tied on behind the wagon.

"He's for sale." Matt jerked a thumb toward the wagon bed. "The saddle, too."

Emma's head shot up, and Matt read the question in her eyes. Why was he selling his horse and saddle?

"A fine piece of horseflesh." Luke walked around the bay, lifting feet, checking teeth. Finally, he named a price.

"You're a fair man, Winchester."

"Yes, sir, I am." He gave Matt the money, counting it into his hand. "I'll take good care of your team, too. You can depend on it."

"Much obliged."

In the distance, a train whistle rent the air. Taking Emma's arm, Matt bid Luke farewell and started toward the depot. With each step down the street, past the barber shop, past the dry goods store, past the apothecary, they were met with the same unfriendly treatment until Matthew felt his blood boil. The storekeeper, O'Dell, had called this a friendly town, but to Matt's way of thinking it was infested with rattlesnakes.

He'd only known Emma two days and they'd known her for years. Yet, not one of them, unless it was the livery man or Maureen, had an ounce of compassion in them. He wondered how they gathered in that church and prayed with a clear conscience.

As they passed the general store where he'd first seen Emma's sign, the shopkeeper's daughter flew out the door and gripped Emma in a fast embrace.

"Emma, I heard. Is Mr. Tolivar the one, then?" Maureen O'Dell's lilting voice talked about him as though he weren't there. "I'd so hoped he was."

Emma took her friend's hands and together they danced in a circle around the boardwalk, drawing scandalized looks from passersby. Emma didn't seem to notice. "The Lord is good, Maureen."

"Aye, He is." The Irish lass tossed her strawberry hair over her shoulder. Her green eyes settled on Matt as she issued a challenge. "And you'd better be the same, Mr. Matthew Tolivar, or you'll be answering to me, you will."

Again, Matt was amazed that news traveled so quickly, but he understood Maureen's concern for her friend. Life hadn't exactly treated Emma well, and if the town's reception today was any indicator, she sorely needed his protection. "You have my word."

" 'Twill have to do, I suppose." Maureen looked none too convinced. "How will you be wed, with the parson so set against it?"

"We're off to Dodge City on the next train." Still gripping Maureen's hands, Emma gazed up at Matt, gratitude in her face. "Matthew sold his horse and saddle for the tickets."

Matt was not surprised that a woman as sensitive as Emma had quickly grasped his reason for selling, but he wasn't prepared for the unexpected rush of pleasure her appreciation gave him.

"Well, God be praised." Maureen looked at Matt anew. "You'll do, Mr. Tolivar. You'll do fine. Now, be off with you. That cranky conductor suffers no late comers, and I've me ma to tend to."

But Emma wouldn't leave without asking, "How is she, Maureen?"

Worry wreathed Maureen's beautiful face. "She's having a hard time of it. Usually by now the sickness is passed and she's fair glowing with health. But this baby is different, draining all the life out of her, he is."

Matt's gut clenched at the switch in conversation. A sick pregnant woman again. He couldn't, wouldn't let himself think about it too much. He was a farmer now, not a doctor. Such things no longer concerned him.

"I'll be praying for her."

"You do that, Emma, darlin'." Maureen released Emma's hands and stepped back. "Ask Him to send us a doctor while you're at it. The way this town is growing. . ."

To Matt's relief, her words were interrupted by another blast of the train whistle. "Emma," he said, "we'd better go."

Amid a flurry of hugs and warm wishes, Matt found himself embraced by the exuberant Irish woman. "I knew you were bringing good the moment I saw you," she whispered.

Puzzling over the curious words, Matt took Emma's elbow and guided her toward the depot. . .and toward a minister who would make them man and wife.

Chapter 3

The preacher wasn't home.

During their delightful train ride, Emma had entertained Matt and two restless children with her songs and stories and frequent exclamations over the marvels outside the train window. Matt's spirits were considerably higher by the time the train pulled into Dodge. Now, he sat in the parlor of the Reverend Tobias Jefferson drinking coffee he didn't want and listening to Mrs. Jefferson regale Emma with details of her own wedding thirty years ago in Boston.

". . .And my dress, dear child, it was the loveliest thing. All satin and lace with tiny pearl buttons." She paused, enraptured by the memory. "I still have it, you know, tucked away in a chest upstairs. My daughter wanted to wear it when she married, but Clara's tall, and we couldn't lengthen it."

Emma, perched on the edge of the settee, touched the woman's hand in sympathy. "You must have been so disappointed."

"Yes." Mrs. Jefferson sighed. "I always wanted to see it on another bride, but only a little thing like you or me could ever fit in it." Suddenly, she gasped, then popped up from the straight-backed chair, her gaze measuring Emma as she walked a circle around Emma's chair. "Emma dear, stand up."

Clearly bewildered, Emma cast a glance at Matt then stood obediently while Mrs. Jefferson continued her assessment. "Yes. . .yes. . .I do believe it would fit. Your waist is every bit as tiny as mine was. And we're almost the same height."

"Oh, Mrs. Jefferson." Emma's hands flew to her cheeks. "You can't possibly mean. . .you couldn't want someone like me to wear your wedding gown."

"And why ever not?"

Emma's eyes found Matt's. In an hour's time, the crazy widow had thoroughly charmed the preacher's wife, and now she didn't know how to react to the woman's kindness. He could see she wanted this. He could read the eagerness in her face. Not that it mattered one whit to him what she wore. After all, this was no love match and not a soul would care one way or the other if they even got married, but after the ugliness in Goodhope, Matt wasn't about to leave Dodge until Emma was in his legal care. If, while they waited, the young girl within Emma wanted to play dress-up in a thirty-year-old gown it was fine with him.

"I agree, Emma," he said. "Why ever not?"

His approval seemed to be all she needed. With Emma-like enthusiasm, she embraced the older woman. "I would be so honored to wear your dress."

Mrs. Jefferson clapped her hands in delight. "Oh,

wonderful! This will be so much fun. Funerals, funerals. That's all we ever have in this town with cowboys shooting each other over everything from whose horse is faster to whose daddy was meaner. You'll be so pretty in that dress. And we'll weave a garland for your hair. And pick some flowers for the church." Excitement seemed to emanate from her every pore. Suddenly, she whirled around and eyed Matt's shaggy hair and whiskered face. "You could use some sprucing up yourself, young man. It's not everyday a woman gets married, and she'd like to see that handsome face of yours, I'm sure."

Surprised by her sudden attack on him, Matt dragged a hand over his prickly jaw. "I suppose I could do with a shave."

"I suppose you could. The barbershop is right down Main Street. You can't miss that red striped pole." With a flap of her hands, she herded him out the door.

As he settled his hat on his head and started down the street, his insides jangling, Matt wondered how the last hour had gotten so out of hand. This wasn't what he'd bargained for, but then, nothing about the crazy widow had been.

❧

When Matthew returned, his face smooth and stinging from the hot shave, he found Emma in the backyard with the parson's wife and a black-suited man he assumed to be the preacher.

"Now, you look more like a bridegroom," Mrs. Jefferson said, approvingly. "And your bride is all ready for you."

The shock of seeing Emma dressed in lace with peach blossoms garnishing her long, flowing hair set his heart to thumping. She waited for him beneath the blooming boughs of a peach tree looking much more like a real bride than he'd expected. Martha had looked like this, radiant, hopeful. He squeezed his eyes shut, bowing his head against the torrent of emotion he did not want to feel and prayed he'd never let Emma down the way he had Martha.

When he opened his eyes again, he noticed what he hadn't seen before, and the sight erased all comparisons to his first wedding. An almost smile threatened his lips. Emma, with her dancing hair and her fancy dress, was barefoot, toes peeking out like a child's, charming him with her sweetness. Peace seeped into him. Taking care of the crazy Widow Russell was the right thing to do. Hat in hand, he went to stand beside his waiting bride.

"Shall we begin?" the pastor asked, opening his Bible.

As the ancient words of faith were spoken, a hush fell over the little gathering, broken only by the hum of insects glorying in the spring. Peach limbs swayed above them, releasing their sweet scent and an occasional shower of blossoms. A pair of robins flitted in and out of the trees tending a nest.

"Will you, Matthew, take this woman. . . ?"

Yes, he would take her as his wife. He would look after Emma and work her land, hiding from his own memories and from the incessant call of medicine on his life. He would promise all that was left of him to Emma

Russell, the orphan, the widow, the crazy woman. From this moment on, he'd look forward, not backward.

Gazing down at Emma's upturned face, seeing the hope and trust in her eyes, Matt felt his throat fill and tightened with some unnamed emotion. Swallowing hard, he answered, "I will."

In a whisper that barely reached his ears, Emma repeated her own vows, and while Matt pondered the odd feeling in his chest, the preacher pronounced them husband and wife.

"You may kiss your bride."

Matt and Emma then exchanged equally startled expressions.

At that moment, a yellow butterfly found the flowers in Emma's hair. Matt almost smiled. Emma Russell—he caught himself and nearly smiled again—Emma Tolivar, in satin gown and bare feet, with a butterfly in her hair, had such a strange effect on him. His chest expanded with a sense of satisfaction so profound that he thought he might, indeed, kiss his bride. But before he could, Emma once again surprised them all as she lifted her clear, sweet voice in a hymn of praise.

When the last pure notes of Emma's song faded away, Mrs. Jefferson dabbed at her eyes with a lace-edged handkerchief. "I felt God smiling down on us the entire time. Truly a match made in heaven."

Matt shoved away the disappointment he'd felt when Emma avoided his kiss. After all, Emma had made it clear that theirs was only a marriage of convenience, and he was certainly in agreement with that.

But in the last few years, he'd had few special moments to enjoy, and regardless of the circumstances, the vision of his beautiful barefoot bride would stay with him forever. Mrs. Jefferson was right. God must be smiling. And as he glanced down at his radiant new wife, Matthew Tolivar did the same.

Emma felt the effect of Matt's smile all the way to her bare toes. With blue eyes twinkling above the flash of white teeth, her new husband was a devastatingly handsome man. After a stern reminder that theirs was a marriage of necessity, she commanded her fluttery stomach to still. She knew about marriage. If they were truly blessed, they'd get along, maybe enjoy each other's companionship, and some day, they might even share a kindly affection such as she'd shared with Jeremiah. But she had no false notions about love. Still, laughter was good for the soul and Matthew needed to smile more. Out of gratitude for what he'd done, Emma made up her mind, then and there, to see that he did.

Chapter 4

S pring gave way to scorching summer as Matt and Emma fell into a comfortable routine. They worked from predawn to nightfall, sometimes side by side, often apart. There was so much to do, so much which had gone undone. Matt felt the constant pressure of time, determined to get as much fence up as possible before the winter. With fencing, he could raise the thousand or more cattle that Jeremiah had left to roam the open range as well as grow plenty of corn and hay to keep them healthy through the fierce Kansas winters. With hard work, he and Emma could have a secure future, and he'd have no time nor need to think about his forsaken medical practice.

When evening came, he sat in the lamplight, exhausted, hot, and filthy while Emma bustled around getting supper on the table. He enjoyed the evenings, enjoyed watching her do the things a woman did— things a man never even thought of doing. And, not a day passed that she didn't do something that made him smile.

As though privy to his thoughts, Emma handed

Matt his meal. A face stared up at him from the blue flowered plate. Two slices of tomatoes formed the eyes. A triangle of ham served as the nose. Thick ovals of bread protruded like ears from each side. And a row of fried okra grinned up at him.

"What's this?" he asked, a half grin tugging his lips.

With a saucy smile, she remarked, "That's the look I'd like to see on your face more often, Mr. Tolivar."

"What!" He returned in mock horror. "Red-eyed? With green teeth? Emma, you have strange tastes in men."

Clearly delighted by the joking reply, Emma threw back her mane of hair, her joyous laugh filling the cabin. Some of Matt's weariness lifted as he dug into his whimsical supper.

When he finished his dinner, Emma's work-worn hands quickly removed the empty plate and set a piece of apple pie and glass of milk in front of him. It was too hot to bake, but Emma had perspired over the stove without a murmur of complaint as though she enjoyed preparing the foods he loved.

"Maureen came out today." Settling into a chair with a pan of freshly picked peas, she began the tedious job of shelling them. He saw that her fingers were stained green, the nails chipped and ragged. It wasn't the first time he'd noticed the condition of her hands or seen her futilely rub lard into the cracked, dry skin. "She helped me pick these purple hulls."

"Maureen's a good friend," he said, savoring the taste of cinnamon-rich apples. "I trust she's doing well."

"She is. Her mother's having a very hard time, though." Emma paused, resting her forearms on the edge of the pan. "I just wish there was something I could do. . . ." She tilted her head to one side and smiled as though someone had whispered in her ear. "How silly of me, Jesus. As soon as You send us that doctor, we'll know just what to do for Kathryn, and all of us can breath a little easier."

Guilt shafted through Matt like a knife. Poor Emma, praying for a doctor, and here one sat. His conscience nearly ate a hole through him.

"Maybe she should rest more, keep her feet up."

Emma glanced at him, eyebrows raised in question. Matt shrugged, purposely nonchalant. "I knew a doctor sometime back. Heard him recommend cutting back on salt and pork and getting plenty of bedrest. She might try that."

"Oh, Matthew, thank you. Maureen will be so relieved, and it certainly wouldn't hurt to try." Emma's ragged little hands resumed their work. "If you're still going into town for supplies tomorrow, I'll send her a letter telling her so."

A measure of relief settled over Matthew as well. He'd helped without revealing his secret, and now maybe he could stop thinking so much about the pregnant woman. *Lord, will the torment never end? Will I never know peace again?*

He swallowed another bite of pie, although the dessert now tasted as bitter as quince. Pushing the plate aside, he leaned his elbows on the table and studied the woman who sat across from him, reviled and scorned, yet filled with serenity. She deserved so much more than public ridicule and a loveless marriage to a man as empty as those pea shells. "Why don't you go into town with me? Visit Maureen awhile. Maybe buy something for yourself."

Her answer was always the same. "No." She shook her head, smiling regretfully. "I wouldn't want to cause trouble."

Though he'd asked her a dozen times, other than the solitary walks she took through the fields and woods under cover of darkness, Emma refused to leave the farm. Having long stopped thinking she was a lunatic crazed by the moon, Matt suspected where she went on those early morning excursions, though she never told him. If he were right, the town's behavior toward Emma was nothing short of hypocrisy.

"Jimmy O'Dell's an ignorant fool," he said gruffly.

"Matthew," she scolded mildly. "He's a good man, doing the best he knows how to take care of his family."

Matt wanted to argue against the people who refused to give Emma a chance, but he knew better. Every time he broached the subject, she sidestepped him, saying something kind. He'd even heard her praying for them, one by one, as she went about her daily tasks. She was a better Christian than he'd ever be. And far better than the residents of Goodhope.

Matt sighed, knowing that he would travel alone tomorrow.

"It's too hot," he complained, drawing a hand down

his gritty neck, "and I'm too dirty to sleep."

With a sudden, merry laugh that startled him, Emma plopped the pan of peas onto the table. She jumped up, dropped her apron over the back of a chair, and flung the door wide open.

"Come on, then," she cried. "I have a wonderful idea."

Having no notion of what he'd said to bring on such a reaction, Matt nevertheless pushed himself back from the table and followed her out into the moonlit night. In their short marriage, he'd come to expect such flights of fancy from his bride. And though others might consider her crazy, Matt found release in the joyful way she embraced each moment. He never knew what to expect, and somehow that added spice to each day.

Once he'd found her lying face down in the backyard and thought she was sick. She shushed him and pulled him down beside her to watch an ant carry a much larger beetle to its hole. Instead of the ant, he'd watched Emma and found the sight of her rapt expression, the glowing golden eyes, and smooth tan skin utterly beguiling. He'd even considered kissing her again, but he'd refrained, remembering their wedding day. That night, he'd lain awake puzzled by the feelings she aroused in him and wondering at the odd sensation hammering in his chest.

"Where are we headed?" he asked. Guided only by the moon and stars, Matt followed her flying hair and billowing skirts to the creek. Beating him there, the ever-barefooted Emma plunged into the cool water.

"Come on. It's wonderful."

Tired as he was, the water would refresh and clean him. And Emma's delightful "craziness" would soothe his weary soul.

As he sat on the rocky bank to remove his boots, Emma waded his direction. By the full moon, he could see she was already soaked, dress plastered to her body, hair streaming. She grinned impishly and flicked water at him. The cold drops felt shockingly good against his parched skin, and he barreled into the creek, splashing and flinging water. Emma laughed and returned fire, soaking him in seconds. Like two otters, they frolicked together, forgetting their aching muscles and tired bodies.

"We should do this every night," he said, shaking back his damp, shaggy hair.

"What? This?" From a running start, Emma gave a shove, pushing him backward onto his backside. Her laughter rang over the tree-lined grove.

"You, dear lady, must be taught some manners." As he groped for a handhold to hoist himself up, Matt made contact with something soft and slimy. Feeling like a schoolboy, he gripped the squirming frog and stalked toward Emma. With a squeal, she floundered toward the bank, but Matt's much longer legs caught her. Holding her captive, he dropped the frog down the back of her dress.

Emma danced around the creek squirming and yelping in mock terror. Her antics brought a chuckle to

Matt's lips. In another moment, he was laughing. At the sound, Emma yelped and jumped all the more, fell backwards into the water, splashing and giggling in delight. Dislodged, the hapless frog croaked and bounded toward safer territory.

Sides aching, Matt slogged over to help Emma up. His courtesy was rewarded with a sharp tug that brought him tumbling down beside her. They sat in the water laughing until they were breathless. When at last the silliness passed, Emma looked up at him, her face golden in the moon shadows.

"Listen, Matthew." The croak of frogs pulsated around them. "Even the frogs are laughing."

"Not the one I dropped down your dress. He's sulking somewhere." The silly answer surprised even him.

With a feather light touch on his arm, Emma said, "I like to hear you laugh, Matthew. And so does God."

Matthew Tolivar wasn't given to fanciful notions, nor was he one to dance and cavort in the moonlight. The people of Goodhope would most likely think he'd gone as crazy as his bride, but none of that mattered one little whit. He felt good—good in a way he hadn't felt in a very long time; a fact that puzzled him no small amount.

The strange sensation in his chest returned, and though he was certain there was no room inside him for love, the feeling stayed with him for days.

❦

Bright and early the next morning, Matt hitched up the wagon, loaded it with Emma's milk, eggs, and vegetables, and headed to town. He'd asked her again to go along, but to his disappointment, she had once again refused.

"The scripture says if something we do offends our brother, we shouldn't do it," Emma had said without rancor. "My presence offends them, Matthew."

"That's their fault," he argued. But in the end, she'd stayed behind, waving him off with her ragged little hands.

During the three-mile drive into town, Matt thought of all the hardship Emma had suffered and determined to try, once more, to make the people of Goodhope see reason. She was the kind of woman who needed people, and though the stubborn townsfolk didn't know it, they needed her zest for life. He was a physician, a trained man of science, who'd lived with Emma for months now. Surely he could convince the people of Goodhope that she posed them no threat. And the best place to start was with her most vocal detractor—the storekeeper, Jimmy O'Dell.

Five minutes into the conversation, Matt knew he was wasting his breath.

"I reckon six sections of land made you an expert on lunatics," Jimmy sneered.

Angered by the insinuation and the man's stubborn refusal to give Emma a chance, Matt was tempted to walk out without the supplies he needed, though it was the only general store for miles. Before he could, Maureen whipped through the curtained door, dragging two redheaded boys by the scruff of their necks.

"Da, it's the woodshed these two are needin' today. Both of 'em running in the house like wild goats, and Patrick here running into Ma and nearly knocking her over."

"I didn't aim to." The accused poked out a defiant lip. "But Danny had a snake!"

Jimmy O'Dell's ruddiness deepened with anger. "You know your ma's not up to such shenanigans from the two of you. Give 'em to me, Maureen. I'll set 'em straight in a hurry if you'll ring up Mr. Tolivar's purchases."

Dragging the recalcitrant boys, the storekeeper banged out the door.

Casting about for a reason to avoid discussing the pregnant woman, Matt spotted a squat white jar on a shelf above Maureen's head. The rose decorated label said Mrs. Parker's Rosewater Ointment. "Is that any good?"

Maureen took down the jar, opened it, and sniffed. "Aye, and it smells heavenly, too. See for yourself."

She stuck it under his nose, and the scent of roses enveloped him.

"Emma's hands. . . ," he started, then stopped, embarrassed. "I'll take it."

Maureen cocked her head to one side and stared at him thoughtfully. Then she pulled a bolt of soft green cotton from the shelf, her golden eyebrows arched in question. "She wouldn't mind a new dress now and again either. This color was made for her, I'm thinking."

Emma loved pretty things. Though unlike the women in his past, she owned so few. Her hands needed tending, and there was no telling when she'd made herself a new dress.

He gave a short, self-conscious nod. "All right, then."

"Don't play coy with me, Mr. Tolivar. You're as transparent as glass." With a twinkle in her eyes, Maureen laid the fabric on the counter, tossing in matching thread and lace. "And it's delighted I am to see it."

While Matt grappled to understand her cryptic comment, a faint call came from the back of the store. "Maureen."

"Coming, Ma, in just a minute." Brow puckering, Maureen shook her red curls and spoke to Matt in an undertone. "Six months gone and she's puffy as one of Danny's toads and weak as water gravy."

The worrisome symptoms filtered through Matt's scientific mind. The woman needed a doctor's care, but it wouldn't be him. He couldn't risk the pain of watching another life slip out of his hands. Not now. Not ever.

His thoughts skittered to a stop when Maureen spoke and he realized he'd been frowning toward the curtained doorway.

"Don't you be fretting now, Mr. Tolivar. The good Lord will provide. With Emma petitioning Him for a doctor, I wouldn't be at all surprised to see one riding into town just any day." Hands and eyes busy with her figuring, she prattled on, unaware of Matt's building anxiety.

Sweat dampened his palms and his heart beat erratically. He needed to get away before he did something irrevocably foolish, like asking to examine the ailing Mrs. O'Dell. Concern for the pregnant woman choking him, Matt managed to gather his purchases, hand over Emma's letter, and make a courteous departure.

❦

"My goodness, you've bought a wagon load," Emma exclaimed, eyeing the bags of flour and meal, the rolls of wire, and buckets of nails. "I'm certain Mr. O'Dell didn't extend credit for all of this."

"It seems Mr. O'Dell is needing meat for his store, so I bartered a bull calf for this and more. He wants me to supply him all through the winter." If there had been any other place to easily sell the beef, Matt would never have bargained with the likes of Jimmy O'Dell. Theirs had been a grudging agreement, brought on by mutual need.

"Praise be to Jesus." Emma ran her hands over the bags, exploring the wagon like an excited child. When she came upon the plain brown package, Matt had a sudden longing to see her reaction. "Open it," he urged.

Eagerly, she released the twine and pulled the paper away. The pale green cloth lay on top.

"Oh, Matt." Her weathered hands caressed the cloth reverently. She lifted the material and held it against her. Maureen was right. The color captured the green flecks in her eyes and turned her hair the shade of ripe wheat.

"Would you look at this, Jesus?" Emma cried, holding the fabric skyward. Suddenly, she began to whirl, spinning, spinning until she became a gold and green blur in the summer sunshine. "Matthew, Matthew, Matthew," she chanted, "you're the kindest man on Earth."

She was a balm for his weary soul, and he laughed to know he could make her happy with such a small gift. Truly it was more blessed to give than to receive, especially when the recipient reacted like Emma.

Breathlessly, she spun to a halt, still clutching the fabric to her chest. Delight shone on her face. Seized by the need to keep it there, Matt said, "There's something else in that package, Mrs. Tolivar."

Back to the wagon she ran, exclaiming over the thread and lace until she came to the jar of Mrs. Parker's Rosewater Ointment. Expression puzzled, she lifted it, turning the bottle in her hands, reading the label, glancing at her mistreated hands.

Seeing her smile disappear, Matt wondered if he'd made a mistake. Was she embarrassed? Insulted? A flicker of anxiety passed over him, but it was short-lived.

Slowly, she uncapped the container, releasing the scent of roses. Eyes closed, she sniffed deeply, head tilted back. When at last she looked at him, tears shimmered above an angelic smile. "Never in my life have I owned anything so wonderful." Swallowing convulsively, she whispered, "Thank you," snatched up the green material, and fled into the house.

That night, long after he'd given up and gone to

bed, he heard her humming and murmuring to the rhythm of the sewing treadle. He fell asleep with a smile on his lips and the scent of roses in his nostrils.

He dreamed he heard her, far off, praying. "I love him, Jesus," she said. "Now, what shall I do about that? Him, who should have a fine lady for a wife, one he could be proud of and take to church on Sundays. And here he is stuck with the village outcast, a worthless orphan. A crazy woman. How can I make up to him for all he's done?"

Straining upward against the dark pull of sleep, Matt wanted to say, "You're the one who's good. You're the one who's given me back a reason to live."

But he didn't, of course. It was, after all, only a dream.

The scents of coffee, bacon, and biscuits drifted into Matt's consciousness, and he rose, chagrined that Emma had once again risen long before him. Darkness still covered the farm, though the rooster was singing his anthem. Bare feet thudding on the wooden plank floor, Matt washed and dressed, then stumbled into the kitchen.

"Don't you ever sleep?" he asked blearily, slouching into a chair.

Ever cheerful, she smiled and slid a coffee mug into his hands. "I'm far too excited to sleep."

Then he remembered the cloth and the perfumed ointment. A proud smile twitched at his whiskered face. "Did you sew all night?"

In answer, she left the room, returning momentarily with a green garment that she held up for his inspection. "What do you think?"

To his utter shock, the garment wasn't a dress as he'd expected. It was a carefully crafted man's shirt, as fine as any he'd ever owned.

"But the cloth was for you, for a dress," he protested.

"There's plenty left for that." Brown eyes danced with eagerness. "Do you like it?"

Fingering the soft cloth, Matt swallowed the lump in his throat. Would she never stop surprising him? Would she never stop thinking of everyone else first?

"Ah, Emma, Emma." He pulled her to him in what he thought was a hug of gratitude. In the next instance, he was kissing her. Her soft sweet mouth parted in surprise beneath his, and an emotion far stronger than gratitude hammered in Matt's chest. When he pulled back, stunned and breathless, a pair of luminous golden eyes measured him. She pressed trembling fingers to rose tinted cheeks, then did the unexpected once again.

"How would you like your eggs?" she whispered, then spun toward the stove, turning her back to him.

Matt blinked, baffled at her response, baffled at the desire to kiss her again, and baffled as to why she was talking of eggs when his insides were twisted in a knot. She cared for him. He was certain. Why had she rejected his kiss?

The answer struck him full in the heart. He hadn't been dreaming when he heard Emma say she loved him. The words had been real. Emma loved him, and she knew he had no love inside to give. Guilt gnawed at him. He'd wanted to heal her brokenness, but he'd only caused her more pain.

Chapter 5

E ven though the calendar said September, the prairie summer continued in full fury: hot and dry and unforgiving. Sweat bathed both people and livestock as an urgent need for rain pressed in.

The kiss was not mentioned again, though Matt could think of little else. Now that the blinders were off, he saw Emma's love in everything she did, and the burden of responsibility weighed heavily upon him.

Late in the afternoon, a cloud appeared from nowhere, dark and heavy with rain. As the shade passed over, Matt and Emma glanced up, then at each other.

"Wouldn't that be lovely?" Emma called from her back-bent position.

Before Matt could reply, the sky opened and the blessed cool water gushed over the land. Emma squealed and straightened.

"Rain. Wonderful rain."

As Matt watched, rain pouring off his hat, his wife began to twirl and spin, arms wide, face turned upward to the heavens.

"Dance, Matthew," she called, her voice full of joy

and laughter. When he only stood with a smile on his face, she ran to him, gathered his hands into her small, rough ones, stood on his boot tops, dipping and swaying. Matt was caught up in her spontaneous delight, her joy too infectious to ignore. To his utter amazement, he wanted to dance and laugh. Emma grabbed his hand and pulled him, captivated, through the mud puddles, stomping and splashing. She could find more happiness in a mud puddle than most people found in their entire lives.

Drenched to the skin, he pulled Emma close to him and looked into her eyes, the urge to kiss her again welling up inside him like an incoming tide. The rain tumbled from his hat onto her face, and she laughed all the more.

"If the people of Goodhope saw us now, they'd say you've gone as crazy as me," she declared, reaching up to swipe a smear of mud from Matt's face.

The cloudburst passed as quickly as it had come and a rainbow split the sky in two.

"Let's chase it, Matthew. And find that pot of gold."

"Ah, Emma. Emma, you're a delight. What makes you the way you are? A woman grown who dances in the rain and lays in the grass at night watching falling stars."

Her laugher ceased and a gentle, wistful sweetness settled over her features. "I thought you knew by now, Matthew."

He could see she was serious, so he waited, holding

her close, feeling the combined heat and damp trans-
ferring from her body to his, smelling the scent of fresh
rain against her skin.

She lay a hand against Matt's cheek and tilted her
head to one side, eyes glowing.

"When I was a child in the orphanage, there was no
frivolity, no laughter. By the time Jeremiah took me in
and taught me of Jesus, all the joy in me was gone. And
then I had Lily. She could chase a butterfly for hours,
clapping her tiny hands, falling, and getting up with a
smile on her face." Emma's voice grew soft with longing. "Oh, Matt, she was my joy. So now, I dance and
laugh and sing and do all those foolish things for Lily."
Tears of remembrance filled the wide amber eyes. "I
dance in the rain for Lily, because she never will."

With his own heart thudding from the poignant
beauty of her admission, he finally recognized the truth.
He'd come here, thinking he was the healer, the man
who could help the poor, crazy widow. But it hadn't been
that way at all. It was he who had been healed by
Emma's simple faith and her magnificent strength. She
had given him back his joy. The truth had been bung-
ing at him for weeks, but now he had to tell her.

"I love you, Emma." Feeling her stiffen with shock,
he held her all the tighter, kissing away a fat drop of
rain clinging to her eyelashes.

"Do you hear me? I love you, Emma," he shouted,
laughing anew at the shock on her face that matched
the surprise in his heart. "Say you feel the same. I know
you do."

And indeed she did. In Emma-like fashion she threw her arms around his neck and kissed him just as the rain began again. Neither of them noticed.

❧

Sunday morning after chores and breakfast, Matthew followed Emma around the cabin, watching her, stealing an occasional kiss, exchanging secret smiles. He was a happy man. Happier than he ever thought possible, and he wanted to be certain Emma was happy too.

"I'm taking you to church this morning," he declared.

Her hands stilled on the towel she was folding. "Oh, Matthew, I don't think so. But if you want to go. . ."

"You once told me how much you enjoyed worshipping with other believers and how much you missed it after Jeremiah died. I think it's time we went together as man and wife."

"But the people. . ." Her throat convulsed, trepidation in her voice.

"I've made a few friends, Emma, and most of the folks are decent. Jimmy O'Dell's the main one who keeps the trouble stirred up. The others just follow along."

"I don't want to upset anyone."

"Once people see you, get to know you again, they'll realize their mistake." Seeing her misgivings, he pleaded, "Please, Emma. If we're going to live and prosper here, we have to find a way to get along with these folks. Both of us—not just me. You're so brave about everything else. Why won't you face this town and make them stop this nonsense?"

"I don't know. . ." She gnawed at her lower lip, clearly weakening.

Matt knelt in front of her, grasping her hand. "What if we have a child together? Wouldn't you want him to be accepted?"

Wonderment lit her face at the possibility, and she capitulated. Drawing in a deep breath, she said, "I'll wear my new green dress."

A dozen or so worshipers had already gathered by the time Matt and Emma arrived wearing their matching green. Tipping his hat repeatedly, Matt wove his bride into the church, nodding and smiling, receiving cold looks in return. Beneath his guiding hand, Emma trembled, though she smiled serenely at all she passed.

Matt's pulse thundered. He prayed desperately that he hadn't made a mistake in bringing her here. What else could he do? Somehow he had to give her back her dignity. Searching the gathering for Maureen or Lucas Winchester, he found instead Jimmy O'Dell, bearing down on them, his face livid.

"What is that daughter of the devil doing in the house of God?" He shouted so loud, every head in the building turned to stare. Except for a few murmurs of agreement, the place fell quiet.

"I've told you repeatedly, O'Dell, Emma is mentally sound. She has as much right to attend church as you do."

"Mentally sound, you say?" Jimmy whirled toward the crowd. "You hear that, folks? This stranger comes waltzing into town and tries to tell us our business. Well, I think we got something to say about that, don't you?"

His statement was followed with rumbles of assent. "Yeah. Sure do. You tell 'em, Jimmy."

"Too many people have seen her do crazy things."

"I say she's moonstruck. Barney Adams saw her dancing in a full moon, singing and waving her arms. The next week his good cow died."

Emma stood in the middle, eyes wide, clinging to Matthew's hand. A bearded man in overalls parted the tightening circle.

"She's a witch, if ye ask me." He pointed a finger at Emma. "Seen her myself sneaking around Floyd Anderson's place in the middle of the night just about the time he got hurt. I figure she hexed him."

Matt seethed inside, wanting to tell the real reason for Emma's surreptitious visits to the Anderson place. But when he looked to her for permission, she shook her head in denial. Filled with both frustration and admiration, Matt kept quiet.

The fine churchgoers didn't.

"Mr. Tolivar, you seem to be a good man, hardworking. I've seen the things you're doing to that farm, and I admire you. Your dealings here in town are honest, and we've come to respect you. But when it comes to the widow, you seem blinded, unable to accept that the woman is unbalanced."

"She's evil, all right." This from a squat man with tobacco stained teeth. "I was there when she chased the undertaker and Parson Jeffers off her place, screaming like a banshee."

"She claimed Jesus came to see her."

"What's wrong with you people?" Matt cried. "Emma was sick with grief then. She'd been locked up in that cabin with her dead husband and child without help. Can't you have a little compassion?"

Some of the women softened and made murmurs of understanding. "Losing a child's a hard thing. Any of us would be sick with grief."

"Yes, and you have other children, other family to comfort you. Emma had no one, nothing left at all."

The church was quiet for a moment, and Matt thought that, perhaps, he'd convinced them. Surely the folks could see that Emma was no threat to anyone. But Jimmy O'Dell wasn't finished. "I want her out of here before my wife arrives," he cried, shaking his fist at Matt. "She'll mark my unborn child." He turned to the shocked crowd. "And if she does, the fault will belong to all of you for letting such as her live in this town."

Barely controlling his temper, Matt shoved the fist aside. "You'll mark it yourself with your own ignorance."

Wrapping Emma in his protective embrace, Matt shouldered his way out of the church and into the wagon. Fury, hot and dangerous, emanated from every pore as he slapped the horses into motion, leaving the good citizens of Goodhope in his dust.

"Matthew, please don't be so angry. It's all right. Truly it is." Voice husky with emotion, she lay a hand on his stiff forearm. Her obvious pain infuriated him even more.

"You'll never convince me of that, Emma. Someday they'll reap what they've sown, and I, for one, will be glad." As town disappeared behind them, he slowed the team to a walk. Tall, dry buffalo grass waved in the fields beside the road, and yellow sunflowers nodded their giant heads. For once Emma did not exclaim about their beauty. They rode in silence most of the way home, hurt pulsating from her, remorse filling him. The big red barn came into sight, then the chimney, before Emma spoke again.

"What if they're right?" She stared off into the wheat fields, eyes unseeing. A frown creased her brow. "What if there is something basically bad about me?"

"Don't be foolish."

She turned to him, tears glistening on her lashes, and the sight tormented him. Why had he made her go? He'd vowed to protect her, and instead he'd escorted her into the lions' den to be devoured.

"I know nothing about my mother or father, Matthew," she continued, sadly. "Perhaps I was born in an insane asylum or to a streetwalker."

"None of that has anything to do with who you are."

Tears trickled down her face as her voice rose in sorrow. "Doesn't it? It's all in the blood, they say. Maybe mine is just bad." A sob broke from her throat. "Bad blood. That's what they call it."

"Emma, no." He'd never seen her like this—weeping, heartbroken. He chastised himself anew for subjecting her to such cruel treatment. Pulling the team to an abrupt stop beside the barn, he turned to her. But before he could draw her sobbing body into his arms, she leaped from the wagon. Chickens squawked in protest as she whipped past, scattering them with her new green skirt as she rushed into the barn. Heart heavy, Matt released the horses and followed after her. He met Emma hobbling out of the barn door, her new skirt drenched in blood.

"Emma!" He rushed to her side. "What happened?"

Her face pale and tear stained, she struggled to regain her composure, but the droplets of moisture on her lip and forehead reflected her intense suffering. "The scythe. I fell."

"Let me see." Behind her thigh, a deep gash bled profusely. "Hold your hand over it. Press hard."

"I've ruined my new dress," she groaned.

"I'll buy you another." Matt scooped her into his arms and charged toward the house, his heart thudding painfully against his ribs. What would he do? How should he handle this? There were no other doctors anywhere around, and Emma needed medical care.

He started for the bedroom.

"Not on the bed. I'll ruin the quilt. The floor is fine."

Relenting, he laid her on the floor in the kitchen. "Now, let's look at this better." Pushing away the cloth, he examined the wound. "It needs stitches."

She groaned, then set her face in determination. "Many's the time I've stitched a horse or a cow. Once I even stitched up Jeremiah. This is no different. I can do it. Boil a thread and a needle."

Matt did her bidding, all the while fighting an inward battle. His mind fought him, but his heart dictated what must be done. When the supplies were ready, Emma sat up, twisting toward the lacerated skin.

With a resigned sigh, Matt took the needle and thread from her fingers. "You can't reach back here. I'll do it."

Tear-darkened lashes lifted toward him. "Can you sew?"

"Yes," he said tersely. "Now lie down on your belly and let's get this over with."

Bits of hay clung to the torn edges of skin, and he frowned at them, concerned about infection. After a thorough washing with soap and water, he took up the needle, working quickly, efficiently, aware that every needle prick brought her pain. Though she never complained, halfway through the procedure, she twisted her head around and watched him. Six years without practice fell away as he neatly pulled the tissues together and sealed them in a long straight line. His hands remembered what his mind had tried to forget.

"That should do it," Matt said as he clipped the last thread and wiped alcohol across the wound. At her sharp intake of breath, he grimaced, grabbed his hat, and fanned at the row of stitches. "Sorry. We don't want that to get infected."

"It's all right." Not waiting for a bandage, she rolled over and sat up, pulling one of his hands into hers. "Where did you learn to sew like that?"

When he remained silent, she turned his hand over and stroked the fingers. "These aren't a farmer's hands."

"They are now." He pulled away.

Clear, amber eyes demanded the truth. "But they haven't always been."

"No." Avoiding her gaze, he began gathering the bloodied supplies, tossing them into the washbasin.

"You're a doctor," she said simply, guessing the truth in her guileless way. "A doctor."

Apprehension flickered through him. He wasn't a doctor. Not anymore. "That's all in the past now."

"If that were true, you wouldn't still be trying to hide the facts. Did something happen? Did you dislike the work?"

Turning his back, he carried the basin to the table and stood staring at the cabin wall, remembering.

"I loved it. And I was good. So good and so confident that I thought I could fix anything and anyone." He pulled one hand wearily down his face. "I was wrong. I couldn't save the two people who mattered most to me in the entire world. My wife and baby."

She wasn't shocked, as he'd expected her to be, just full of compassion and understanding. "And you feel guilty."

"Yes."

"So you've punished yourself by leaving the profession you love. By hiding from God's call on your life."

"No!" But hadn't he? He shrugged. "Perhaps."

"Then it's time to stop, to lay down your guilt. Your skills are needed, desperately needed, right here in this town."

Even if he could lose the guilt and fear that plagued him, he'd never considered practicing medicine in

Goodhope. He faced her, incredulous.

"How can you even suggest that I help anyone in that town? After the way they've treated you, they all deserve to suffer."

Emma started awkwardly to her feet, shaking her head. Rushing to assist her, Matt pulled her upright.

"When Jesus came," she said, holding Matt's hand against her heart, "everyone rejected him. He had reason to hate them, to punish them. Yet, He loved them so much—even those who crucified Him—that He prayed for them as He died."

Gripping her shoulders, Matt couldn't decide whether to shake her or hold her. "But they hurt you."

"Yes, they did. But I have you, and I have Jesus. That's all I need to be happy." Arms wrapped around his waist, Emma pressed her head against his heart. "I want you to be happy, too, Matthew. I don't think you ever will be until you can forgive yourself and resume your true life's work."

Dread rose in him like a sickness. He couldn't go back. Another failure would be the end of him.

Matt clasped Emma tightly against him, holding fast to the strength she offered. "I'm a farmer now, Emma. That's enough for me."

But the words rang false even to his own ears.

Chapter 6

A flock of geese winging its way southward caught Matt's attention as he labored in the field north of the house. He tossed a pile of fresh-cut hay into the wagon bed, then leaned on the pitchfork, gazing upward. A year ago, he wouldn't have cared about a flock of birds, but now he could enjoy the sight, thanks to Emma. The geese were the very kind of thing she loved. He thought to go and tell her about them, but before he could, the cabin door burst open and Emma rushed out.

"Did you see them, Matthew?" she called, pointing to the heavens. "They're waving at us."

Shading her eyes against the blue-gray glare, Emma hopped up and down, waving back at the honking geese.

With a smile, Matt watched Emma watching the geese. His heart filled with gratitude for this special woman God had sent his way. Her leg had healed well, he thought with relief, in spite of his concerns over infection. That was due in part, he knew, to the care he administered. He'd cleaned and dressed it three times a day, finding a measure of satisfaction in the familiar task.

Emma said little else about his abandoned profession, but she watched him with a quiet compassion that was more bothersome than nagging would have been. On the day the stitches came out, she lifted his palms, kissed each one, and said, "God has blessed you with a special gift, Matthew. Healing hands."

He'd not known how to reply. She'd asked for so little. And yet, he couldn't give her this one thing she longed for.

"Do you love me, Matthew?" she'd gone on, taking his face in her rough little hands.

"You know I do," he replied almost desperately.

"Yes, you do. But it isn't enough. You'll never be truly happy until you give in to God's calling on your life."

He'd crushed her to him, holding her against his throbbing heart, knowing she was right. The heaviness lay on him even now as the geese disappeared overhead. Emma turned his way, blew him a kiss, and started back to the house.

"Someone's coming," he called, catching sight of a copper-colored head bobbing through the south fields.

"Maureen!" Emma's bare feet churned the ground as she flew toward her friend.

Though her visits were infrequent, Maureen came when she could, bringing bits of town news but, most of all, giving Emma her friendship. While they talked and prayed, their fingers would fly: braiding rugs, piecing a quilt, peeling apples. Matthew liked Maureen as much as he disliked her father.

On his occasional trips to town, Matt was forced to

patronize the general store, though he dreaded each encounter. Dreaded the arguments with Jimmy. Dreaded the thought of encountering the pregnant Mrs. O'Dell. Dreaded the longing he felt to practice medicine.

The rest of the town had warmed a bit toward him, though few ever mentioned Emma and none invited the Tolivars to social functions. He knew the other farmers helped one another during harvest. There would be husking bees and threshing parties—none of which the Tolivars would attend. He'd even had a talk with the parson, quite by accident, one day outside the blacksmith shop. Parson Jeffers had apologized for the incident at the church, saying, "The Lord would be displeased if we turn away any who seek Him, Mr. Tolivar. You and your wife are welcome anytime."

Though his anger toward the austere parson had lessened, Matt had no intention of subjecting Emma to another scene like the last.

Matt resumed the task of filling the wagon with hay, glad that the constant toil kept him from thinking too much. Another fork or two, and he'd head to the barn to unload, then start the process all over again. In the distance, beyond the acres and acres of corn and grass yet to be harvested, a spiral of dust rose. Curious, Matt paused in his work again. Two guests in one day?

A horse pounded into the yard, its rider leaping from the saddle and running toward the house.

"Maureen! Maureen! I know you're in there." The panic-stricken voice of one of the O'Dell boys carried all the way out to Matt's hay field.

Maureen came rushing out the door. After a muffled exchange of words that Matt couldn't understand, she mounted the horse behind her brother and the pair raced away, leaving Emma alone in the front yard.

Something had happened. Something bad. Matt's gut knotted with dread. Was there a sickness? An accident? Or was it the pregnant mother?

He hadn't long to wait before the questions were answered. Emma hastened toward him, hair and skirts flying out behind her. Dropping the pitchfork, he rushed to meet her.

"What is it?"

Breathless, her chest rising and falling rapidly, Emma pressed a hand to her heart. The anxiety in Matt's stomach was reflected in her face.

"It's Kathryn O'Dell. Her baby is coming now."

"Babies are born all the time." He wanted to turn away, to run back to Texas or Colorado, anywhere but here with this oppressive sense of duty clawing at him.

"Matthew, please." Emma gripped his arm. "You don't understand. It's too early, and Mrs. O'Dell is so terribly weak."

"No, Emma." Shaking his head, he backed away, knowing what she wanted. "Don't ask this of me."

"I know you, Matthew. You're a good, good man who could never live with himself if something happens to her and you didn't even try."

"How can you say that?" he cried, despairing of making her understand. "My own wife and baby are dead because of my incompetence. Don't you think I tried then? But I couldn't save them. Why do you think this time will be any different?"

"Please. Please, Matthew." Emma slid to her knees before him, the hay stubble crackling under her weight. "I beg of you. Maureen is the only friend I have."

In a posture of pure supplication she knelt before him, ripping his heart in two.

"Stop it, Emma. Get up." He gripped her narrow shoulders, tugging, but she only bowed deeper into the hay. When she began to pray, Matthew almost collapsed beside her.

"Heavenly Father, You know everything. You know why Matthew's wife and baby died. You know how he's suffered over their loss. And You know how desperately Kathryn needs him right now. Please, dear Lord, take the scales from his eyes. Let him recognize the calling on his life to minister to the sick. Give him the strength and courage to fight through this fear of failure and come out victorious. I love him, Jesus. I want him to be happy, to have the peace he lost when Martha died. It means so much to him, and he's fought it for so long. Please, Lord, Open his eyes." And she began to weep.

The gaping wound inside Matthew began to bleed afresh. He'd thought he could lose himself here on the farm with Emma and never have to think of medicine again. Instead, it haunted him, the only unresolved need in his life.

"Emma, I'll go." Bending, Matthew lifted her trembling body and held her close, murmuring against her hair. "If it means that much to you, I'll go. If you'll go with me."

Stiffening, she drew back, regarding him with anxious eyes. Though for different reasons, she was every bit as afraid as he.

"I need you, Emma. I can't do it alone."

Drawing in a deep, shuddering breath, she lifted her chin, aiming it toward Goodhope. "All right, then. I'll pray. You drive."

Drying her eyes, she clambered aboard the loaded hay wagon.

❦

Stomach churning, pulse pounding, Matthew hammered on the back door of Jimmy O'Dell's general store, the portion of the building where the family resided. Emma stood beside him, her face pale, gripping the medical bag he'd dug from its hiding place in the barn.

"What are you doing here?" The disheveled Irishman opened the door. "The store is closed for the day."

"I'm a doctor, Mr. O'Dell. I've come to help your wife."

"A doctor, you say?" His astonished blue gaze went from Matt to the bag in Emma's hands.

"Yes. A doctor. I understand your wife is having the baby."

A muffled cry from the room's interior turned O'Dell around. "Aye. Aye. She's trying." In agitation, he ran a hand over his balding head. " 'Tis a bad time of it she's having, too. Worst I've seen."

"Are you going to let me help her or keep us standing out here while she suffers?"

"You're really a doctor, then?" O'Dell asked, his expression dubious.

"I said I was." Annoyance rapidly replaced Matt's fear. If O'Dell didn't let him in soon, he'd turn around and go home, his conscience clear that he'd tried.

"Da, what's going on?" Maureen's worried face appeared behind her father. "Emma! Matt! Whatever are you doing?"

"Claims he's a doctor. Wants to see your ma."

"For pity's sake, Da. He's the answer to our prayers. Let him in."

"It's little choice I have, but he comes alone. Not with her. I'll not have that crazy woman in my house. We've trouble enough as it is."

Matt's patience snapped. With teeth gritted he leaned toward the storekeeper. "You self-righteous man. After all you've done to hurt her, it was Emma who convinced me to come. Now, you can either let us both in, or we'll get back in that wagon and leave you to manage on your own."

"Da, we've prayed and prayed for a doctor, and now that he's here, you're wanting to turn him out? When Ma is needing his help so badly?" Maureen elbowed around her father and grabbed Emma's hand, pulling her inside. Matt followed, feeling the anger of Jimmy O'Dell as he brushed passed.

"If anything happens to Kathryn and me babe, I'll have your hide, Matthew Tolivar. And that loony wife of yours will be locked away like she should have been long ago." His venomous tirade was cut short by a cry from the bedroom. In a rush of concern, Matt and Emma left Jimmy to fume and hurried into the bedroom where an older version of Maureen writhed on the bed.

Sweat broke out on Matthew's palms as the image of Martha flashed through his mind. If he failed again, if Kathryn died, he didn't know if he could go on.

Emma, feeling his tension, lay a hand on his. "Guide him, Jesus. Give him wisdom."

The simple prayer lifted him. He wasn't in this alone.

"Mrs. O'Dell," he said, going to her side. "My name is Matthew Tolivar. I'm a doctor. I'm going to help you deliver this baby." He turned to his two assistants. "We'll need boiled string and scissors, lots of towels or rags, and some warmed blankets for the baby."

" 'Tis ready and waiting whenever you say, Doctor."

The title sounded good, stoking his courage. He was a doctor, a trained physician with the skill to do this. Emma and Maureen bustled around the room, doing his bidding, praying out loud, while he examined the patient. To his horror, something was amiss. The baby was there, ready to be born, but even a strong contraction didn't push the infant forward. The mother worried him, too. Except for an occasional moan or the sudden arch of her body, Kathryn was listless. Her eyes were closed, her face pale and moist.

"She's give out, Doctor. I don't know how she'll manage the strength to finish."

Matt rummaged in the worn medical bag. It had been so long since he'd opened it, but the familiar tools were all inside. Struggling not to think of the last time he'd used them, he handed a pair of forceps to Maureen. "I'll try not to use these, but I want them boiled just in case."

Not every physician agreed that cleanliness was important, but Matt subscribed to Dr. Lister's notion that invisible microbes spread infection. Though he had no carbolic for disinfectant, the boiling water would help. He just wished he had some ether. Taking a baby with forceps was a difficult procedure, but under the circumstances, he was afraid it might be the only choice he'd have. Mrs. O'Dell had given up the battle and the baby would suffer damage in the birth canal if he waited too long.

Taking out his stethoscope he listened to Kathryn's chest.

"Her heart is strong," he said with relief. "If she just has the strength to help us a few more times. . ."

Quietly, Emma eased to the bedside and grasped Kathryn's pale, puffy hand. "Kathryn, dear, do you remember how you helped me when Lily was born?"

Matt's head whipped around in surprise. She'd never told him that.

Emma's sweet, gentle voice continued, "I couldn't have done it without you. Now I've come to return the favor. You're almost there, my friend. Just a little more and you can hold your sweet, precious babe in your arms."

The pale eyelids fluttered upward.

"That's right. We're going to do it together. Maureen

and I will lift your shoulders and Dr. Tolivar will do the rest."

With a flicker of resolve, Kathryn nodded slightly. As the contraction began, Matt reexamined his patient, ready to forcibly deliver the child. What he felt sent a jolt of panic shooting through him.

"Stop!" he cried. "Don't push." Tension knotted his neck and shoulders. His breath grew short and perspiration bathed his face.

The cord was wrapped, not once, but twice around the baby's neck. Any further pushing would strangle the child to death. He remembered this terror all too well. Only extremely skilled hands and the grace of God could save the O'Dell baby. Matt squeezed his eyes shut for a moment.

Please, Jesus, help me to help her.

When he opened his eyes, a strange sense of calm came over him. Moving quickly and efficiently, he worked the tightly wound cord over the slippery little head with one hand while holding back the force of nature with the other. It was difficult, tedious work and time was against them.

The string of tension in the room bound them all, so that when, at last, the noose was removed, a collective sigh of relief issued from Emma and Maureen. Matt knew better than to relax. At the next contraction, the tiny infant slid into the world, blue and flaccid.

"Oh, no," Maureen cried, hands grasping for Emma.

"Breath, baby girl." Matt ran a finger inside the lax mouth, then placed his own lips over the child's and blew gently. The baby gave a shudder, then sucked in a chest full of air. Matt swatted her bottom twice and received a mewling cry in return. The wonder of it brought tears to his eyes.

"Thank you, Jesus," Emma whispered. Matthew's heart echoed the sentiment. He rubbed the baby's back, checking her over, waiting until the even breathing and pink hues of health assured him that she was all right. Then, he wrapped her in a warmed blanket and handed her to Maureen.

"She's a little thing," he said as he turned back to the exhausted mother. "We'll have to watch her close, keep her good and warm, but I think she'll make it."

"I'll go and tell Da. He's worried sick."

During Maureen's absence, Matt and Emma cared for their patient and were immensely relieved to know that she'd weathered the delivery with no further ill effects. Rest and good food would soon have her well again. Matthew knew a sense of accomplishment he hadn't felt in years.

"I'll be back to check on you first thing tomorrow," Matt promised as he carefully placed the tools of his trade back inside the black bag. "You stay in that bed and let the rest of the family look after you for a while."

"Aye, she'll do that. I'll see to it meself." Jimmy came into the bedroom, cradling the tiny bundle in his arms. He shifted nervously from one foot to the other. "I'm a proud man, Tolivar. Apologies don't come easy. But you've got one coming, so I'm giving it to you. We needed you here today, and you came, knowing I'd fight you tooth and toenail. Still, you came. I'm grateful."

"You can thank Emma for that," Matt said stiffly, not ready to forgive the man who'd caused his wife so much grief.

"Then, I do." He turned to Emma, expression sheepish. "Maureen told me how you helped the missus. Thank you."

"I'm the one who's grateful, Mr. O'Dell," she said in her sweetest voice. "Seeing that little girl of yours come into the world was a special privilege."

Jimmy cleared his throat. When he spoke again, his voice was gruff. "If you folks want to come to church on Sunday, I'll stand up for you."

Matthew watched the change come over Emma's face. Unlike Matt, she bore her detractors no animosity, no bitterness, just a Christ-like love he still didn't understand. But after today, he wanted to learn.

❦

By the time Emma and Matt arrived at church on Sunday morning, the service was about to begin. As they slipped quietly into a back pew, heads turned to stare. Tensing, ready to take Emma and escape before any trouble began, Matt glared back at the people of Goodhope. A few tentative smiles and a head bob here and there told him that, today, the crowd was friendly. He relaxed, squeezing Emma's cold hand. No one was going to hurt her anymore.

As the organist began to play, the O'Dell family filed in and, seeing the Tolivars, slid onto the bench beside them.

"How's your mother?" Emma whispered.

"Getting stronger. The baby, too." Maureen whispered in return.

Matt leaned forward. "We'll come by after church."

Maureen smiled and nodded as they all quieted, turning their attention to the service. The song master led them in hymns that seemed especially sweet to Matt that morning. His prayers seemed to go straight up to heaven, so thrilled was he to worship freely with other Christians and the woman he loved.

When Pastor Jeffers took the pulpit, his sermon, not surprisingly, was on forgiveness. "Now, you folks all know what I'm talking about today," he said toward the end. "We all need forgiveness from the Lord and, at times, from each other. Things have happened this week to wake us up to the fact that we've done wrong by a young couple in our community."

A few dozen pairs of eyes swiveled toward the back pew. Emma sat with head down, an almost holy smile on her lips.

"For months," the reverend went on, "we've prayed for a doctor. Finally, the Lord sees fit to send us one, and we treat his wife so badly, he's not even willing to tell us who he is. We've been stiff-necked, passing judgment on Emma, when who better to judge her mental state than a doctor who spends every day with her? If any of you still have doubts, I believe Floyd Anderson has a word or two to say about it."

Near the front, a man with a noticeable limp stood and hobbled forward. "I wasn't here the last time the

Tolivars came to church, or I'd a-told this then." He scratched at his beard and went on. "All of you know the hard time me and the wife had after I busted my leg. I'm a proud man, don't like to ask for help, but if it hadn't been for Emma Tolivar, I reckon we would've starved. All them times someone saw her sneaking over to my house, she was bringing groceries. She didn't want to cause me no embarrassment. That woman's heart is gold, I tell you. She's a pure saint if ever there was one."

With an expression that dared anyone to argue, Floyd clumped back to his pew. Matt was hard-pressed not to smile at the man's feisty attitude even while he was grateful for what was said. Now, he knew for certain where Emma went on her early morning walks. No doubt, the Andersons weren't the only recipients of her generosity.

"I got something to say myself, Parson." Jimmy O'Dell rose. "Most of you have already heard about my wife and baby, and how the doctor here and his little wife saved their lives. If it wasn't for them, I'd be in mourning. That's all I got to say." With a self-conscious swipe at his nose, he sat down.

Emma's eyes shone suspiciously as she listened to the total change of public sentiment. More powerful than any medicine, acceptance was a healing balm.

"Dr. Tolivar, this town needs a man of your skills." Parson Jeffers's boots thudded softly on the wooden floor as he came to stand beside Emma and Matt. Every person in the building either stood or turned to watch.

"Could the two of you find it in your hearts to forgive us? And, sir, would you consent to be our doctor?"

Pulse pounding, Matt rose to his feet, pulling Emma up beside him. "My wife is the most forgiving person I know. She's never borne you any resentment for the way she was treated. I, on the other hand, have had a bit more difficulty." He gazed fondly at his wife. "Emma here tells me I'll never be content until I let the past go and get back to medicine. Emma's a wise woman." He extended a hand to the preacher. "I'd be proud to serve as Goodhope's physician."

Rousing applause echoed through the room until the organist struck a jarring chord, then stood and said, "Thank the good Lord for that. I don't know what we'd do with all the food we cooked if you refused us. You young folks didn't even have a proper shivaree when you was wed, so we figured we'd have us a town celebration in your honor and cover the whole shebang, new doctor, new married couple, and the O'Dell's new baby all in one whack."

The congregation laughed and began to rise, filing slowly out onto the lawn where makeshift tables were set up beneath the trees. As they followed, talking with the well-wishers, the joy on Emma's face was reflected in Matthew's heart. This was what he'd been looking for, what he'd longed for, and the crazy widow of Goodhope had been the answer to his prayers.

Filled with the kind of happiness he'd never thought possible, Matt took Emma's hand and started across the grass. Halfway to the shade trees, right in view of the whole town, Emma stopped. "Wait."

She pulled off her shoes, then whirled her husband in a circle, laughing. Matt smiled at his beautiful barefoot wife.

"You think I'm crazy, don't you?" she teased.

"That's not what I think at all."

"What then?"

"I was thinking of the day I came here, bound by my own guilty past, unable to laugh, a lost and wounded man. And you showed me a better way."

Relishing the brand of freedom she'd taught him, Matt removed his own boots and tossed them high into the air with a exultant shout. A moment of stunned silence settled over the churchyard.

"Well, what are you looking at? Ain't you all got feet?" Jimmy O'Dell plunked himself down on the ground and yanked off his boots so fast the socks came with them. With a cry of delight, Maureen mirrored her father, kicking her shoes into the tree overhead.

The startled looks turned to chuckles. Then, one by one, the people of Goodhope followed suit, discarding boots and slippers, until the whole town was barefoot, and laughing, and dancing. . .and crazy with the joy of the Lord.

LINDA GOODNIGHT

Linda and her husband, Gene, live on a farm in the beautiful rolling hills of southern Oklahoma. Her hobbies include music, reading, spending hours in the woods and fields, and anything that involves her six young adult children. Following a serious illness which she considers a spiritual wake-up call, Linda left her dual career as a teacher and nurse. She is now in her fifteenth year as an elementary schoolteacher. Though she's published many magazines stories and won awards for her writing, *The Barefoot Bride* is her first published novella. Readers can contact Linda at gnight@brightok.net

A Homesteader
A Bride
and
A Baby

by JoAnn A. Grote

Dedicated to my grandniece and grandnephew,
Alexis Olsen
and
Brett Olsen
who are descended from Minnesota pioneers

Chapter 1

Minnesota prairie, 1878

I didn't even have a chance to say good-bye."

The prairie wind snatched away the whispered words as soon as they left Lorette Taber's lips. The ever-present breeze swept through the tall prairie grasses that surrounded the four fresh graves, as though asking, "Why are their deaths more important than those of the thousands of other creatures I've seen die in this land?"

The wind whipped waving strands of prairie grass around the simple wooden crosses that stood at the heads of the graves. *Already reclaiming Bess and Tom and swallowing up their dreams for this place,* Lorette thought.

The earthy smell of freshly turned graves and wild grasses, the rough untamed land beneath her feet, the forlorn whistle of unceasing wind, all joined in concert to punctuate nature's power and man's helplessness in attempting to conquer these lands.

Viney stems of tiny pale pink wild roses were

wrapped about each cross. The meaning of their presence came through the fog of Lorette's loss and pain. Someone else missed her sister and family.

The child in her arms stirred, rubbing his eyes against the shoulder of her once-crisp blue traveling suit. He uttered tentative cries, pausing briefly between each, waiting to see whether the comforting presence of the parents for whom he longed would be given before he began crying in earnest.

Lorette's heart crimped. She rubbed one hand lightly over the nine-month-old baby's back, pressed her cheek gently against his soft, short baby hair, and murmured, "Poor Samuel. Your mommy and daddy still love you. They'll always love you. You'll never be alone, I promise. I'll always be with you."

Her eyes blurred. Could Samuel comprehend that he'd never see his parents and older brother and sister in this world again? Of course he was too young to understand their deaths in terms of logic and words, but did his infant spirit sense his loss in some mysterious way known only to God? Over the last twenty-four hours, had he felt abandoned by the four people who had cared for him all of his short life?

"Miss Taber?"

At the sound of a man's deep voice, she swung around, pulling Samuel protectively closer. She didn't answer, only stared at the blond man whose steady gray gaze met hers.

The wind didn't blow away the powerful odor of dirt, sweat, and kerosene emanating from him. He wore the flour sack shirt and heavy denim trousers of a farmer. A wide soft-brimmed hat, a sweat ring about the crown, hung from one hand.

"I'm Chase Lankford, your sister's neighbor. I helped out on their farm some."

A bit of tension left her muscles at his gentlemanly manner and the knowledge of his name. "Bess mentioned you in her letters. She said you were a good friend to her and her husband."

He nodded once, briskly. "Yes, Miss. They were good people. I'm sorry for your loss."

Samuel pushed himself away from Lorette with his tiny fists, then with pudgy arms outstretched leaned toward Chase. "Uh. Uh."

His sudden, unexpected movement threw Lorette out of balance. She leaned with him, attempting to adjust her hold.

Chase grabbed him. "Careful there, big boy."

Lorette caught her breath as she watched him swing the baby to his side. She started to reach for Samuel, hesitated, then let her hands drop to her sides. Chase looked comfortable with the child, she realized, as though he'd held Samuel many times.

Watching them, Lorette pushed from her blue eyes a strand of black hair, which the wind had tugged from the thick figure eight at the back of her head. She thought it a wonder the wind hadn't blown off her dainty traveling hat.

Chase lifted Samuel until their eyes were on the same level and grinned. Samuel grinned back. Giggling, he touched his round little fingers to Chase's unshaven cheeks.

Lorette smiled. Obviously Samuel and Chase were friends, the boy happy with someone he knew. Her heart ached with the thought that Chase might be the only person left whom Samuel truly knew.

She turned back to the graves, blinking away tears. "It's so hard to believe they are gone. I got off the train expecting them to meet me. Instead I was met by a woman I didn't know who told me they were dead and handed over Samuel." She spoke painfully around the lump that had formed in her throat. "Diphtheria, she said."

Lorette was aware he stepped up beside her, that he swallowed as though he had a lump in his own throat. "Yes, diphtheria."

"It was so sudden. How could it happen so fast?"

"At first they thought they only had sore throats. When Bess and Tom realized that their sickness was more serious, Tom went after the doctor. Doc was miles out in the country on the other side of town on a call. By the time Tom found him, Tom was so weak himself from the diphtheria that Doc insisted he stay where he was while Doc came here. He was too late. Aaron and Liza, Bess and Tom's oldest children, were already dead. Bess died within hours. Tom never made it home again. He died at the farmhouse where he found Doc."

"Samuel never took the disease?"

"Hasn't shown any signs of it. Doc thinks the others

caught it through contaminated milk, and Sam wouldn't have had any, him being. . ." Chase's tan took on a dusky tint.

Him being still at his mother's breast, Lorette completed silently, feeling her own cheeks heat.

"Bess had her hands full taking care of herself and the sick children," Chase continued, "so Kari Bresven offered to care for Sam until they were better."

"She was the one who met me at the railway station."

"Yes."

"Why couldn't the funeral have waited until I arrived? They only died yesterday."

"The bodies had to be buried right away to keep others from getting sick."

"I didn't even get to say good-bye." Her voice broke. Sobs welled up inside her, forcing their way through her chest and throat. She pressed a hand to her mouth, desperate to hold back what she feared would be a flood. A shaky gasp escaped.

A curious frown drew Samuel's blond eyebrows together. The fingers that had been playing with the top button of Chase's shirt stopped, and Samuel stared at her. She turned away, not wanting the boy to see her break down. "P—please, may I have a few minutes alone?" The strangled sobs mixed with her words, and she wasn't sure Chase could understand her.

She was relieved when he said, "Sure. Sam and I will be waiting in the yard."

Soft swishing sounds told her Chase was walking away through the tall grass. Lorette sank to the ground beside the black dirt covering her sister's grave. "Oooh, Bess!" Realization of her loss cramped her stomach. She wrapped her arms about her middle, bent into the pain, and let her sobs flow onto the prairie winds.

❦

Lorette hesitated at the yard's edge and surveyed the house. The two-story white frame building was simple in design. It looked like many others she'd seen in the nearby town and passed in the country on the way here. A porch ran across half the front of the house. The paint looked new, glistening merrily in the sunlight. Lilac bushes, past their blossoming season, waved near the corner of the porch. What Chase had referred to as a yard was swept dirt and poorly cropped prairie grass.

Chase and Samuel sat beside the well. It was topped by a twirling windmill that made Lorette think of a misshapen steeple. She could hear Samuel's baby laugh as a black and brown dog with a waggling tail poked its nose into Samuel's face. Chase grinned down at the two. Lorette smiled at the sweet picture they made. Then her eyes misted. No one looking at this cheerful home and the man, baby, and dog would suspect the life-and-death struggle that had so recently transpired here.

She took a deep, shaky breath and started toward Chase and Samuel. A strong odor caused her to wrinkle her nose. What was it? Nothing that smelled like any farm she'd ever been on.

Chase looked up as she neared. The gray eyes set in

a spray of wrinkles were laughing. She assumed the wrinkles came from years of squinting against the sun. He nodded at the dog. "Meet Curly. He and Sam are great friends."

She smiled in return. "I can see that."

Samuel buried his head in Curly's fur and rubbed his face back and forth, a funny little baby growl in his throat. Curly just wiggled. Chase and Lorette laughed together at the sight.

Chase stood. Without his support, Samuel tipped from his sitting position to his side in the grass. Curly stuck his nose in Samuel's stomach, instigating a delighted giggle.

Chase reached for a dipper tied to the well, dipped it into the wooden bucket, and handed it to Lorette.

"Thank you," she murmured. The cool water felt good. It tasted more metallic than the water back in Philadelphia. She handed the emptied dipper back to him. "I'd like to see the inside of the house."

"That's not possible."

His quick response startled her. She drew herself up, squaring her shoulders beneath her wilted traveling jacket. "You might recall that I am Bess's sister." She whirled about and started toward the house.

"Lorette! Miss Taber!"

She ignored him. A moment later she felt his large hand on her shoulder. She kept walking, and the hand slid away. Chase fell into place beside her, with Samuel caught securely about the middle in one strong arm.

"I apologize, Miss Taber. I'm not trying to order

you about, but the house is being disinfected."

She stopped short. "What?"

"Doc said it had to be disinfected with sulfur smudges. After everything was washed down, that is. You'll barely be able to breathe if you go inside now. It needs to be aired out."

"Oh." So that was the strange odor she'd smelled, sulfur. She felt ashamed for her hasty conclusion that he considered himself in a position to tell her what she could and could not do. Lorette tipped her head to one side, studying Chase's earnest face. "Are you saying you did this yourself, disinfecting the house?"

"Well, yes." He shifted Samuel's position. "I hope you don't feel I was invading your family's privacy. I didn't think you should have to clean up after. . .everything. . . ." His usually strong voice tapered off.

Lorette could think of nothing to say. This stranger had taken upon himself the task of cleaning up after the death of his good friends in order to spare someone he didn't know the unpleasant experience. Surely such a chore had been difficult for him. "Thank you." Her gratitude hoarsened her voice on the inadequate words. "The crosses. . .did you make them, too?"

"Yes. You'll want to replace them, I'm sure, but it didn't seem right, nothing marking the graves."

No wonder there were deep gray circles beneath his eyes. He must have been up all night taking care of things that would normally have fallen upon her shoulders. "And the wild roses on the graves?"

"Mrs. Bresven brought them. They grow wild on

the prairie. Neighboring farmers dug the graves, and their families came for the service, those who weren't sick themselves. Bess and Tom were special people. Everyone liked them."

A cloud of helplessness enveloped Lorette. The house with its sulfur fumes was not available to her. There was nothing more she could do at the graves.

Chase cleared his throat. "What are you planning to do now?"

She tried to focus her thoughts. "Bess arranged a position for me as a governess with a family in town."

"The Henrys. She told me."

"I suppose I should speak with them next. I'm not certain they will welcome another child in their home." Her gaze shifted to Samuel, who was beginning to struggle in Chase's arms, impatient for release and new experiences.

"I'm sure the Henrys will understand if you take a day or two to get your bearings first, all things considered. The Bresvens would welcome you at their place for a few days, until you get things straight in your mind."

She remembered Kari Bresven, the plump, middle-aged Scandinavian woman who had met her at the station, had extended that offer when she drove them out to the farm in the Bresvens' buckboard, but Lorette had been too much in shock to register her need at that time. "I couldn't impose on strangers. Isn't there a hotel or boardinghouse in town?"

"Yes, miss, but I think you and the boy would be more comfortable at the Bresvens', if you don't mind my saying so. No one's a stranger to Mrs. Bresven. She likes having children around. She must. She has a passel of her own."

Lorette brushed the back of her hand across her forehead, noting with mild surprise that her skin was not only sweaty but also gritty from the dust blown about by the wind. She felt weary to her bones. She shouldn't accept a neighbor's hospitality when there was a hotel in town, but the town suddenly seemed a continent away. "If you're certain Mrs. Bresven won't mind—"

❦

Bouncing on the hard seat of a buckboard beside Chase Lankford on the short ride to the Bresven farm, Lorette ran quickly through possibilities for her immediate future. They appeared dismally few in number. If the Henrys would not take her on because of Samuel, what would she do? She no longer had a position to return to in Philadelphia. The family for whom she'd worked there had already hired a new governess. Finding another position anywhere would be difficult. Parents who hired a governess usually wanted all the governess's attention given to their own children.

Lorette drew the boy in her lap into a quick hug. Abandoning him to strangers wasn't to be considered. He was the only family she had now, and she was his only family. They needed to stick together.

Standing beside the rough driveway on the Bresven farm, Lorette watched Chase drive away on the clattering buckboard, dust rising in small clouds from beneath the wooden and metal wheels. Samuel whimpered in her arms, already missing Chase.

"It's all right, Samuel," she whispered in his ear. "I'm not going anywhere. It's you and me now."

The Lord always makes a way.

The words she'd heard her mother repeat hundreds of times spoke softly in her mind. Lorette's gaze swept the prairie. In the distance she could see Bess and Tom's house. A couple other farmhouses stood on the horizon. There were no trees, only fields, and a seemingly endless ocean of undulating prairie grass, amongst which Chase and the buckboard and the dust clouds were already lost to her view.

Could the Lord make a way for her and Samuel even in such a place as this?

❧

The wagon jolted along over the road that was barely more than two deep ruts in a prairie that had been unbroken and untamed ten years ago. Chase felt as jolted emotionally as he did physically, bouncing along on the leather cushioned scat.

He'd been working without sleep since he'd discovered the deaths of his friends. He closed his mind now as he had again and again to the horror of discovering Bess and the children and hearing the story of Tom's desperate and futile search for the doctor before Tom succumbed to the disease himself. Helping with the graves, putting together the makeshift crosses with shaking hands, disinfecting the home—he'd worked through it all grateful to have someplace to put his energy, grateful for the reprieve from the depths of grief he knew were to come.

He was teetering on the edge of grief's abyss now, he knew. He recognized the place and dreaded it.

It was the realization that Sam, the last living part of Tom and Bess, might soon also leave his life that brought him to the edge. The hardest thing ever required of him was to ride away leaving that little boy in a stranger's arms, even though that stranger was Bess's sister. Even though he knew from everything Bess had told him of Lorette that Bess would completely trust Sam to her sister's care.

Chase didn't trust anyone but himself to care for that boy. Lorette hadn't even laid eyes on Sam until a couple hours ago. How could she possibly care for the boy as much as Chase cared?

He wished it were possible to keep the boy from missing his parents. He wished he could bring him up with laughter and love and a respect for the land and hard work and faith in God, the way Tom and Bess would have raised him. He wished. . . .

"I just want to protect him," he whispered fiercely.

There was no reply to the words, which had been a prayer. Only the insects that dwelt in the prairie grass and cornfields spoke, creating the incessant music of the homesteaders' rolling land.

He hadn't been able to protect Tom and Bess and the kids from diphtheria. Now he couldn't protect their son from grief or from anything else. He had no right. It was Lorette who would decide Sam's future.

The pain that had been building inside him burst.

The tears he hadn't had time to shed flowed down his cheeks.

Chase flicked the reins, urging the horses into a canter. He longed to escape the pain that engulfed him. He wanted to run. But he knew that there was no hiding place from this sorrow.

Chapter 2

Lorette sat beside Mrs. Henry in church, the service going by in a daze. She sang the hymns and responded with the rest of the congregation to the readings without comprehending the words. Her only communication with God was the constant cry in her heart and mind, *What now, Lord? Help us!*

Mrs. Henry had drawn her aside right before they left for church. The scene replayed through her mind. It had started with a compliment. "You are wonderful with our children," Mrs. Henry had said. "The two weeks you've been with us have proven that. There's no question of your ability or dedication, but we hired a governess because we want our children to have that person's undivided attention. You must admit that with Samuel here, you are unable to give my children your first duty. Mr. Henry and I would like you to stay on as governess, but it will only be possible if you find another home for Samuel."

Lorette's fear for her and Samuel's futures swirled through her. On her meager salary, could she possibly afford to pay someone to care for Samuel while she was at work each day? Not likely.

When the service was over she followed the rest of the congregation outside into the early summer sunshine. All around her people chatted in friendly groups, but she knew only the Henrys.

"Good morning, Miss Taber."

She blinked in surprise at the masculine voice and looked up at the tall man beside her. He looked familiar, but she couldn't place him. Samuel, who had been watching the crowd from the safety of her arms, lunged for the man. Lorette gasped and leaned with the boy.

"Whoa, there, fella." The man grinned as he effortlessly lifted Samuel from Lorette's arms.

"Why, Mr. Lankford, I didn't recognize you." Lorette pressed gloved fingers to her lace-covered throat, realizing too late that he might take her comment for an insult. The man wasn't covered with sweat and dust today. He was dressed in a simple brown suit and was as clean and close-shaven as any of the other men in church.

"There's a number of churches out near the farm site, but their services are in Norwegian or Swedish or German due to the immigrant settlers. I try make it into town for services whenever I can."

Lorette relaxed slightly. She rather liked it that this young man would make the uncomfortable trip to church without prodding from a mother or sister or wife.

Samuel bent forward and put his lips about the brim of Lankford's hat. "Samuel, don't." She tried to pry the brim from Samuel's busy mouth and tight grip. "That's all right, miss. It's an old hat."

Lorette tried not to cringe, realizing it was the same sweat-stained hat the man had worn the day they met, though it looked as though the worst of the dust had been knocked from it. She gave Mr. Lankford a wavering smile and continued with her attempts to release the hat. "Just the same, it's best he not try to eat it."

Lankford cleared his throat. "I was wondering if you'd like to see your sister's house. I've been airing it out and the sulfur smell's gone now. Well, mostly gone. I thought perhaps you'd have the afternoon free, since it's Sunday and all." He nodded toward the dirt road where a couple dozen buggies, carriages, and wagons were lined up behind tethered horses. "I brought the wagon and would be glad to drive you out to the farm."

The fog of confusion that had hung about her since Mrs. Henry's announcement lifted momentarily. What a welcome break it would be to have a couple hours away from the Henry home and the talk she must eventually have with Mrs. Henry. "Thank you, Mr. Lankford. That would be lovely."

❧

The smell of sulfur still lingered strong in the home when Lorette stepped over the threshold in spite of Mr. Lankford's assurances. Her nose wrinkled in reaction to the spoiled-egg odor. Samuel squeezed his eyes shut and screwed up his face in distaste. Lorette and Chase burst into laughter, and the protective shell of fear and grief that had encased Lorette's heart began to crack.

Sunshine poured through white curtains with blue and yellow embroidered flowers, cheering the large, high-ceilinged kitchen. Blue and white dishes brightened an open cupboard along one wall. The nickel plating on the combination cooking and heating stove glistened as if polished yesterday. A cast-iron teakettle sat atop the stove ready for use.

Lorette ran a gloved fingertip lightly across the top of the rectangular wooden table where the family had shared meals. Except for a kerosene lamp, which needed cleaning, the table stood empty. It was as if the room waited for Bess to enter again and bustle about caring for her family. "Bess was so excited about this house."

"So was Tom."

Chase's words startled her. She hadn't realized she'd spoken aloud.

"Bess and Tom spent a winter planning this house," Chase continued. "When the snow is covering the ground for months, a farmer has time to make repairs and plan for spring. Every time I'd stop over that winter Tom and Bess were seated at this very table in their soddy pouring over their sketches of this house, arguing good-naturedly over the size of rooms and where to try and save money."

Lorette shook her head. "I could never imagine my sister living in a sod house."

"She never complained." Chase swung a hand casually toward a window through which Lorette could see the barn. "They turned the house into a barn after they moved in here."

Lorette felt her cheeks blanch, not only appalled that her sister had lived in a dirt home but one that had become a home for farm animals. Yet Bess's letters had always been filled with plans and hopes and dreams and the excitement of her life with Tom in this land.

Chase indicated a doorway with his hat. "Sitting room's this way."

Lorette moved to the doorway and stopped, surveying the second of the two first-floor rooms. Just as Bess's kitchen took the place of both kitchen and dining room, the "sitting room," as Chase called it, combined both parlor and family room. She knew Bess had hoped to eventually add on a parlor and dining room.

Blushing tan roses on a rich brown background papered the walls. Maroon velvet draperies framed the tall windows. In the center of the room stood a large round table of dark wood, a kerosene lamp with a painted glass shade in the exact middle of the table's marble top. A gentlemen's chair, an armless ladies' chair and camel-back sofa, all framed in intricate carving and upholstered in plush fabric which matched the draperies, were set about the room with small marble-topped tables beside them. Dainty, snowy white crocheted pieces protected the furniture from hair oils.

"I remember how proud Bess was when she wrote of buying this furniture," Lorette said.

A bittersweet sadness twisted inside her. Everything in the room shouted its newness. To Lorette, the room seemed a pitiful attempt to capture the beauty of a parlor from back East, an impossible task in a four-room house on the prairie.

Samuel was poking with a pudgy finger at the watch which hung from a silver breast pin on Lorette's green swirled gingham dress. After a moment of observation, he flopped his head forward and tried to put the watch in his mouth.

"No, Samuel." Lorette pried the strong little wet fingers from his mouth and the watch from his fingers, then set the boy down on the floor. He immediately crawled toward the sofa.

The most comfortable looking piece of furniture was a rocking chair that didn't match the fancier pieces. Before it was a low footstool, just high enough to keep a woman's feet above the drafts that run along floors. She wondered whether Bess had made the embroidered footstool cover and the matching sewing bag that hung beside the chair.

Chase must have seen her looking at the rocking chair. "Tom surprised her with that chair right before their oldest, Aaron, was born. Nearest railroad station was at Benson back then, thirty miles from here, so that's the closest he could have the chair shipped. Tom and me took a buckboard to pick up a load of wood and came back with the wood and the chair both. There was no road between our settlement and Benson back then. Just ruts across the prairie." A grin split his wide face. "That chair rocked so hard it had twice as many miles as the buckboard by the time we reached here. Tom nearly burst with anticipation. All he could talk about was what Bess would say. Wish you could have seen Bess's face when we pulled up in front of the soddy with that chair."

Lorette tried to will away the knot that caught high in her chest. Chase's grin had gentled into a shadowy smile, and his eyes had the faraway look that eyes take on when one is watching memories. Lorette wished desperately that those memories were hers. She forced herself to smile. "I expect Tom wasn't disappointed in Bess's reaction?"

Chase chuckled, and she found her smile widening at the sound. "No. He surely was not. I can see her now, standing in front of that soddy with her apron and hair blowing in the wind. She took one look at the chair and her eyes grew as large as buggy wheels. Then she came across the yard as fast as her delicate condition allowed. Tom's boots had barely touched ground when her arms went around his neck. She like to squeezed the living daylights out of him."

Lorette studied his face, curious at the way his voice had softened at the end.

A large picture in an oval tortoise-shell frame caught her eye. She walked toward it slowly. It hung above a sideboard, another reminder that the little house did not have a proper dining room.

She hugged herself tightly as she stared at the family photograph. Bess's face, her beautiful, thick brown hair pulled severely back into a bun, stared back at her. Tom stood behind Bess with one hand on her shoulder, a proud young family man. Samuel's older brother and sister stood one on each side of Bess, leaning against their mother's lap. Bess held Samuel, his long embroidered gown cascading like a beautiful waterfall over Bess's dark tailored skirt. The children all had blond hair like their father. Lorette shivered and hugged herself even tighter.

"That was taken a couple months ago." Chase spoke from behind her in a low voice.

"I know." Her voice came out in a hoarse whisper. "She sent me a small copy of it."

Between Chase and Lorette hung a heavy, awkward silence, so common when one has lost a loved one and there is nothing anyone can say or do to bring them back or prevent the grief of their loss. Lorette stared at the picture, trying to absorb everything she could about her older sister. Bess had looked so different when she left Boston years ago as a young bride.

"She was happy." Chase's voice was gentle in its masculinity. "She loved being a mother and she loved Tom. She even loved this impossible-to-tame prairie."

"Her letters were filled with her joy."

Crash!

Lorette whirled about. Samuel was proudly surveying the sewing basket he'd tipped over. He reached eagerly for a ball of pale blue yarn stuck through with knitting needles that had tumbled from the basket. Lorette darted forward, but Chase reached the boy first.

"That's not a toy, fella." Chase righted the basket and began replacing the spilled objects. "I'll keep him entertained if you want to look around a bit more."

A dainty ladies' desk stood beside a window. Curiosity stirred within Lorette. What reminders of herself had her sister left in that desk? Lorette crossed to it.

"Bess wrote her letters to you seated there."

Lorette took a bundle of envelopes from a cubbyhole, recognized her own handwriting on the top envelope, and quickly returned them to their keeping place. She pulled out a drawer. She didn't know what she expected to see there, but what she found was a book bound in rich brown leather. Curious, she removed and opened it.

This will be our first night sleeping in our new home. It's been a long day and my eyes are closing in exhaustion as I write, but I could not go to bed without recording the great joy Tom and I are feeling this day.

Tears blurred the script. Lorette returned the journal to the drawer. She knew that later she would read and cherish this record of Bess's thoughts. Yet Lorette's pain was still too new to read it now. She closed the drawer and turned her back to the desk.

Chase was on the floor beside Samuel. Four wooden blocks sat in a row on the thick brown rug. Chase slowly balanced a block on top of the others. "See, Sam? It's easy." He placed another block.

Samuel stared, his brown eyes wide below lifted blond brows, his little bow mouth open slightly.

"Going to help me, Sam?" Chase placed one of Samuel's hands on a block. Together they lifted and placed it.

Chase's tanned hand seemed to swallow up Samuel's

tiny white one. Lorette smiled at the sweetness of the moment. With a pleasant start she realized that for the first time in days she was genuinely smiling inside, too. The smile loosened somewhat the painful knot that had existed in her chest since hearing of Bess's death.

Lorette wasn't accustomed to seeing men play with their children. The fathers of the children for whom she had cared in Philadelphia had been reserved with their offspring. Had Tom played with Samuel, Aaron, and Liza as Chase was playing now? If so, the children had indeed been blessed.

"We did it, Sam," Chase congratulated.

Samuel stared at the blocks a moment longer. Bending forward suddenly he pushed the block they had so carefully balanced in place with the palm of his hand. The block went tumbling. Samuel giggled and slapped his hands on his chubby knees, his face filled with glee.

"Hey!" Chase's face registered disbelief.

Lorette burst into laughter at his chagrin. Chase looked up in surprise. Meeting her gaze, he joined in her laughter.

He stood to his feet, bending over to swoop Samuel into one arm. "Guess the fellow isn't into building yet." He disentangled a hunk of his hair from one of Samuel's fists. "How are things going at the Henrys'?"

"They are no longer 'going' at all." She held out her arms for Samuel.

Blond brows met above troubled eyes. "Haven't they treated you well? Mr. Henry has a fine reputation—"

"Oh, yes," she hurried to assure him. "They simply wish for a governess who can give all her attention to their children." She touched her lips lightly to Samuel's temple. "I can't do that." She glanced into the boy's bright eyes and smiled. "Thank God, I cannot do that," she whispered.

Chase stuffed his hands into his trouser pockets. "Will you be taking Sam back to Philadelphia?"

He stood in an easy manner, but she sensed a tension about him. Was he afraid she would take the only remaining member of his friends' family away?

"Maybe," Lorette responded. "But parents back East don't care for governesses who come with nephews any more than parents here. I'll need to find another way to support us."

"So. . .what are you planning?"

"The attorney read the will to me yesterday. He said Samuel inherits this house and farm."

"And?"

Lorette shrugged. "My first thought was to sell the farm. The money from the sale would be Samuel's, of course. It would all go for his support."

He nodded, his gaze on hers.

"If I can't find another position where I can keep him with me, I can use the money to pay someone else to care for him properly while I work. Or perhaps the money would allow me to stay with him until he is old enough to begin school before I accept another position as a governess."

She waited, hoping for a response from him. He'd

been Tom's best friend. Wouldn't he know what Tom and Bess would have wanted her to do?

"I'm afraid the farm wouldn't bring as much money as you think." Chase sounded as though he spoke with reluctance.

Unease quickened her heartbeat. "Why not?"

"Tom made a good start developing this place, but it took a heap of money to do it. Sam must have inherited Tom's debts. Selling the farm would barely pay them off."

"How can that be? They homesteaded the land. It barely cost them anything." Lorette spread her free hand to indicate the home within which they stood. "They had enough money to buy and furnish this new house."

"He used the land and future crops to borrow the money to pay for the house, and for farm machinery to run this place, and to buy another section of land."

His words sent goose bumps running along her arms, and she shivered. "What about the crops? Won't they help pay the debts?"

"It's not as simple as it sounds. Farmers live on credit all year. It's not only the house and machinery they pay for after harvest. If the crops are poor, prices will be good—that is, if you're one of the fortunate farmers with crops to sell. If the crops are good, prices will be low because everyone has a lot to sell. Either way, there won't be enough to pay off normal living debts and the loans, too. 'Course if you're thrifty, there may be enough to pay off this year's loan payments."

The hope in Lorette's chest was rapidly sinking. "I suppose I could rent the farm out. It wouldn't support

Samuel and me, but it would help pay the debts and let us keep the farm for Samuel."

"Sure. 'Course, if the renter doesn't pay up or the crops aren't good in the future, you'll need to find another way to make the loan payments or lose the property."

Lorette closed her hands into fists in frustration. "How do farmers manage to live at all?"

He grinned. "Tom always said the only way was by depending on God and using a man's brains and brawn. I'd say he's right."

"But what am I going to do?"

"If you don't mind a suggestion—"

"Mind? I'm pleading for one."

"You don't need to decide this minute. You can stay here while you figure things out. You and Sam would have a roof over your heads and a garden and chickens and a cow for your meals."

"I don't know anything about running a farm. I wouldn't have one idea of what to do with the crops."

"I do."

She stared at him a moment, not comprehending his quiet reply. Understanding dawned rapidly. "Oh. *Oh.* The chickens. . .the cow. . .the other animals. . .*you* have been caring for them the last couple weeks."

Chase shifted his feet and glanced at the floor. "Yes."

"And the crops?"

Chase nodded.

"Oh, my." Lorette moved to the dainty rocking chair and sank onto the tapestry covering. "My thoughts have been only on my grief and Samuel's, and on how I am going to care for Samuel. I've been incredibly selfish, leaving the care of this place on your shoulders. I'll pay you for your trouble. I have a little money coming from the two weeks I spent with the Henrys."

He shook his head vigorously. "I couldn't take the money. I've done what I've done for Tom. He was a good friend. If you decide to move in here for a while I'll be more than glad to continue helping you out."

Everything in Lorette's nature went against accepting such a huge gift, but she knew she must accept it out of concern for Samuel's future. If what Chase said about the crops and debt were true, she'd need her meager funds.

"Thank you. I accept your kind offer." She forced a smile. "I'm afraid you've no idea how much your advice will be needed. I know nothing of life on a farm. In Philadelphia my food came from merchants, not from the land just outside my door."

"You'll catch on."

He sounded as though he had no doubt at all. She wished she were as sure of her capabilities.

At least for the moment, she and Samuel had a roof over their heads and food for only the price of her labor. She needn't worry immediately about finding a position, nor must she rely on Kari Bresven's or the Henrys' charity to meet her own and Samuel's needs. Some of her trepidation at staying on the farm melted away. Depending on Chase Lankford to help her with the farm, she felt as secure as Samuel obviously felt when in Chase's arms.

Chase rolled over, grunting when his shoulder hit a raised nail. He shifted. The wooden floor he'd put in his sod house was a pleasure to walk on, but there was no way to make it comfortable for sleeping. Still, he didn't regret giving the feather mattress from his bed to Lorette. He smiled into the night, playing her name over in his mind. Manners might demand that he refer to her as Miss Taber, but in the privacy of his thoughts he loved the sound of her name.

He hadn't told Lorette that the mattress was his. She'd assumed Mrs. Bresven had lent it, along with the Swedish woman's pillow, sheets, and quilts. He hadn't informed her otherwise. The bedding had been necessary to replace that which the doctor had ordered him to burn.

Chase rolled over again and groaned. He'd order another mattress next time he was in town. At least he still had a pillow.

He let the events of the afternoon roll through his mind. Since their deaths, it had been difficult to be in the home of Tom and Bess. He still missed them sorely. He supposed he would feel that way for a long time.

Still, the sound of Lorette's laughter rang in his memory, and he pictured her face when he'd looked up from playing with Sam. It had been a perfect moment.

The picture was replaced by the sadness he'd caught in her blue eyes. Seeing that pain, his instinct had been to try to protect her, the same way he wanted to protect Sam. It was then that the thought of marriage first crossed his mind.

Foolish thought. Pity was no foundation for marriage. Besides, he couldn't protect her. Not by marriage or any other way. Not only hadn't he the right, the same as he hadn't the right to protect Sam, but grief wasn't a pain from which anyone could be protected by another human being.

When Lorette said she might take Sam back East to raise, he'd felt a pain in his stomach worse than the worst sickness he'd ever known. He'd had to all but bite his tongue to keep from asking her to marry him right then.

He snorted and drew his quilt up to his chin. Didn't make any sense to ask a woman he barely knew to marry him, even if Bess had been telling him about Lorette for years. He might not have known Lorette long, but he'd seen enough to admire her pluck. He was glad she wasn't the kind of woman who'd consider Sam's inheritance something to feather her own nest. And she sure wasn't sore on the eyes.

The only other woman he'd ever thought of marrying was Anna, and he'd known her for years before he asked. She had turned him down flat. A life of a farmer's wife was too hard, she'd said.

So he'd taken up his homestead claim and closed his heart.

Until now. Until Lorette.

He snorted again. No reason in the world to believe she'd have said yes to his proposal even if he'd been rash enough to make it.

He dug his head deeper into the pillow and muttered, "Must be lonelier than I realized to even invent such a thought."

While the vision of Lorette's eyes played in his thoughts, Chase drifted into sleep.

Chapter 3

The dawn streamed through the lace-covered windows as Lorette arose early the next morning. The sweet music of Samuel's baby jabberings drifted from his cradle beside her bed, providing a pleasant start to her day. She talked with him while she dressed, glad he never seemed hungry until he'd been up for a while.

"You're such a good-natured little boy." She ran a hand over the cradle's hooded bonnet with its carving of roses. The wood was butter smooth. Tom must have sanded it for hours and hours. "Your mother wrote me about this cradle, how your father made it and gave it to your mother the Christmas they were expecting Aaron."

Samuel grinned and kicked his feet.

Lorette wondered whether Samuel could feel his father's love surrounding him when he was in the cradle. Her eyes misted over, and she brushed at them with the back of her hand.

Putting behind her fanciful thoughts, she picked up Samuel and started downstairs. The two rooms behind closed doors across the hall were hard to ignore. She had peaked into them last night. They felt forlorn with mattressless bedsteads and deserted toys: one of Liza's dolls, a slingshot of Aaron's, and a pile of pebbles and arrowheads Aaron had collected. More than anything else, those rooms told the extent to which death had filled this house.

Lorette found Bess's aprons hanging on pegs on the pantry door. She reached for a crisp white apron, then selected a tan plaid which wouldn't show the inevitable results of a day's work as easily. Besides, it complemented her brown-checkered gingham dress, the simplest she owned.

While Samuel played with spoons on the floor, Lorette searched the pantry, discovering what she did and did not have available to prepare meals. She looked in wooden boxes, colorful tins, glass containers, cupboards, and drawers.

Finally she settled her hands on her hips. "Well, Samuel, the only loaf of bread is moldy. Chase must not have thought to clean out the pantry when he disinfected the house. I find flour, but no yeast. We'll have to do without bread this morning. Rather, I will. Milk will satisfy you for a while."

She grunted as she lifted Samuel. "My, you're a big boy."

He grinned as though he appreciated her comment, then leaned forward and gave a harmless bite to her shoulder.

"You must be hungry. Or your new little teeth are bothering you." She picked up a small tin pail and he transferred his attention to it. "It's a good thing Chase showed me last night where the milk was kept or you'd miss breakfast, too," she continued, carrying him out to the well. "I'd never have guessed to look in the well. In Philadelphia, a delivery man brought milk to the house each day."

She set Samuel down in order to free both hands to raise the covered tin bucket of milk from the well. She poured enough milk for Samuel and to make pancakes for herself, then lowered the bucket back into the well. "I hope Chase. . .Mr. Lankford stops by this morning. This milk won't last you the day, Samuel."

She swung the boy up to her hip and groaned. His navy blue dress was covered with dirt. She'd been so intent on getting the milk she'd forgotten to pay attention. "At least it's not mud," she muttered, brushing him off.

Her stomach was growling by the time he'd had his fill of breakfast milk and she'd laid him in the crib in the corner of the kitchen for a nap. In the pen were a tin rattle and a rag doll which had seen better days, likely because it was well-loved.

Ready to make her own breakfast, she sighed. She couldn't make buckwheat cakes without eggs, and the eggs were in the sod barn beneath chickens. Lorette straightened her shoulders. "Trying to avoid the task, aren't you? What is so scary? Hundreds of women collect eggs every day. Thousands, maybe. Children, too." She picked up a basket from the counter and groaned. "Why doesn't that make me feel any braver?"

Lorette started across the yard, swinging the basket,

deliberately putting a bounce in her step, and began singing "Oh, Susannah." Her spirits actually lifted until she opened the door to the sod barn.

"Oh! No! No! Oh!" Chickens and a rooster rushed at her, their cackles and feathered bodies filling the air. She threw her arms up, dropping the basket.

Strong arms drew her back. "Don't be afraid, Lorette. They only want to get outside and have their breakfast."

She clasped her palms over her racing heart. "Chase . . .Mr. Lankford, I'm so glad you're here. I. . .I don't know anything about chickens and. . .and eggs and. . . Can you show me what to do?"

She hated her breathlessness, but considering that a feathered army had just attacked her, she felt she was doing quite well.

Then she realized one of his large, strong hands was against her back, steadying her. A flush seemed to rise from the soles of her feet and spread upward to her hairline. She felt herself stiffen as though she were a statue.

He didn't appear to notice. With one easy movement, he leaned down, picked up her forgotten basket, and handed it to her.

"You'll be an old hand at egg hunting in no time."

Strong barnyard smells that she knew must be from the chickens, cow, two oxen, horse, straw, and things she didn't want to think about hung about them as they entered the building.

Even with his help, she definitely did *not* feel like an old hand at egg-gathering after they had collected eight brown eggs. "I feel like I've spent a week trying to keep a room full of eleven-year-old boys still and teach them arithmetic." It was the most tiring experience she could recall.

His laugh rang out clearly in the morning air.

Cheered, she tucked back a strand of hair loosened by the battle with the chickens and started toward the house.

"Uh. . .the chickens need feeding, Miss Taber."

She stopped short. "Oh. Of course."

"I'll show you where the feed is kept. You'll be giving them table scraps, too, naturally." He led her to a large wooden covered box, which stood along one wall.

"Naturally." Her ignorance was beginning to overwhelm her.

"Not everything, of course, but things like potato skins."

"Of course." Behind his back she rolled her eyes. She assumed he meant no meat scraps.

"Moo-oo-oo."

He turned to the cow. "Pansy." His face had the strangest expression.

"Is something wrong?"

He avoided her gaze and kept his own on the cow in the nearby stall. "Have you given Sam any milk yet today?"

"Yes. I'm glad you reminded me. I've used almost all the milk from the bucket in the well."

"There's more where that came from." His voice tangled with laughter, and his mouth twisted in a vain effort to avoid grinning.

Embarrassment flooded her. She felt so inadequate for the demands of farm living. "I know." She straightened her shoulders, attempting to retain a little dignity. "The trouble is, I don't know how to. . .to get at it."

Chase shouted with laughter. Within moments he was doubled-over in his mirth.

Lorette's embarrassment multiplied one hundred fold, but Chase's laughter was contagious, and soon she was laughing along with him. By the time their laughter had dissolved into chuckles, her sides hurt and she was wiping tears from her lashes.

"Let's feed the chickens," Chase said when they were both able to speak again. "Then I'll show you how to milk Pansy. She needs to be milked twice a day, every day. Each morning after milking let her out to pasture. You'll bring her in every evening and milk her again."

She recalled his milking lesson two weeks later while leaning against Pansy's side, feeling the occasional swat of Pansy's sharp, scratchy tail against her cheek and listening to the satisfying sound of milk entering the pail. Deep satisfaction filled her upon mastering this task, which people had been performing for thousands of years. She'd been surprised at the strength it took. Her wrists had been swollen at the end of that first day.

The milking done, she stood stiffly, put her hands on her lower back, and stretched. The gardening, housework, and care of the animals were all taking their toll on her body. Her work as a governess seemed idle by comparison.

She pulled the heavy pail to safety. "We did well this morning, Pansy." The cow turned her huge head and eyed Lorette.

"Glad to hear it."

Lorette jumped, sloshing milk from the bucket onto her shoes. "Chase Lankford, you shouldn't startle a body so!"

"Sorry about the milk." Chase's grin showed he wasn't too sorry. He jostled Samuel, who was struggling unsuccessfully to get out of the man's arms and into the straw with the cats now winding about Chase's legs. "Stopped by the house. He was a bit perturbed at being there alone. Sounds like you're handling the milking just fine."

"Pansy didn't kick the bucket or step in it this morning. The cats didn't tip it trying to drink. Pansy didn't step on my foot or bump me off the stool. It's been my best milking yet." It was absurd how pleased it made her to tell him so.

"I knew you'd make a great milk maid." He ignored Samuel's continued efforts to get down.

Does he think I'm not caring for Samuel properly? she wondered uneasily. "I hate to leave Samuel in the crib while I do the chores, but it's too dangerous for him in the barn. One of the animals might kick him, or the chickens peck him." She shuddered at the things the straw hid. "I hate to think what he might try to put in his mouth." She poured the milk into the nearby strainer, then set down the empty pail and reached for the boy. "He does love to be close to the animals."

"Maybe I can make a small pen where he can play while you work in here, something smaller than his crib, maybe without legs. For now, if you want to give him breakfast, I'll finish up here for you."

Guilt and thankfulness braided together in an unlikely mix as she crossed the yard in a slow, stumbling gait with Samuel in one arm and a tin pail of milk in the opposite hand. She hated to allow Chase to do any of the chores she could do. He had so much to take care of with Tom's crops, as well as his own. Still, she was glad to be relieved from wiping that fierce-smelling concoction onto the animals. Chase said it helped keep the cow flies from biting them. She did pity Pansy, the oxen, and the horse, Boots, their constant battle with those creatures.

Lorette and Samuel had their share of the bites. She tried keeping herself and Samuel well-covered to prevent the bites, despite the summer heat. She resisted rubbing kerosene on herself and Samuel to keep the flies at bay as Chase and other farmers did. That was more than her Philadelphia-bred genteel self could bear.

At the porch outside the door, she slipped off her shoes. She had learned her first day on the farm what awful, smelly things her shoes accumulated in the barn. Today one of her shoes sloshed with spilled milk, too.

The fragrance of rising bread greeted her as she entered the house. Another lesson from Chase. When she'd told him she needed yeast to bake bread, he'd shown her Bess's supply of sourdough starter and how to make bread with it.

"Seems that man has had to teach me everything but how to change your diapers," she told Samuel, setting him on the kitchen floor.

She hadn't even known Bess had stored canned meats, vegetables, and fruit in the cellar until Chase told her so. She especially appreciated the canned meat. She hadn't been able to bring herself to kill a chicken yet. That was another thing Chase did. So far he had refrained from insisting she learn to do that herself.

She started a fire in the stove, then let it burn down to cooking and baking temperature while she fed Samuel. He was still fussy while he fed. He hadn't liked being weaned suddenly after his mother died. As she usually did, Lorette kept up a steady conversation with him while he drank the warm, fresh milk.

Samuel fell asleep with his blanket on the kitchen floor while she was putting the bread in the oven to bake. It was an overcast morning, and the baking wouldn't heat the house as unbearably as it did some days. Ready to begin breakfast for herself and Chase, she looked around for her eggs.

"I know I collected them. Where are they?" she muttered, glancing about the large kitchen. Then she remembered. Her hands full with Samuel and the milk, she hadn't had enough hands to carry the eggs from the barn to the house. She hated to leave Samuel, even when he was sleeping. But it would only take a moment to run to the barn.

She saw Chase turn about at the sound of her entering the sod barn. "I forgot the eggs." She headed quickly to where the basket sat on the straw-covered floor. She reached for the handle and saw something move quickly beneath the straw.

With a screech she leaped back. "A snake! It's a snake!"

Fear tore up through her like a living thing. She couldn't seem to move fast enough. Her feet felt as though they were in buckets. She couldn't take her gaze from the yellow form gliding through, blending in the straw. Her screams filled the barn and her ears and she couldn't stop them.

They continued while Chase grabbed a pitchfork, stabbed the wriggling form, and rushed outside with it. To Lorette it appeared he was moving at a snail's pace.

Lorette's screams turned into shaky gasps. She stumbled to the door, watching the floor the entire way, certain other snakes must be hiding in the innocent-looking straw covering. From outside she could hear Curly the dog barking excitedly.

She'd barely crossed the threshold when Chase's arms surrounded her, drawing her quivering body close. "It's all right," he whispered into her hair. "I killed the creature. It can't hurt you now."

Her fingers clutched at his shirt. "I've n—never seen a s—snake before. I didn't know there were s—snakes in the b—barn."

"It's just a corn snake."

Lorette thought it absurd to refer to any snake as "just" a snake.

One of Chase's large hands rubbed her back firmly

but gently, and her shaking began to lessen. "Corn snakes are common in the fields, but they seldom come into the barn. The cats keep them away."

Even so, Lorette wondered how she would dare set foot in the barn again. . .or take the animals to pasture. . .or bring Chase his lunch in the fields. She didn't know how to tell him the extent of her fear. Bess and other women had lived with the reality of snakes in their world. Somehow she would have to find the strength to do so, too.

Chase's arms were so comforting. She had only experienced a man's arms about her a couple of times before. Never had they felt this strong, this gentle. Held close, her cheek against his shoulder, she could hide her embarrassment at the way she'd reacted, but she could not stay there. Reluctantly, she pushed herself away.

He released his hold immediately.

She wished he hadn't. *Don't be a silly goose,* she reprimanded herself. "Thank you for killing the snake. I'm afraid I'm rather timid when it comes to them. I never saw a snake in Philadelphia."

"Everyone jumps when they see a snake. It's human nature. Corn snakes aren't poisonous. There aren't any poisonous snakes hereabouts."

She appreciated his attempts to reassure her, but they weren't working. She glanced back at the sod barn door. Apprehension sent shivers through her. "Would you mind? The egg basket is still in there."

He retrieved it for her.

Her knees felt as pliant as corn silk as she walked to the house. Her hands shook when she slipped her shoes off on the porch.

Once inside, her hair stood on end. "Samuel! No!"

Chapter 4

Samuel was crawling across the kitchen floor, headed for the hot stove. Lorette dropped the basket and rushed for him, grabbing him up in a bear hug just as he reached out for the silver filigree on the oven door.

Samuel let out a squeal.

She only hugged him tighter. She took two steps back from the dangerous stove and dropped to her knees. Samuel squirmed. She didn't let go. "That's hot. Samuel must never touch the stove. Hot!" The words trembled, but no more than her heart. If she had been a moment later returning from the barn—

She couldn't let herself think of the "what-ifs." Thank God she'd returned in time. Her heart went out to all the mothers who hadn't.

Tears rolled over her cheeks. She rocked herself and Samuel back and forth, trying to comfort herself. *I can't do this,* she thought. *I can't live like this. It's too much. It's too hard, too dangerous.*

Eventually her sobs stopped, her breathing became normal, and her thoughts less wild. Hot stoves were in every house, not just prairie farmhouses, she reminded herself. There was no place she could take Samuel where there would not be dangers. Besides, she should not have left him alone on the floor, even though she had been certain he was sound asleep.

When her legs would hold her again, she put Samuel in his crib in the corner of the kitchen. He howled in protest until she brought him a pan lid and spoons to pound together.

Lorette rinsed her face with cold water, trying to wash away the vestiges of her crying jag, and straightened her hair, which had been mussed from rubbing against Chase's shirt. She felt her face burn at the memory.

Only then did she remember the egg basket. Most of the eggs were broken. A sticky yellow mess covered the bottom of the basket. She picked up the three eggs that remained whole, lifted her chin in determination, and began breakfast for herself and Chase.

She'd insisted Chase take his meals with them and that she would do his laundry in partial payment for all the work he did on the farm. She'd learned quickly that he liked a big breakfast after he'd done chores and before he left for the fields. Today she made fried potatoes, bacon, and the three eggs. Fresh warm bread and her own butter would round out the meal.

Truth be told, she enjoyed the time that she and Chase shared at meals. His companionship kept some of the loneliness of farm living from overwhelming her. She was accustomed to spending most of her days with children, but not to the exclusion of adult companionship.

Determined to put the morning's frightful memories behind her, she forced herself to sing. "What a friend we have in Jesus," she started, her voice quavering, "all our sins and griefs to bear." Before long, the quavering ceased. Samuel kept up a beat on a pan lid that was like no accompaniment Lorette had sung to in the past. By the time Chase came to the house for breakfast, Lorette had herself well in hand.

"It's nice to hear singing in this house again," Chase said when they sat down to eat. "Your sister sang while she worked, too."

Lorette's smile was genuine. His memories of Bess were different than Lorette's, but she was glad they shared memories of her. "Tell me more about her, the way you knew her."

He did. The things he remembered might have seemed insignificant to others, but to Lorette they spoke loudly of Bess's love for Tom and the children and her joy in the life she lived.

Lorette wondered silently whether a corn snake had ever surprised Bess, and if so, how she'd reacted. Lorette doubted her older sister had fallen apart and ended up in the arms of a man to whom she wasn't married for comfort.

The thought brought back the wonderful sense of rightness and security she'd felt in Chase's arms, the strength in the arms hidden beneath the brown cotton shirtsleeves. She had to lower her gaze to her plate to keep her eyes from revealing her thoughts to the man across the small table.

He didn't appear to notice anything unusual in the atmosphere between them. His mind was apparently on more practical things.

"Looks like it might rain later today. Might take advantage of the weather to drive into town and take care of some business. You're welcome to join me, if you'd like."

Lorette looked up in surprise. "In the rain?"

He shrugged. "If it's raining more than a drizzle, I can't be in the fields. If you'd rather not ride in the rain, you can give me a list of things you need and I'll pick them up."

"Oh, no, I don't mind the rain." She wasn't about to pass up a trip to town, regardless of the weather.

After the breakfast dishes were cleared, she examined the items in the pantry and made a list, just in case the trip became reality. Her mood lifted by the minute. She'd taken to wearing Bess's housedresses, as they were more suitable than most of the clothes she'd brought from Philadelphia. Now she changed from Bess's worn housedress to one of her own simple gowns, one that wouldn't be ruined by a little rain. Even Samuel had a change of dress.

Her spirits continued to lighten as the sky grew darker and sprinkles pattered against the windows. She stood in the kitchen doorway and watched the clouds tumble over each other across the sky, glorying in the vast distance she could see above the rolling prairie lands. The smell of rain and wet earth and grasses was refreshing.

In an effort to still her impatience and to keep Samuel entertained and clean until they left, she settled herself and Samuel in Bess's rocking chair with Bess's journal. Lorette had begun the practice of reading aloud to Samuel from the journal the first full day she'd spent in the house.

A small crocheted white cross marked the place she'd left off at the last reading. She started the chair in its gentle rocking motion while she opened the book.

Mr. Lankford had dinner with us today following church services. Afterward, while I cleaned up the kitchen, he and Tom rolled about the floor with Aaron and Liza for all the world as though they were children themselves. Aaron and Liz love Mr. Lankford as though he were one of us. He is a hard-working, responsible man, a church-going man, gentle yet strong in his ways.

Lorette was glad for the journal's glimpses into Bess's view of Chase. Her mind drifted to the man who had become such a large part of her life in such a short time. She might as well admit that she not only relied upon him, but she was beginning to care deeply for him—and as more than just a friend.

"Don't fool yourself into thinking he helps out for you," she admonished herself. "He does it for Samuel and because Tom was his friend."

She started as the kitchen door slammed. "Miss Taber? Are you ready to leave for town?" Chase called as he entered the house.

When she and Samuel joined Chase, she was surprised to see a buggy drawn up to the porch. "I didn't know Tom and Bess had a buggy."

"I borrowed it from the Bresvens. Figured you and Sam would get soaked riding in the wagon."

Even with the covered buggy, their ride was a damp one. She was glad for the oilcloth Chase provided to cover their legs and laps.

Bess's journal entry and the minutes Lorette spent in Chase's arms that morning made Lorette all the more conscious of every bounce of the wagon that jostled her shoulder into his. Her heart kept an erratic pace during the journey. She couldn't help but wonder whether the simple, innocent contact reminded him of the time they'd spent in each other's arms, too.

The muddy roads made the journey longer than usual, and Lorette thought they made the ride bumpier than usual, also. Conversation with Chase was somewhat limited. It took all of Chase's concentration to drive as the road grew worse.

The simple general store with its narrow aisles and one room of goods piled upon goods from floor to ceiling looked as wonderful to Lorette as a large emporium in downtown Philadelphia. Chase introduced her to the owner, a middle-aged Swedish man named Larson. Chase explained that she was Tom's sister-in-law, and Larson agreed to extend her credit against harvest.

Lorette and Chase went about the store gathering items from their separate lists. Chase completed his within minutes. "I'm having a leather harness repaired at a shop down the street. I'll run down and pick it up while you finish here."

She agreed and went happily back to examining the bolts of fabric piled on a table in one corner of the store. Samuel was growing fast. He would need new clothes soon.

"How nice to see you, Miss Taber."

Lorette turned to the woman at her elbow. "Mrs. Henry, what a pleasant surprise."

Mrs. Henry leaned forward and tickled Samuel's cheek with a gloved index finger. "Hello there, Samuel. My, aren't you the big boy." She straightened and smiled her formal smile at Lorette. "I hope things are going well for you on the farm, my dear."

"Yes, everything is fine." *Mrs. Henry's words are always right,* Lorette thought, *but somehow her manner makes them sound all wrong.* "How are the children?"

"Fine, fine." Mrs. Henry waved her hand in a dismissing manner. A frown marred her features. "There's something I must tell you." Her voice had dropped a degree.

At her tone, Lorette's stomach turned queasy. She tried to ignore it. What could the woman possibly say that could justify such a feeling? Lorette barely knew the woman. "What is that, Mrs. Henry?"

Mrs. Henry laid a hand on Lorette's forearm. "My dear, I hardly know how to say this."

Lorette wished her former employer would stop calling her "my dear." "Say what?"

"I understand Mr. Lankford spends a great deal of time at your farm."

"Yes. He's been a marvelous help. As you know, I know nothing of running a farm."

"He was a friend of your brother-in-law's, of course."

"Yes. They helped each other with their fields, so Mr. Lankford knows all about Tom's crops."

Mrs. Henry bit her bottom lip for a moment. "People say Mr. Lankford spends a *great* deal of time at your farm." She hesitated, staring directly into Lorette's eyes. "An inordinate amount of time."

The woman's meaning began to sink in. Lorette could hear a roaring sound in her ears. "What are you saying?" Her lips felt numb, but she knew she had asked the question. If Mrs. Henry was saying what Lorette thought, she needed to hear it in plain English.

"People are saying he is living at the farm with you, that you are living together. . .inappropriately."

Chapter 5

The ride back to the farm was the longest Chase could ever remember. The man at the saddle shop had told him of the ugly rumor going about town. Chase knew there were men who found such tales amusing, but he could hardly believe the townspeople he knew and respected thought him capable of such gross conduct.

Worse, they thought sweet Lorette would descend to such an arrangement.

The entire situation made him sick.

He'd told the leather worker, in no uncertain terms, that the rumors were not true. Chase had no illusions that he would be able to squelch the rumors or convince everyone of their untruth. He knew enough about human nature to know he could not work such miracles.

Anger at what the rumors would mean to Lorette's reputation made him drive Boots harder than he normally would under such poor road conditions. His thoughts swirled in a vicious circle. What was he going to do? What could he do? Did Lorette know? Had she, too, heard the rumors in town? She seemed agitated, avoiding his glance, barely speaking, but perhaps she was only responding to his temperament, which he admitted to himself was anything but friendly and easy-going.

❦

Lorette was glad when they finally arrived back at the farm and Chase headed to the Bresvens's with the buggy. The ride had seemed unendurable. The rumor had shouted through her mind the entire time.

Had Chase heard the awful accusations?

"Oh, no." She stopped short. Did he think she had staged her fright at the snake that morning, had purposely found a reason to throw herself into his arms? The possibility was too horrible to consider.

"How can people be so terrible, making up stories like this about people?" she asked the Lord, unpacking the goods from the wooden box Chase had carried into the house for her.

It was awful enough for her and for Chase, but it almost broke her heart to think what the rumors would mean for Samuel. The sins of the fathers did follow the children. The untrue rumors would follow Samuel if he grew up here. What would Bess think if she knew the disgrace Lorette and Chase had inadvertently brought upon her youngest son? The thought twisted Lorette's heart like a cloth being wrung.

"I thought You would make a way for Samuel and me, Lord. Is this hurtful rumor Your way of telling me that Samuel and I are to move back to Philadelphia? Please, make our path clear, so I do not make any more missteps."

The next morning Chase arrived as Lorette was headed to the barn to care for the animals. Did she only imagine that his face looked grim and gray circles underscored his normally smiling eyes?

"I'll take care of the animals this morning." His tone sounded curt.

She longed to take him up on his offer but knew she didn't dare. "If I don't find the courage to go back in the barn today, I might never find it."

For a moment she didn't think he was going to accept her decision. Then he nodded. "We'll work together. You collect the eggs and milk Pansy while I rub the animals down with the fly ointment."

Gratitude flooded her. In spite of her brave words, she was terrified to step into the straw that hid snakes and other creatures so well. "Thank you."

He glanced at Samuel, who was seated on her hip, and raised his eyebrows.

Lorette explained about the stove incident from the day before. "I don't dare leave him alone in the house anymore. He's not satisfied with crawling any longer. He pulls himself up on everything. Any day now he'll be walking."

When they were done with the chores Chase carried the milk to the house while Lorette carried Samuel and the eggs. "I won't be needing any breakfast this morning," he said without meeting her gaze. "Fields are too wet to get into today. I'll be using the time to mend some things about my own place."

He turned abruptly, leaving before she could say good-bye.

The day wore on drearily long. Lunch and dinner seemed too much work to prepare for only herself. She settled for bread with butter and sugar and didn't bother to cook. She was glad when it was time to bring the animals back from pasture, even though it also meant entering the barn again, and this time without Chase's comforting presence.

She was inordinately pleased to find Chase's wagon in the yard and Chase in the barn when she returned. He was raking an area clear of straw. With a wave of his hand he indicated a legless wooden pen similar to the crib in the kitchen. "Thought we'd better set up a safe place for Sam in here right away."

"Thank you. I know how difficult it must have been for you to find time for this."

"Needed doing."

She set Samuel in the pen and went to get a pail of water from the well. The animals' legs and undersides were mud-caked from being in the pasture after yesterday's rain. Pansy's udders needed washing before milking.

Once she started milking, Lorette was so busy watching the floor for snakes that the milk bucket was missed as often as it was hit. She gritted her teeth and forced her attention on her work.

She and Chase worked in silence, at least in as much silence as one could find in a barn with a cow, oxen, a horse, chickens, insects, a woman milking, a man raking and tossing straw, and a ten-month-old boy trying to get anyone's and anything's attention. Lorette wondered how one small earthen building could hold so much tension. Then she wondered how her much smaller body could contain that much tension.

Still in silence, Chase accompanied her and Samuel to the house. He set the milk down on the porch. "We need to talk."

His demanding tone surprised her. "All right. Let me get a shawl to protect Samuel from the gnats."

He was pacing the porch when she returned. He stopped a foot from her. In the twilight the lines in his face looked set in stone. "I don't know if you heard the rumors in town yesterday—"

She nodded, too embarrassed to answer.

His shoulders lowered slightly, and she knew he was relieved not to have to put the rumor into words for her. "I haven't been able to think of anything else since I heard them."

"It's been the same for me," she admitted.

"I think I have a solution."

Immediately her spirits brightened. "Yes?" She should have known he would come up with something. Hadn't he had an answer for all her problems from the very beginning?

He took a deep breath. His hands formed into fists at his sides. "Marriage. I mean, I think we should marry. That is, will you marry me? Please, Miss Taber?"

Shock rolled through her. Her mouth dropped open. She couldn't make her throat work. Her first thought was to blurt out that of course she could not marry him, but something within her checked the words. It couldn't have been easy for him to offer this proposal. Her answer should be as kind as she could make it.

Lorette had to swallow twice before she could speak. She lifted her chin and straightened her shoulders in an attempt to gather as much dignity as possible about her. "It's kind of you to try save my reputation from the rumors, Mr. Lankford. However, I assure you—your generous sacrifice is not necessary."

"I'm not asking because of your reputation. Well, not entirely, though I've seen how easy it is for a woman's reputation to be ruined. I'm thinking mostly of young Sam. His life might be affected by these rumors, too."

Lorette turned and stared out over the farmyard to keep him from seeing that she recognized the truth of his words. "I can take him back East."

She felt his hand firm and gentle on her shoulder and caught her breath sharply.

"Miss Taber." His voice was as gentle as his touch. "Together we can make good parents for Sam, and if we're married, I can stick around to help you run Sam's farm."

Unexpected pain ripped through her. His arguments were true, but they weren't what her heart wanted to hear. She had always dreamed of her future husband expressing undying love for her when he proposed marriage. This man only wanted a ready-made family, and a housekeeper, and maybe Samuel's farm.

No, that's not true, her heart forced her to admit, *not the part about Samuel's farm.*

Lorette wished Chase would remove his hand from her shoulder. His touch made it more difficult to think clearly. But what was there to think about? There could only be one answer.

She pulled her shawl more tightly about her and Samuel. The boy nestled against her chest, his eyelashes resting against his fat cheeks as he drifted off to sleep. If only she were as restful.

"I know you love Samuel, Mr. Lankford, and it's a fine thing you are willing to raise him as your own." She did love the way he loved the boy. "Even so, my answer to your proposal is. . .no." It was harder to say than she'd anticipated.

He took a deep breath. "I understand your reluctance, Miss Taber, but my proposal stands, should you change your mind."

His boots clumped against the porch's wooden planks as he left. She watched him, barely more than a dark shadow against the twilight skies, as he walked down the rutted dirt road toward his neighboring farm. Finally, as he crossed a cornfield a bend hid him from sight.

She lowered herself slowly onto the top step. Her thoughts reeled. The same questions and the same problems and the same possibilities replayed over and over while the twilight faded into night and the nighttime insects' songs grew loud. Samuel's breathing grew slower and more even, his tiny chest rising and falling rhythmically against her own. Curly laid down beside her, resting his head against her thigh with a melodramatic sigh.

Like most unmarried women her age, Lorette had dreamed for years of marrying. Even in a large city like Philadelphia, a governess had few opportunities to meet marriageable men. Properly chaperoning and teaching children did not include becoming overly friendly with vendors and clerks. The few men who had asked to escort her she had met at church. Most were widowers looking for someone to care for their homes and raise their children. She'd wanted more in a marriage. She'd wanted a man who wanted her for herself. "Is that so much to ask, Lord? Is it terribly selfish to want to be loved for me?" she whispered into the night.

Curly stirred, looking up at her with a soft whine. She smiled down at him. "It's all right," she assured him quietly. "I'm only indulging in a little self-pity."

The night was clear and the stars sparkled with more brilliance than a Philadelphia jeweler's window. She loved the prairie sky. She couldn't remember it ever looking so large back East. It reminded her of the entry she'd read in Bess's diary that day.

Each day as I look out over this vast land, I am amazed anew at what Tom and I and others like us are accomplishing, the homes and communities we are building on this prairie. The sky, the fields, the prairie grasses seem to go on forever.

When our children are grown, will there be any
wild land left to tame? I hope the children will
still be able to feel the wonder of this place. Today
when Tom came in from the fields, Aaron ran to
greet him and asked when he can be a farmer. I
thought Tom would burst from pride that his son
at even such a young age wants to work alongside
him. Will our boys still want to work beside Tom
in the fields when they are grown? At least in this
fine land they will have the opportunity to do so if
they choose.

Lorette had told Chase she could take Samuel
back East to protect him from the rumors about her
and Chase. If she did, would Samuel have the opportunity to choose the life of his father, as Bess and Tom
wished for the boy? Could she deny him the opportunity to claim the heritage for which they'd fought so
hard for him?

If her refusal to marry Chase was the right thing,
why didn't she feel at peace? Instead she felt restless
inside.

Lorette pressed a soft kiss to Samuel's head. She
loved the way he rested against her with complete
abandon, with complete trust. She couldn't imagine a
better man than Chase to raise him. She hadn't a doubt
Tom and Bess would approve. Chase would make an
honorable and faithful husband. "But, Lord, I don't
know if I can give up the dream of marrying a man
who loves me."

Even for Samuel? The words whispered through her mind.

She'd asked the Lord yesterday to make clear the best path for her and Samuel. Was marriage to Chase His answer?

Chapter 6

Chase risked a glance at Lorette over the break-fast table. She didn't meet his glance. Her gaze was on her plate, where she idly pushed a piece of sausage about with her fork.

Gray circles shaded the area beneath her eyes. She looked like she hadn't slept any better than he had last night. Could she have reconsidered his proposal? He didn't have the courage to ask, and she didn't mention it.

They barely spoke two words to each other all morning, not during the barn chores and not since. The silence between them was thicker than cream, and not nearly so pleasant.

He glanced down at his own plate and realized he hadn't eaten any more than Lorette. He took a bite of fried egg. Cold fried egg.

Misery slithered through his chest. He'd enjoyed Lorette's company almost from the beginning. Had he ruined all chance of friendship between them by his proposal last night? He had convinced himself it was the sensible thing to do.

Lying in bed last night he finally admitted the

truth to himself. He was falling in love with Lorette. He admired that she hadn't for a moment considered the possibility of not raising Sam, that she was willing to do anything necessary to care for him properly. He liked the courage with which she took to farm life. He enjoyed her cheerful companionship at meals each day.

And he couldn't bear the thought that not only Sam but Lorette might move east, out of his life forever. That fear had been behind his proposal. Had he been a fool to broach the subject of marriage?

Lorette cleared her throat.

His gaze darted to her.

She was still staring at her plate. "About last night. . ."

He waited.

She took a deep breath, not lifting her gaze. "I've been thinking. If I take Samuel back East, I'll likely have to sell the farm." Her words began to come in a rush. "I know from Bess's journal and letters that it was important to her and Tom that the children grow up out here. The farm is Samuel's heritage. I want him to have the choice of living here when he's grown. I know Tom and Bess would want that for him, too. I can't take that away from Samuel."

She paused again, pressing her lips together so hard they turned white. He could barely breathe for waiting for her to finish.

She took another deep breath. "So, if your offer still stands, for Samuel's sake, my answer is yes."

"Yes?"

Lorette nodded, lifting her lashes but not her head

to peer at him, as if to judge his reaction.

"Yes." Joy relieved the pressure in his chest. "You said 'yes'?"

A smile tugged at the edges of her lips. Her gaze darted from one side to the other and back to him in an embarrassed manner that delighted him.

He reminded himself that she wasn't marrying him because she loved him, but for Sam's sake. It surprised him that the knowledge only slightly diminished his joy. "When?"

She shrugged, looking confused.

"It should be soon. To squelch the rumors, I mean."

A shadow passed over her face. He could have kicked himself. How could he be so insensitive? They both knew the rumors were the reason he'd proposed. No need to keep dragging them up. "Is this evening too soon?"

"This evening?" Her voice sounded small and frightened.

Was she frightened to marry him? The thought dampened his spirits. "We can go into town this morning for the license."

"What about the crops?"

"They'll have to do their growing without me this morning. Get yourself and Sam ready. I'll hitch Boots up to the wagon. I want to stop by Bresvens' on the way."

By the time they were ready to leave, Lorette had changed into a slim peach-colored dress with lace trim and a matching bonnet. The dress was much fancier than the calico and gingham dresses covered by aprons she normally wore about the farm. She blushed prettily when he complimented her.

Lorette waited in the wagon while he went to speak with Mrs. Bresven. When he told her of the marriage, the Swedish woman hesitated only a moment before her round face burst into a smile. Her plump hands clasped his arms. "The Bible says it's a good thing when a man finds a wife. You've found yourself a good one in Miss Taber. I'm happy for you both," she congratulated in her singsong accent.

The reserve with which he'd been protecting himself fell away. "Thank you. We want to get married right away. Tonight. I was wondering—could we be married in your parlor? I know it's a lot to ask on such short notice, but I want it to be special for her, and—"

"A wedding in my own parlor!" Her eyes sparkled. "Yah, I should say you can marry here."

She insisted on going out to the wagon to congratulate Lorette. They found the future Mrs. Lankford in the wagon bed finishing up changing Sam's diaper. Chase watched Lorette's face anxiously as Mrs. Bresven eagerly congratulated Lorette and told how honored she was that Chase and Lorette wanted to be married in the Bresvens' home.

Lorette's surprised gaze met Chase's over Mrs. Bresven's head, but she answered with only a slight stammer that it was very kind of Mrs. Bresven to agree to their request.

As they continued their journey Lorette said, "I

thought we would be married by the judge in town this morning."

Chase didn't want to tell her that he thought such a marriage would appear clandestine, an admission of guilt to the gossiping townspeople. He looked right into her eyes and said, "A marriage should be a joyful occasion. I want it to be a nice memory for you."

He allowed her to study his eyes, knowing she was searching for the truth. Finally her face lost a little of the tension he'd seen in it all day. Her smile was soft. "Thank you."

Chase smiled back, his chest expanding beneath his clean brown work shirt. He felt like he'd just been handed the world.

Sam, who was the cause of the marriage and was seated on Lorette's lap, giggled for no apparent reason and clapped his baby hands with glee.

❧

That evening Lorette was surprised and humbled when she entered Mrs. Bresven's parlor. The room wasn't fancy. The furniture wasn't as new or as beautiful as Bess's. Yet Lorette's heart was touched by the effort this newfound Swedish friend had gone to on her behalf.

Vines of pale pink wild roses stretched delicately across the tops of the windows and door. They wound among the items on the lace-covered table at one end of the room, in between a huge bowl of punch, plates of angel food cake, and delicate china plates and cups that Lorette knew Mrs. Bresven must count among her treasures.

"Everything is beautiful, Mrs. Bresven. Thank you so much."

Her neighbor beamed. "Please, call me Kari. If you are to be married in my home, we must be good enough friends to call each other by our first names."

"Yes, and I am Lorette."

"Your dress is beautiful."

"Thank you." Lorette looked down at her emerald green silk gown. The dress did not have the trim silhouette that was currently popular. She ran a gloved hand lightly over one hip, feeling the skirt's fullness. The long train caught up on the sides with silk flowers adding an elegance to the gown. "It was Bess's wedding dress."

She had found it in Bess's trunk. It had taken hours this afternoon to iron out the wrinkles.

"You look beautiful in it."

Lorette looked up in surprise at Chase's gravelly voice. She hadn't realized he was so close.

He cleared his throat. "Bess would have been happy that you chose to wear her wedding gown."

Lorette smiled at him, glad he recognized that wearing the dress made her feel closer to her sister.

The Bresven children rushed about alternately helping their mother prepare for company and reluctantly obeying her orders to keep away from the food and to be careful of their Sunday clothes. They all wanted to hold Samuel and play with him. Lorette enjoyed the bustle. The conversation with the children kept her mind off the enormity of the event ahead.

She was surprised when neighbors began stopping.

"I thought only the Bresvens would be at the wedding," she said when she and Chase had a rare moment alone.

"I wanted my friends to celebrate with us. Do you mind very much?"

"No."

He touched her cheek softly with the back of one hand. "I wish your friends could be here."

At the gentleness of his touch and his thought for her, sweet pain throbbed in her chest. Her gaze caught in his and she forgot there were other people about them.

"Here comes the minister," someone shouted.

The announcement jolted Lorette back to the parlor.

The ceremony was simple and solemn. Lorette was thankful that Chase had arranged for the minister to perform it, rather than the judge she had at first thought would marry them. She believed deeply that marriage was not only a legal but also a spiritual union.

It was frightening saying the vows, pledging to spend her life with this man she'd known such a short time. But working on the farm together, didn't they know each other better than most couples who courted in the prescribed manner?

She barely noticed the ring when he slipped it on her finger. When the ceremony was over and his friends were toasting them with Kari's punch, Lorette realized she was twisting the ring nervously and looked closer. She gasped at the beautiful jewelry. The stone was a large, rectangular blue sapphire mounted in a delicate, intricate setting. She looked up at Chase and saw he was watching her. He seemed to understand her question.

"The ring was my mother's," he said in low voice for her ears alone. "If you don't like it, we'll buy you another."

"No." She slid her right hand over the ring. "I'll cherish it."

He took her hands between his own and squeezed them lightly. Then he raised an arm and waited for the crowd to quiet. He thanked them all for sharing the special day. He slid an arm around Lorette's shoulders and looked down at her. "And I thank God for bringing the gift of Lorette into my life."

Lorette's heart stumbled. He seemed so sincere. She wanted to believe he thought her a gift, but it felt like trusting in daydreams. Hadn't she given up the dream of marrying a man who loved her?

The ride back to the farm wasn't nearly long enough, Lorette felt. Chase had explained that as a bachelor, he hadn't put time and money into building a 'real' house yet. He lived in a one-room soddy. They had agreed it was best to live in Tom and Bess's home.

She was trembling when he helped her down from the wagon. He kept his hands lightly on her waist. She didn't dare lift her gaze to his but stared into his shoulder.

"If you want, I can spend the night at my soddy."

She shook her head. "No," she whispered. What if the neighbors spotted him heading to Bess and Tom's from his own place in the morning? It would be terribly embarrassing.

He bent his head and touched his lips to hers, quickly and lightly. Slowly his arms slid around her waist, drawing her closer. Her heart tripped over itself. He kissed her again, his lips soft, lingering, questioning, sweeter than she'd imagined a kiss could be.

Lorette wanted to abandon herself to his arms and kisses, but her chest burned. How could she give herself freely when he hadn't said he loved her? She pushed lightly against his shoulders.

He pulled his lips from hers immediately and rested his head against hers. His breath was coming quickly and unevenly. They stood that way for many minutes, until they heard Samuel fussing in his makeshift bed in the back of the wagon.

Lorette felt cold when Chase released her to pick up the boy. He placed Samuel in Lorette's arms. "I'll put Boots away while you put Sam to bed."

She nodded and started up the porch steps. Her heart hammered in her ears. What would happen when Chase came inside? Would he expect. . .

"Lorette."

She couldn't see his features as he stood in the late evening shadows beside Boots.

"It's all right, Lorette." His voice was gentle. "I'll sleep in one of the other rooms."

Lorette wasn't sure whether she felt relief or regret as she carried Samuel up to her bedchamber.

Chapter 7

T he first few days after their marriage, things felt strained to Lorette between herself and Chase. Marriage hadn't changed their daily lives much. Chase had been an integral part of her life and Samuel's before the marriage; now they just lived under the same roof.

That they no longer referred to each other as Mr. Lankford and Miss Taber, but as Chase and Lorette, was only a symbol of the true changes. Her emotions were vulnerable in a new and terrifying way. She was self-conscious about every look between them, every casual touch. Her life and Samuel's were no longer hers alone to control. She was tied to Chase and this land forever.

One rainy evening in late July Chase took a fussy Samuel into the family room while Lorette cleaned up after the meal. She shaved soap into the enamel dishpan and poured in hot water from the steaming teakettle. Setting the kettle back on the stove, she paused at the sound of Chase's deep voice singing a lullaby.

Smiling, she tiptoed to the doorway and peeked in. Chase was seated in Bess's tapestry covered rocker, dwarfing the delicate chair. He didn't notice her. His attention was on Samuel lying on his lap in total trust, his eyes closed. The hominess of the scene was endearing.

When Chase finished the simple melody for the third time, she cleared her throat to get his attention. He looked up with a silly grin that showed her he was embarrassed.

Not wanting to awaken Samuel, she walked softly until she was close enough to whisper. "My mother sang that to Bess and me when we were little."

"Tell me about your childhood."

She lowered herself to the small crewel-covered footstool and told of growing up in Philadelphia. It had been a happy life until her parents were killed in a train accident. Soon after, she'd found a position as a governess, and Bess married Tom and moved to the Minnesota prairie.

Inclement weather made the room darker than usual for the hour, and Lorette hadn't lit the lamps yet. Perhaps the atmosphere made it easier for them to confide in each other in new ways.

Chase told her about his own life, his early childhood years in the East, coming west to Wisconsin with his parents to farm, then moving here to homestead as a young man. He hadn't as much land under acreage as Tom. He'd begun assisting Tom for money, working his own land at the same time. It was a long, hard road, but Chase didn't mind.

"Tom used to talk about when Sam and Aaron

would be old enough to work beside him in the fields. He hoped to eventually buy more land so he could help them get started on their own farms."

"Bess spoke of that, too, in her journals." *I made the right decision, marrying Chase,* Lorette thought. *He understands and shares Bess and Tom's dreams for Samuel. It's obvious he loves the boy.*

"By the time Sam is grown and claims his inheritance, we'll have a real house on our land."

This was the first time either of them had spoken of their distant future together, when it would be just the two of them in a marriage without the boy who had brought them together. She'd been too busy with everyday life to consider that such a time might come. The thought was a disturbing one to Lorette. "I'd best get back to the dishes before the water gets cold."

His words stayed with her. "*We* will have a real house on *our* land."

Always in the back of her mind she'd wondered whether Bess and Tom's land and their new house had been important factors behind Chase's proposal. The way he spoke tonight, it didn't appear so. "*We* will have a real house on *our* land." His words seemed filled with promise, as though he believed one day their marriage would be beautiful and rich in its normalness.

For days his words came back to her at odd times while she played with Samuel, or cared for the animals, or worked about the house. Weeding in the garden two weeks later the picture of Chase rocking Samuel and singing the lullaby filled her mind. "Oh, my!" Her hands stilled the hoe as a surprising and dismaying thought struck.

"This is the life I wished for when I was back in Philadelphia," she told an uncomprehending Samuel, who sat in the dirt happily yanking at a stubborn weed.

Wonder filled her at the realization. She hadn't wished to be a farm wife, she thought, placing a hand on her lower back and stretching stiff muscles. But she'd wished for her own family. Bess's letters, which had bubbled over with love for Tom and the children, had stirred embers of envy in Lorette's heart.

"Now I have my own family—and all because Bess and Tom died." She looked across the land to where the crosses were barely visible through wind-whipped prairie grass. She didn't believe God allowed Bess and Tom to die in order to give Lorette a ready-made family. But living on the prairie, she saw that nature and God waste nothing, even death. In one way or another all death brought new life out here.

Her gaze dropped to Samuel. "No!" She darted to him, bending over and pulling his hand from his mouth. She opened the sticky, dirty fingers and removed a granite colored stone with a sigh of relief. "I have to watch you every minute."

"Uh! Uh!" He made grasping motions with his fingers.

"No."

Samuel struggled to his feet and started down the row, trying out his newfound independence in walking. Three steps along he tumbled into the dirt. Curly, who was never far away when Lorette was outside with Samuel, stuck his nose in Samuel's face to be sure he was okay. Samuel pushed himself up on his forearms and shook his head until his curls shook, too. "No. No, Da."

Lorette laughed. Samuel's vocabulary only included four words: mama, papa, no, and da for dog. Sometimes he called her mama and Chase papa. It was hard to hear. She and Chase agreed Samuel would always know who his parents were, but he wasn't old enough to understand yet.

She took his hand as he struggled to his feet. "Let's go back to the house and get dinner ready."

Contentment filled her as they walked slowly along with his little fingers clutching hers. Every few steps he'd fight for balance, sometimes winning, sometimes losing. "You're getting better at walking every day," she told him.

Like she and Chase and Samuel were getting better at being a family every day. She knew Chase loved Samuel. She was pretty sure Chase liked her. But liking wasn't loving. *That's the part of my dream that's missing*, she thought, her heart twisting, *a husband who loves me.*

❧

Lorette stole a moment to look out Kari Bresven's kitchen window at the late summer fields bathed in sunshine. The crops were abundant and beautiful, but they wouldn't be standing long. Harvest was going well. Chase, like most of the area farmers, had hired men to help. The neighbors were helping each other out, too. Harvest on Chase and Lorette's crops had been completed yesterday. Today Chase was helping in the Bresvens' fields, and Lorette and other neighbor women were helping Kari in the kitchen as the women had helped Lorette previously. Kari's children watched Samuel and some of the other wives' young ones so the women could work unimpeded.

Throughout the last week Lorette had fried chicken, peeled potatoes, and baked ten loaves of bread and a dozen pies. Now she was peeling potatoes again and wondering whether she would have any skin left on her fingers after harvest.

"Watching for a glimpse of that good-looking husband of yours?" a voice teased behind her.

Lorette turned with a smile but ignored the jest. "Catching a bit of breeze." She liked Susan, a dark-haired young farm wife. Lorette thought Susan seemed much younger and more carefree than herself, though she was only a year younger and had been married five years.

Lorette stepped back to the worktable and glanced in dismay at the pile of unpeeled potatoes on which she and Susan were working. It looked like it had grown in the few seconds she'd spent at the window. Already she missed the breeze. She'd grown accustomed to the prairie winds. They were quieter than usual today, and the house was hot from the oven that had been going since before dawn. The smell of fresh-baked bread and pies didn't make the heat any easier to bear. Her dress stuck to her and her hair itched.

Susan finished peeling another potato and continued her teasing. "A number of young ladies had their bonnets set for your husband when he was single."

Lorette glanced at her in surprise. Unmarried men greatly outnumbered unmarried women in the area. Why hadn't it occurred to her to wonder before why Chase, who loved children and family, hadn't married before she came along?

"Good thing he waited." Kari set a kettle of cold water on the table for the peeled potatoes.

Lorette began to feel uneasy with the turn in conversation. The women were talking as if they didn't remember the rumors that precipitated Chase's proposal. She shifted her worried gaze to Kari.

The practical woman said quietly, "I've known Chase a long time. It's easy to see you make him happy."

Her words warmed Lorette's heart. She knew the hasty wedding hadn't fooled Kari, but the dear woman believed she and Chase could make a happy marriage even with such a beginning.

"He's not as good-looking as my husband of course," Susan continued with a laugh, "but he's a good man."

Lorette smiled. "Yes."

Kari brushed her hands down her apron. "There's nothing wrong with Chase Lankford's looks that I can see."

Susan shrugged good-naturedly. "I guess handsome is in the eye of the beholder."

Lorette shared in the laughter Susan's misquote

brought. It was fun to be teased about Chase. She thought him by far the best looking man she'd seen since her arrival from Philadelphia, but it wouldn't have mattered if he was bald and had to bend over to see his boots. It was Chase's heart she loved.

Out in the yard, large pieces of wood were set on sawhorses and barrels to form a long table. At noon when the men came in from the fields Lorette watched eagerly for Chase while carrying food from the house to the table. They only shared quick smiles as they passed. Lorette enjoyed the visiting that went on with harvest time, but she missed the family meals with just her, Chase, and Samuel.

The table almost groaned under the heavy load of food. Lorette walked down one side filling coffee cups while the men loaded their plates. Each of the men had washed up at the pails of water on the back porch before sitting down, but it seemed to Lorette that the washing hadn't decreased the smell of sweat and kerosene one iota.

When she came to Chase he lifted his cup for her. "Things going all right this morning?"

She met his gaze, found him smiling into her eyes, and returned his smile. "Yes, fine. How are things going in the fields?"

He hadn't a chance to answer. Susan's husband, Ben, seated across from Chase, spoke first in a loud voice meant to draw attention. "Can sure tell yer a newlywed, Lankford. Come from a hot morning in the fields and yer more interested in speaking to yer wife than eating."

Ben's eyes sparkled with fun, but Lorette knew her cheeks flamed from his comments. She went on with her work.

Susan didn't ignore him. "Stop your teasing, Ben. Every man should look at his wife the way Chase looks at Lorette."

"Better listen up, Ben." Laughter threaded Chase's words.

Lorette darted a surprised look at Chase. He grinned at her in a manner that was downright flirtatious. Flustered, she murmured something about getting more coffee, though the pot still felt heavy, and retreated to the hot kitchen.

During the afternoon, Chase's looks and words danced through Lorette's mind. Ben's comments hadn't appeared to embarrass Chase at all. Still, she tried to avoid giving cause for further comments at the group supper and was glad when they finally left for home.

Chase brought in the large tin tub from the shed to the kitchen and Lorette heated water for their Saturday night baths while Chase took care of the animals. Samuel was the first to be bathed. Lorette had hoped the long day with the other children would have tired him, but it seemed to have energized him instead. She was glad Chase offered to watch the boy in the sitting room while she bathed.

The change into clean clothes felt good after the long hot day. She towel dried her hair and combed it out, letting it hang loose to dry.

When she entered the sitting room, Chase was holding Samuel and standing in front of Bess and Tom's family picture. Chase glanced at her. "Sam looks more like his father every day."

Lorette compared the boy to the image of the man. "Yes." Even in the lamplight the similarity was noticeable. So were the lines in Chase's face. He looked weary. She was sure he was wishing Tom and his family hadn't died. He would think it no use saying so; his wishing wouldn't bring them back.

Samuel wriggled and pushed at Chase's chest, and Chase set him down.

"I'll watch him now," Lorette said.

"He's mighty full of life for so late. He's trying to climb up on everything, when he's not chewing it."

"I'll rock him and read to him. I read to him every day from Bess's journal. I like knowing he is hearing his mother's words, even if he doesn't know they are hers." She shrugged, self-conscious at her revelation, half expecting him to laugh.

Chase touched her cheek, brushing his thumb slowly and gently over it. "When he's older, I'll tell him you did this for him, and he'll read her journals himself."

His sweet intimacy was unexpected. He never touched her in such a personal manner. His understanding made it a moment she knew she would cherish. "Thank you," she whispered.

A frustrated grunt cut the moment off as effectively as a slamming door.

"No!" They hollered at the same time. Both lunged

for Samuel. Chase reached the boy first, swinging him up with only an inch to spare before Samuel would have grabbed the fringed table covering beneath the fancy lit kerosene lamp.

Lorette was shaking when Chase put the boy into her arms. "Close call." Chase shook his head before heading for the kitchen and his bath.

Lorette had to rock the struggling youngster for a few minutes to calm herself before she could read. She and Samuel had read almost the entire journal; they were up to the last entry. Lorette looked at the date and a sadness welled up in her. The date was the day before Bess died.

> *Aaron and Liza are complaining of sore throats, and mine is feeling a bit scratchy. Such a time to come down with something, with Lorette coming in a couple days. I can barely contain my excitement at seeing her again! I keep thinking of things I must tell her, and must ask her, and memories I want to relive with her. I do hope she will be happy working for the Henrys, though I confess another fantasy has crossed my mind a few times since she agreed to come out west. I like to pretend she and Chase fall in love. . ."*

Lorette's voice stumbled. She glanced at the closed kitchen door. Had Chase heard? She lowered her words to barely a whisper.

I like to pretend she and Chase fall in love and marry. Tom tells me to quit being fanciful, but it would be such fun to have my sister and Tom's best friend for neighbors. Our children could grow up together.

She closed the book. "That's your mother's last entry, Samuel."

He plopped both hands on the leather cover. "Mama."

Tears leaped to her eyes and she hugged him close. "Yes."

The door opened and Chase stuck his wet head into the room. "I'm going out to check on the animals one last time." A moment later she heard the outside door squeak open and close again.

In a shaky voice, she began singing a lullaby. After what seemed a long time, Samuel fell asleep. She placed him in his crib and went to stand on the porch.

The weather was pleasant, having cooled off after the sun went down. An orange harvest moon brightened the landscape. In the pale light she saw Chase walking back from the graves.

"I was thinking," he said when he arrived at the porch, "that we should use some of the money from the crops to buy headstones."

Gratitude flooded her. "I'd like that. You were wonderful to make the crosses, but. . ."

"They aren't permanent like a headstone."

"No."

255

He came to stand beside her, leaning against the rail and looking out over the land.

"I'm going to miss the crops," she told him. "I liked watching them grow and change. As they grew they changed the landscape. Sometimes the colors changed from hour to hour, depending on the height of the sun, and the movement of the clouds, or the wiles of the winds."

He chuckled. "They'll be back next year."

Lorette looked down at the wooden rail and ran her fingers lightly along it. Her heart beat hard against her chest as she built up her courage to ask the question she'd been wondering about since morning. "Why didn't you marry before you met me?"

He was silent so long that she finally looked at him. His face looked taut in the shadows cast by the moon.

"Never mind. I shouldn't have asked."

He took a deep breath. "You have every right to ask. You're my wife. You can ask me anything."

Lorette tried to drink in the wonder of his words before he continued.

"I'd been courting a girl when I decided to move out here and homestead. Thought I loved her. Thought she loved me, too. When I told her my plans and asked her to marry me, she said she'd never marry a farmer."

Lorette didn't know what to say. She reached out and tentatively laid a hand on his forearm. He covered her hand with his own and went on with his story.

"Gave up on the idea of love and marriage after that. Then I met Tom and Bess. Tom, he sure was crazy in love with your sister. After awhile, seeing them together, I began to have second thoughts about getting married, but I didn't meet anyone I wanted to spend my life with." He squeezed her hand. "Then God brought you into my life."

Her throat tightened. Was he saying he truly cared for her?

"I saw the sacrifices you were making for Samuel, the hard life you took on without a whimper of self-pity. Every day I found myself liking you more, and then it was more than liking."

Lorette could barely breathe. Was he saying he loved her?

He slid his hand from hers, and her fingers felt suddenly cool in the night air. "It was wrong to ask you to marry me the way I did." His voice sounded hard.

"Wh. . .why?"

"You were grieving for Bess and you'd just found out about the rumors. No one could be expected to think clearly about what they want and need at such a time." He shoved both hands through his hair and turned to her. "I was so terrified you might move back East that I was glad for an excuse to press you to marry me. But maybe I've ruined your life. Maybe you would have been happier back East, and now I've tied you to me and to this land."

He'd wanted to marry her for herself, not only for Samuel! Joy flooded her at the realization, but he still hadn't said he loved her. She chose her words carefully.

"I'm beginning to understand Bess's love for this

land. When I first came here, I thought the prairie was a threatening place. Living on the farm has made me aware of nature's life, death, life cycle. I'll never stop missing Bess, but I'm able to accept her death better now. I realize the land isn't the enemy. We aren't in battle against it. We're in partnership with it." Lorette could feel his gaze on her.

"We?" His tone was wary.

Lorette met his gaze. "I've no desire to move back East. Every day when you leave for the fields or chores, it seems all Samuel and I do is wait for you to return."

His hands lifted slowly and framed her face. "I love you, Lorette. I've loved you almost since you moved out to the farm, but I didn't think you'd want to hear it."

"I do want to hear it. I want to hear it every day."

He pulled her into his arms and whispered against her hair, "I love you, Lorette. I love you. I love you."

She relaxed against him, drinking in the words she'd waited so long to hear. "I love you, too," she replied shyly, whispering the words she'd been waiting all her life to say.

He chuckled, lifting her in his arms and swinging her around in a circle again and again, his boots thunking against the porch boards. "I want to hear it every day, too," he demanded.

He kissed her soundly on the lips, his arms tight about her waist, then lowered her slowly until she stood on her own feet. His kisses didn't stop. They grew sweeter and lingered longer and longer and longer.

"I should get you inside before it gets too cool out

here," Chase finally said.

Lorette nodded against his shoulder. Her last thought as they walked into their home wrapped in each other's arms was that the Lord had indeed made a way for her and Samuel; He'd made a very nice way indeed.

JOANN A. GROTE

JoAnn is an award-winning author from Minnesota. Her first novel, *The Sure Promise*, was published by **Heartsong** in 1993. It was reissued in the best-selling anthology *Inspirational Romance Reader, Historical Collection #2* (Barbour Publishing). JoAnn has published historical nonfiction books for children and over twenty historical novels for adults and children, including several novels with Barbour Publishing in the **Heartsong Presents** line as well as the American Adventure series for kids. She contributed novellas to the anthology *Prairie Brides* and to the best-selling anthology *Fireside Christmas* (Barbour Publishing). JoAnn's love of history developed when she worked at an historical restoration in North Carolina for five years. She enjoys researching her books and weaving her fictional characters' lives into historical backgrounds and events. Her latest **Heartsong Presents** novel, *Come Home to my Heart*, is an exciting departure from the past for her as it is her first contemporary novel. Once a full-time CPA, JoAnn now works in accounting only part-time and spends most of her "work" time researching and writing.

A Vow
Unbroken

by Amy Rognlie

Prologue

A bby Cantrell stared at the date at the top of the letter, her eyes widening.

April 29, 1881. Why hadn't Aunt Caroline told her it would be so soon? Dropping down into the chair, she smoothed the crisp paper, reading again the telltale words.

Dear Miss Peters,

I can't tell you how happy I was to receive your letter this past week. I trust that you, as do I, look forward to the approaching day when we shall meet here in Littleton. Enclosed is the train ticket, as well as a little extra money in case you have need of something. I will be waiting for you on the appointed day. Until then, I remain yours truly,

James Parrish

Abby jumped as footsteps sounded in the tiled hallway. Slipping the letter back into the Bible where she had found it, she stood and ambled over to the library window. The fading sunset cast shadows on the budding trees, holding her gaze until she heard the footsteps behind her, their sound muffled by the plush carpet.

"Beautiful evening."

The softly spoken words invaded the tumult in Abby's mind. She sighed, turning slightly to drape her arm over the shoulders of the small woman beside her. The comforting scent of roses embraced her. "What am I going to do, Mama?"

Hazel Peters smoothed her daughter's dark hair. "I don't know, dear. Surely God has a plan. . . ." She fell silent as Abby turned away to gaze out of the lace-framed window. The silence stretched, broken only by the sound of the mourning doves getting ready to roost. "But I do know this," Hazel whispered. "He said He would not give us more than we could bear."

Abby eyed the darkening sky. Her mind acknowledged the truth of her mother's words, but her heart felt the shadows of night moving slowly and surely, threatening to plunge her into a darkness unlike any she had ever known.

Chapter 1

J ames Parrish gripped his cap tightly at the sound of a distant train whistle. He scarcely noticed the porters checking the luggage or the scampering children. His concentrations focused upon the tiny, moving speck in the distance. Perspiration prickled at the nape of his neck.

Would she be on the train, as she had promised? He had waited so long, had poured over her letter, had dreamed of what she would look like. *Miss Caroline Peters.* He liked the sound of it as he rolled it around in his mind. He stared at the train, now close enough for him to read the letters on the side. The Denver Rio Grand Railway. He peered anxiously at the windows, straining to see as the train squealed to a stop. Was she finally here?

He watched the passengers as they disembarked. Most were Denverites coming to Littleton for a day in the country. He kneaded his cap, his eyes locked on the straggling line of people. There. Was that her? His heart leapt as he spied a dark-haired woman coming toward him, a welcoming smile on her lovely face. She had almost reached him, when an older gentleman brushed past him and grasped her arm.

James exhaled forcefully and turned his attention back to those still struggling down the narrow steps, their valises bumping their sides. He wished that he had a more detailed description, but the brief one she had sent him would have to do. He would find her, if it was the last thing. . .wait. There. That had to be her. One of the last passengers to came down the steps, she paused at the platform as if unsure of herself. He watched her glance about, the fetching pink feather in her hat softly dancing, her arms full. He couldn't see her face very well, until her gaze fell on him.

The woman smiled tentatively and he started toward her as if in a dream, his gaze locked with hers. Finally, he stood in front of her. Her hazel eyes reminded him of the first greening of spring. She was beautiful. And so small. She barely came up to his shoulder. . . .

"Mr. Parrish?" At her softly spoken words, James realized that he had been staring.

"Yes, I'm Mr. Parrish." He winced at how stiff and formal he sounded. He had wanted to greet her warmly. Welcoming. But meeting this way was just so awkward.

"I'm glad to finally be here. And to make your acquaintance," she said.

Her voice sounded weary, and as James continued to study her face, he noted the purple shadows under those beautiful eyes. Her journey had been a long one,

he realized. But did her eyes reflect more than weariness? Sorrow, perhaps?

He watched her out of the corner of his eye as he
collected her trunk. She was so beautiful; he could
scarcely believe it. Of course, he had made up his mind
the he would love his new bride, no matter what she
looked like. Yet, the Lord had chosen to bless him with
a beauty of a wife. He smiled at her tenderly, then offered his hand to help her into the wagon. For the first
time, he found himself wishing he had a nice carriage.
Still, she knew he was a farmer. Surely she hadn't expected anything fancy.

He watched her gather her skirts to climb into the
wagon. As she leaned into his grip to hoist herself up,
her foot slipped. Instinctively, he caught her as she fell
backward, catching a whiff of her perfume as well. He
set her carefully on her feet, his heart pounding at her
nearness. He wanted to hold her in his arms and never
let her go.

She stammered out an apology, bending laboriously
to retrieve her shawl from the dusty street. Straightening
up, she met his shocked gaze. She was with child!

*Dear God, what kind of cruel trick has this woman
played on me?* He gaped at her in silence. *How could she?*

Vulnerability briefly shimmered in her eyes before
a glaze of weary resignation replaced it. "I suppose she
didn't tell you."

"Who?" he croaked.

She raised her eyebrows.

"Who didn't tell me what?" He swallowed against

the sudden dryness in his throat, trying to gather his thoughts and steel himself for whatever explanation she would offer.

"My. . .aunt. . .Caroline. . ." Her shoulders drooped and tears filled her eyes, threatening to spill over.

James reached out to her instinctively, as he would to a forlorn child. He put his hand under her chin, marveling at how soft her skin was against the roughness of his own. "It's all right," he whispered. "Can you just explain. . .I mean. . .I. . .don't understand."

She swallowed hard but didn't pull away from his touch. "My aunt Caroline. She didn't tell you that I was in the family way." Her words formed a statement rather than a question.

Silence settled between them as James struggled to comprehend her words. Why had Caroline's pregnant niece come, and not Caroline? Were they trying to trick him? If so, why? Was this all a big joke on him—the dumb farmer out in cow country? The heat began to rise in his face. How could he have been so idealistic—so hopefully stupid—to believe that he would finally have wife?

He glanced back down at her, his mental tirade ceasing when he met the misery in her eyes.

"I'm so sorry," she whispered. "She said she didn't think you'd mind if I came in her place. She. . .I should have known she wouldn't have told you. But I can still work. I'll do anything you need me to do. I don't know how to do anything on a farm, but I can cook and clean, and. . ."

Her words trailed off as he scrutinized her. He couldn't believe someone so small could carry such a large child. He doubted she'd be doing much cooking and cleaning for quite awhile. He shook his head in disbelief at this bewildering situation. "If you are not Miss Caroline, then I suppose I don't even know your name."

"Abigail Cantrell." She gave him a faint smile. "Most people call me Abby."

What else should he say? "Well, Abby. . ."

Her face clouded. "I guess I'm just not what you were expecting, Mr. Parrish. I'm so sorry. . . ."

He made an effort to grin, but failed. "Can I ask you. . .why Caroline didn't come?" Did she decide that life on a farm would be too dull, so she sent her niece instead?

Abby looked pained. "It's a long story, Mr. Parrish. However, I assure your arrangement wouldn't have worked out anyway. Caroline is. . .would not be suited for the work."

Why does she keep talking about all the hard work? Sure, it is work to be a farmer's wife, but that's not the reason I searched for a wife. Only God knows how long I've yearned for a companion, someone to share life's sorrows and joys. James cleared his throat, hoping for some inspiration to seize him. What was he supposed to do with a pregnant woman? He couldn't very well marry her now, could he? But, what else. . .?

"Might there be somewhere I could get a drink of water?" she asked.

Abby's soft voice pulled his attention back to her. The look of utter exhaustion on her face smote his heart with regret. How long had he kept her standing outside in the blazing sun, and in her condition? "Forgive me," he said, giving her his hand.

She sighed with relief as she sank down onto the wagon seat, closing her eyes as if she would fall asleep right there. James clucked to the horses then glanced at her in concern. "Are you all right, ma'am?"

Guiltily, her eyes popped open. "I didn't sleep very well on the train, I guess." She gazed at him. "How far do you live from town?"

James swallowed hard, feeling slightly addled. *Surely she doesn't think I am going to marry her!* "Uh, not too far. I hadn't planned on us going home until to-morrow. . .but I guess. . ."

She bit her lip, obviously sensing his turmoil. "It's all right, Mr. Parrish. I should have known. . . ." She straightened her shoulders. "I don't want you to feel beholden to me. If you'll just let me off at a boarding-house, I'm sure I can find some other work."

He gaped at her. What kind of man did she think he was? True, she didn't know a thing about him. But, surely she didn't think that he would just dump her in a strange town. He was responsible for bringing her here, wasn't he? "I can't do that, ma'am," he said softly. "I'm sure we can work something out."

The relief in her eyes spoke volumes. After all, what kind of "work" could she find in her condition? The thought made him cringe.

"I'm a good cook," she offered timidly.

He smiled then, his first real smile since this peculiar situation began. "Well, I like to eat. So I guess we're off to a good start." *But what do I do now?* He glanced at her small, glove-covered hands clasped demurely in her lap. Or what was left of her lap.

"When is. . .I mean how long until. . ." He felt his face redden at his clumsy questioning.

"The child will be born in about six weeks, Mr. Parrish." She didn't smile, but he thought he detected a glint of humor in her large eyes.

"Ah, I see. Well. . .I. . ." *Dear Lord, help me*, he pleaded silently. *I'm in over my head, and I don't know what to do.*

The voice in his heart replied, *Show her the way to Me.*

James swallowed hard, then made up his mind. "Ma'am, I know that you're very tired. I'm going to take you to the boardinghouse, and we can talk more in the morning."

"Thank you," she said, giving him a small smile.

They drove the rest of the short distance in silence. James pulled up in front of his sister's house, jumping off the wagon seat as soon as the horses came to a halt. Abby was looking paler by the minute. Lifting her gingerly down from the wagon, he escorted her to Iris's door. "Hope you got a room ready, Sis," he hollered in through the screen door.

Iris came running, her eyes widening as she took in the couple standing on her porch. Her gaze flew to

James's face. He frowned slightly and shook his head, and she nodded, turning her attention to Abby. "You look worn out, dear. Come in and let me fix you a cup of tea."

James silently blessed his sister for not questioning him. He released Abby into her care with a sigh of relief. "Miss. . .uh, ma'am, this is my sister Iris." He pasted a smile on his face. "I'll be back in the morning, ladies." Turning, he strode back to the wagon as fast as he could without actually running. What kind of a mess had he gotten himself into?

Chapter 2

Abby stared after him for a long moment, wondering what was going through his mind. He had seemed to be such a gentleman, although she was obviously not what he had expected. What in the world had Caroline told the poor man?

He was a lot younger than Abby had expected. *Yes, quite a bit younger,* she mused. *And handsome, too. With hair the color of sun-kissed wheat, eyes—*

"Come on in, dear," Iris repeated, breaking into Abby's wandering thoughts. "I guess James forgot to tell me your name."

Abby looked up to find Iris's brilliant eyes, eyes the same bright blue as her brother's, fastened on her face. "Abby Cantrell. I'm so sorry. . . ."

"Nonsense." Iris gave an unladylike snort, accompanied by a friendly grin. "You're tired from your long trip, and James brought you here so you could rest. That's no reason to be sorry."

Abby sighed as she slogged into the house after Iris, feeling as if she might collapse if she remained on her feet much longer.

"Now, you just sit down here and put your feet up on this stool," Iris commanded. "I'll bring you a cup of tea."

Abby obeyed, her heart warming at the genuine friendliness of the woman.

Iris reappeared with two steaming cups. Handing one to Abby, she settled herself comfortably on a floral tapestry settee. "Now, tell me all about yourself, Abby."

James clenched his teeth against the jarring of the wagon as it bumped over the dirt road. How could the day's events have taken such an unexpected turn? He sighed as he pulled up in front of the farmhouse. He should have been bringing a bride home. But, instead of a bride, he had a problem. A big one.

He did his chores mechanically, then sank down in his favorite rocker in front of the hearth. Since she—no, since Caroline—answered his newspaper advertisement, he had dreamed of his bride sitting next to him in this very room, sharing treasured moments from the day, just being together. Now that's all it was—a dream.

God, I thought you were leading me. I thought I was doing Your will. He pictured Abby's face. She was all he had hoped for in a wife. Even in the short time he was with her, he could sense her gentle spirit. And she was beautiful, too, of course.

But what of the child? He wished he'd had the presence of mind to ask her more questions. How could she possibly even think that he would marry her?

It wasn't just the fact that she was carrying a child, but that he felt somehow deceived. Had it been their plan all along? Was she running from some sort of trouble? *Maybe her family sent her away when they learned the shameful truth of what she had done—or had done to her,* he thought.

He felt his head begin to throb. What did she want from him? A sudden horrifying thought came to him. What if there really was no Aunt Caroline, and what if Abby was already married? Maybe she was running away from her husband. He had heard of such things happening. But then. . .he thought again of the wounded look in her expressive eyes, her shy smile, the way she carried herself with womanly dignity, and he couldn't believe anything sordid about her.

"Well, Lord, I guess You will have to show me what to do with this young lady," he said aloud. "All I know is, I prayed long and fervently for a wife. . .and Abby Cantrell is the one that arrived on the train." He picked up his well-worn Bible from the hearth. "If she's the one You sent me, I need to know."

"Lean not unto thine own understanding. In all thy ways acknowledge him, and he shall direct thy paths." The oft-read verse from Proverbs jumped out at him. He closed his eyes, remembering the still, small voice that had spoken earlier.

Show her the way to Me. Show her the way to Me.

After a long while, James rose and went to bed. Tomorrow should prove to be a day he would remember for years to come—his wedding day.

His heart began a slow thump when he saw her sitting on Iris's porch steps, the morning sun glinting off her dark, shiny hair. She smiled at him, and he couldn't seem to remember anything he had planned to say.

He swiped his hat off as he neared the porch. "Good morning, ma'am. Did you sleep well?"

She nodded. "Yes, thank you."

He gestured to the step. "May I?" At her nod, he seated himself next to her, immediately assailed with her scent that he remembered vividly from yesterday, from that brief intoxicating moment he had held her in his arms. She smelled like a sun-drenched field of wildflowers. He scooted a little farther away, trying to regain his train of thought. "I, uh, thought we'd better discuss a few things," he said, feeling like an awkward schoolboy.

She darted an amused glance at him. "I'm not going to bite you, Mr. Parrish."

He grinned sheepishly, fascinated with the way her hazel eyes were smiling at him. "I've decided that we can still get married," he blurted.

Her mouth dropped open. "M–married?"

What is going on here? Surely she—

"Isn't that why you came here?" he asked cautiously.

She stared at him wordlessly for a long minute. "I. . .no. I did not come here to get married. Caroline told me. . ." Her voice trailed off, and her gaze turned compassionate. "That's why you were so disappointed when you saw me."

Disappointed? That wasn't the word I would have chosen.

"No, no," he said hastily. "Not disappointed. Just. . . surprised."

She didn't look convinced.

"I just never imagined—" He stopped as he noticed her lips beginning to twitch. Was she. . .laughing? He smiled into her eyes, a chuckle working its way up to his throat. "I guess it is kind of funny," he said.

She glanced back down at her protruding belly, but not before a soft giggle escaped. "Forgive me. It's just that—" She giggled again, and this time he laughed with her. Soon they were shaking with laughter, tears running down their faces.

He finally caught his breath. "Perhaps we should introduce ourselves all over again," he suggested.

She dabbed at her eyes with a lacy handkerchief. "All right." Her eyes still danced with laughter as she gave him her hand. "I'm Abigail Cantrell, your new housekeeper."

He bowed over her hand then captured her gaze with his. "Pleased to meet you, Abigail Cantrell. I am James Parrish, your future husband."

The light in her eyes dimmed, and he felt her small hand tremble beneath his. "I'm not so sure that's such a good idea, Mr. Parrish. You see, I'm not a free woman."

She felt him start. "I wasn't going to tell you all this, but I guess I owe it to you." She gently withdrew her hand from his. "I suppose you'll put me back on the train once you hear my story." It had taken all the courage she possessed just to leave home and all she had known to come west. And now—

He shook his head. "I don't think so."

She moved restlessly, feeling the weight of the babe in her womb, and the still greater weight of her guilt bearing down on her. Why, oh why had she gone against Papa so willfully? Then none of this would have happened. She would still be enjoying the peaceful life she had always known.

She finally remembered the silent man sitting next to her, and she turned to gaze at him. Why couldn't she have met someone like James before—? She noticed the tiny laugh lines around his eyes and the gentle peace written there, drawing her like a magnet. Something deep within her reached out to him, as it had from the first moment they had met.

He watched her quietly as she studied him, and suddenly she knew that she could trust him with her life. "I'm not sure where to begin," she said, searching his blue eyes again, just to make sure. "I guess I should tell you that I'm widowed."

He nodded, an unreadable expression on his face.

"My husband died six months ago." Her flat, emotionless voice matched her feelings. "We were just suspecting my condition at the time of his death." Shifting her weight, Abby tried unsuccessfully to find a comfortable position on the hard porch step.

"But if the truth be told, I don't regret the fact that Charles never knew about our child. You see, when my husband died, I learned that he wasn't the man

I thought he was. . . ."

James frowned. "I'm afraid I don't understand."

She smiled ruefully. "I'm not sure I do, either, Mr. Parrish. And I'm not sure I'm up to explaining it all to you now. Perhaps some other day. But, suffice to say, my husband. . ." She stumbled over the word, then began again. "My husband was involved in something. . .unlawful."

"And so?"

Abby raised her eyebrows, wondering why he hadn't made the obvious connection. How could she make it plainer? "My husband committed some crimes. Then he died. Someone has to pay for what he did."

He frowned again. "Pardon me for saying so, ma'am, but as much as I know about the law, I don't think that a widow is expected to be punished for her husband's crimes."

"Oh no. Not the law." She took a deep breath. "It's God that I'm concerned about."

"God? But God doesn't require—"

"I, too, did some things that I regret. And so I made a vow to God, Mr. Parrish, the day that Charles died. It cannot be broken." She could see the shock written on his face, but she plunged ahead, wanting to get it over with. "I will not allow someone else to be hurt because of my sins." It sounded so stark, so melodramatic. But it was the truth.

"And the vow was?" His voice was grave, his gaze unwavering.

The question reverberated in the quiet morning air,

a cricket chirping under the porch the only sound for a long minute.

She closed her eyes briefly, then opened them to look directly into his. "I have vowed that I will never love anyone again."

❧

James took in the earnestness of her sweet face, and his heart ached for her. How had she missed the fact that love is the very essence of God? How could she think that a loving God would want her to live life without love?

He gently reached for her hand, holding it firmly between both of his. "Abby, I would be honored if you would accept my hand in marriage."

She stared at him as if he had suddenly gone daft. "But I just told you—"

"You didn't promise God that you would never let anyone love you, did you?"

She dropped her gaze, but not before he saw the blush that colored her smooth cheeks. "No," she whispered.

"Then there's no problem. You need someone to love and care for you and your child." He smiled. "And I've been praying that God would send me a wife who I could love forever."

She met his gaze for an instant before staring down at her swollen belly again. "But I wouldn't be your wife. . .really."

He felt the back of his neck grow hot at the thought of it. He couldn't deny that he wanted her to be his wife in the fullest sense of the word, but until she was ready for that. . . "Look at me, Abby," he commanded gently.

He waited until she lifted uncertain eyes to his. "I promise you that I will take care of you and your baby to the best of my ability. I will honor you, and I promise you that I will never take advantage of you."

She swallowed hard. "Why?"

Why? Because I love you already, he thought, wishing he could take her in his arms and show her. "Because I asked God for a wife and he sent you, Abby."

"I don't deserve someone like you."

Her words were whispered, but the force of them nearly took his breath away.

God, please shine your grace on Abby, he prayed silently. *She's like a lost little girl.* "We all deserve to be loved, Abby."

"Are you sure?" A tiny spark of hope glinted in her eyes. "A lifetime is a long time, you know."

Long enough to convince you of my love. And long enough for you to return my love. He squeezed her hand. "I'm sure."

She gave him a small smile. "I hope you like my cooking."

*

An hour later, they stood in front of the justice of the peace. Iris had picked a huge bouquet of wildflowers, and Abby held them tightly now in her shaking hands. James stood beside her, his hand warm on the small of her back. "Just a few more minutes, Abby. Then we can go home," he whispered in her ear. She looked like she was about ready to keel over in exhaustion. Yet to James, she was the most beautiful bride he had ever seen. A shaft of late afternoon sunlight found its way into the dim parlor, illuminating her delicate face. Though some might say he was getting a bad deal, he confidently believed that this woman would hold his heart for eternity.

Chapter 3

W ell, this is the old homestead," James said. Abby allowed him to help her down from the wagon, then gazed at the farmhouse appreciatively. It wasn't very big, but the place looked tidy and snug. Newly whitewashed and the wide front porch swept clean, her new home was a welcoming sight. She smiled up at him. "It's very nice, James." It still felt awkward to call him James instead of Mr. Parrish, but he was her husband, after all.

Could it have only been yesterday that she had arrived on the train from New York? Now, here she was— a newlywed. She still felt slightly stunned at the events of the last few hours. Yet, somehow, she was at peace.

It wouldn't be hard to live with James, she decided, watching as he hefted her trunk out of the back of the wagon. She had never met a more caring, gentle man. Before she could pull her satchel from the wagon seat, James took the bag, then led her down the well-worn path toward the house. In pleasant surprise, Abby stopped by the front porch. The sweet-spicy fragrance of a beautiful pink rose in full bloom enchanted her.

"Do you like roses?"

James's low voice broke into her thoughts as she bent slightly to sniff a large blossom.

"This is exquisite." She glanced up at him, then swept the arid landscape with questioning eyes. "Wherever did you get a rose bush way out here?"

He shrugged. "I have friends who just made a trip back East. Had them bring it back for me." He smiled down at her. "I thought my new wife might like something pretty to welcome her."

Her eyes widened. What a thoughtful man! "How very kind. . .I don't know what to—" Her sentence ended in a shriek as something cold and wet pressed into her hand. She whirled around, her heart pounding as she came nose to nose with the largest dog she had ever seen. She backed up a step, her legs shaking.

Where had the dreadful creature come from? She cast a pleading glance at James. "Can you get it away from me?"

He chuckled, reaching for the dog's collar. "Sit, Frank," he commanded.

Abby sighed in relief, sinking down onto the porch steps. "Is that yours?" she asked.

James grinned. "Now, that's no way to talk about a family member, Abby," he drawled. "This is Frank. He's quite a feller."

"I'll say." Abby eyed the panting animal distrustfully. "So, he's a male dog?"

"Yep."

She swallowed hard, almost afraid to ask. "Does

it. . .live in the house?"

James appeared to be trying not to laugh. "No. Frank is a farm dog." He scratched the dog's floppy ears. "Though he does sneak in at night every once in awhile when it's cold out."

"Oh." Abby peered at the dog again. Was he smirking at her? She didn't like the look in his eye. "I haven't been around dogs very much," she said.

"I kind of figured that." James plunked down next to her on the step. "But Frank won't hurt you. He likes you. See, just let him sniff your hand, like this." He reached out a hand, which Frank obligingly covered with dog kisses.

Be brave, Abby, she told herself. She reached her hand out toward the dog, stopping midway. "Why is it thumping its tail?" she whispered to James nervously. Maybe dogs thumped their tails right before they pounced on their prey.

James sighed, but she could still see the laughter in his eyes. "Frank is a he, not an it. And he's thumping his tail because he's happy."

"Oh." Abby folded her hands safely under her watermelon-sized stomach. "I'm very pleased to meet you, Frank," she said. "I'm sure we'll be friends," she added, fervently hoping that it would be so.

She glanced up at James, frowning. Why was the man making such strange noises?

The look on her face must have been the last straw, because his suppressed chuckles suddenly broke into hearty laughter.

"What is so funny?" she demanded. "All I said was—"

"I know!" James grinned. "I've just never heard such a polite speech to a dog!" He chuckled again. "I like you, Abby," he said, taking her hand.

She smiled back at him, her heart warming at his sincerity. "I like you, too, James," she said.

Frank gave a hearty woof and Abby jumped. She would have to get used to the creature, she supposed.

James pulled her to her feet, keeping her hand in his. "Come on, Mrs. Parrish. I'll show you through your new home."

It didn't take long for Abby to get settled. She hadn't brought many things with her, since she had thought she was coming to be a hired housekeeper. A few dresses, her Bible, and a few items she had sewn for the baby.

James sat watching her one night as she hemmed yet another tiny garment. "Is it a boy or a girl?" he asked.

She glanced up at him. "Only the good Lord knows that," she said. "But I like to think that my baby is a girl." She studied his face in the flickering light of the fire. "Why do you ask?"

He shrugged. "Just curious, I guess."

She smiled then turned her attention back to the soft white material.

He settled back in his rocker, watching her. She seemed happy enough, he thought, noticing the adorable way she held her lips in a slight pucker while she worked. He had memorized every line of her lovely face in the past few weeks, often watching her when she was unaware.

They had fallen into a comfortable routine. He would spend the days out in the wheat fields, while she tended the house and garden. She hadn't been exaggerating when she said she was a good cook. It was comforting to know that when he finished with his chores, she would be waiting for him with a smile and a delicious meal.

Yet, she had withdrawn from him since their wedding day. He had given her his bed, while he slept on a bedroll in front of the fire. She had seemed distressed that he had to sleep on the floor, he remembered with a smile. With such a kind and gentle spirit about her, how could anyone help but love her?

His eyes roamed to her stomach, and he watched in amusement as it moved with the baby's antics. He wondered if Abby were afraid. He had heard so many terrible stories about the travails of childbirth. Even his own mama. . .he sighed. They would simply have to face any problems should they come and trust the Lord to protect Abby when her time of delivery arrived. Stewing about tomorrow's problems would do no good.

In the meantime, he wanted to get to know Abby a little better. She seemed so remote since that first day when they had talked and laughed so easily. Oh, she was friendly, but aloof. Distant. He had hoped that at least they could be friends, even if they couldn't be lovers. He sighed again. Maybe he had been dreaming to think that this marriage, a marriage in name only, could really work.

Father, I was so sure I heard Your voice that day, he prayed inwardly. *Please show me what to do. I want to love Abby and care for her, but I feel like she regrets marrying me.*

Show her the way to Me. The still small voice echoed in his heart, reminding him of the first day they had met. Wasn't that what God had told him that first day? But how could he accomplish the task?

He glanced over at her bowed head. Her dark hair glinted in the light of the oil lamp beside her.

"Abby."

She looked up, her hands resting on her stomach. "Did you need something?"

Yes, I need you, he thought, his heart suddenly pounding. What he wouldn't give right now to have the right to take her in his arms. However, he must be patient. "I was wondering if you would like to have a time of prayer together in the evenings."

She looked surprised, and his heart sank. "I'd like that very much, James," she said quietly.

"You would?"

She nodded. "My mama and my sisters and I used to pray together every night. I've missed that since Charles and I. . .since. . .for a long time," she finished quickly.

One of these days he would ask her to tell him the whole story, James decided. But not right now. Reaching for his Bible, he laid it on his knees. "Would you like me to read anything in particular?"

She thought for a moment, her head tilted to one side. "I guess my favorite has always been the psalms," she said. "Maybe Psalm 91?"

"That's one of my favorites, too," he said, smiling into her eyes. In fact, he could have recited it from memory, but he lowered his gaze to the page, deciding it would be safer to read than to lose him in her large, hazel eyes.

" 'He that dwelleth in the secret place of the most High shall abide under the shadow of the Almighty. I will say of the Lord. . . .' " Before he was halfway through, he heard her reciting it softly with him. Closing the Bible with a soft thud, he laid it back down on the hearth then scooted his chair closer to hers. He reached for her hand, gently kissing her work-roughened fingertips before enfolding them in his grasp.

"Father God, Abby and I come before you tonight as your humble children. Lord, You have searched us and known us. You know our downsitting and our uprising and are acquainted with all our ways. There is not a word in our tongue, but Thou knowest it altogether. Thou hast beset us behind and before and laid Thine hand upon us. Such knowledge is too wonderful for us, it is high, and we cannot attain unto it. For where shall we go from Your presence? Where can we flee from Your spirit? Even if we take the wings of the morning and dwell in the uttermost part of the sea, even there shall You be. When we awake, we are still with Thee. Thank You, Father God, that by Your Holy

Spirit, You are present with us always. Please teach me how to be a good husband to Abby, Father. Bless her and the child abundantly. We thank You, Father. In Jesus' name, Amen."

He raised his head, his heart too full for words, and saw the same written on his wife's face. And his soul rejoiced within him.

Chapter 4

Abby lay in bed, feeling her spirit moving within her as much as the child who kicked in her womb. She had never heard anyone pray like James had prayed tonight. Of course she recognized that he had borrowed a portion of his prayer from Psalm 139. Yet the way that he had prayed, with such assurance and fervor, amazed her. It had been so long since she had allowed herself to think of God as anything other than a tyrant. What used to be second nature now seemed unreal.

James was such a good person. She could tell from that very first day that she would face a constant battle to keep her vow. How easy it would be to love James, and let him love her. She couldn't help but notice the way his eyes followed her around the kitchen. And he always remembered to thank her for the meals she prepared.

"Mmph!" The baby gave a hard kick, and Abby grimaced. It was getting harder and harder to find a comfortable sleeping position. She rolled over on her side, trying to concentrate on the soothing smell of lavender that wafted from the fat bouquets she had hung in the attic to dry.

The fire had died down, but in the moonlight she could see enough to make out the features of James' face as he lay asleep on his bedroll. How many times had she caught herself in the last few days, just before she reached up to caress his cheek or to smooth his fair hair off of his forehead?

He was becoming dear to her. But that must not be. She would not allow it. If she started to love him, he would be taken away. Just like Papa. Just like Charles. Just like—she wrapped her arms around her stomach, hugging the babe to her in the cold night. No, she wouldn't even think it. Not her child, too. Even God wouldn't be so cruel, would He?

She squeezed her eyes shut against the pain and fear that threatened to overwhelm her. But her efforts did no good. The fear was like a living thing, threatening to squeeze the very breath out of her body.

"Abby! What's wrong?"

Her eyes flew open to see James standing over her. She must have cried out. She shook her head, taking a couple of deep breaths.

He sank down on his knees next to the bed and laid a cool hand on her forehead. "What is it, love?" he whispered. "Are you in pain? Is it the child?"

She shook her head again, tears welling up into her eyes. Swallowing against the lump in her throat, she grasped his hand and clung to it. Slowly the bands of fear loosened from around her chest.

"I'm sorry," she whispered. "It's just that sometimes I'm so afraid."

She felt him nod.

"Do you want me to sit with you for a while?" he whispered.

No, she wanted him to take her in his arms and hold her until she felt safe again. She wanted him to lie next to her, so she could feel protected. Loved. Secure. But that could never be. She was being weak to even let him sit near her and hold her hand.

She sighed. "I know you're tired. I'll be fine." She thought, if he could have seen her face, he would have known she was lying.

He sat still for a few moments, then brushed his lips across her forehead. "He will never leave you nor forsake you, Abby," he whispered.

The outdoorsy smell of his warm skin lingered in her senses as he returned to his makeshift bed to lie back down. She squeezed her eyes shut against the lonely tears that seemed determined to fall. Surely morning would come soon.

Morning did finally dawn, and with it a new resolve. She would gather the eggs today, no matter how the task frightened her.

James had shown her how to do it once or twice, but she still felt intimidated by the chore. The very idea of reaching under a squawking bird into its warm nest was unnerving, not to mention the possibility of roosters pecking at her shoes and fluttering in her face.

James had chuckled at her timidity, and told her he'd take care of it. But egg gathering was really woman's work, she knew. Besides, he already had enough to do.

She timidly approached the front of the coop, basket in hand. She had first made certain that the hound, Frank, was nowhere in sight. She wasn't quite so afraid of the dog now, but her heart still skipped a beat when he came galloping up to her. She hoped he was as nice as James said he was, because he had awfully big teeth.

As the sun beat down on her head, Abby decided she had procrastinated long enough. "Well, little one, it's now or never," she said to her unborn child. Flinging open the door of the coop, she hollered, "Rise and shine!"

The startled birds flew everywhere, and Abby backed out of the coop, flailing her arms. "Shoo! Shoo!" she yelled, feeling ridiculous.

"I've never seen it done quite like that before," came an amused voice behind her.

Abby turned with a groan. "Hello, Iris."

James's sister grinned. "What are you doing, Abby?"

"Gathering eggs." She tried to keep a straight face, then gave up. "I thought maybe if I made them all get out first, it might be easier."

"Hmmm." Iris made a comical face, and both women giggled. "Didn't your know-it-all husband show you how to do it?"

"Yes, but I can't stand reaching under those poor hens." Abby grimaced. "Besides, the smell makes me feel ill."

"You do look a little green, dear," Iris said. "Why

don't you go put the tea kettle on the stove. I'll gather these eggs."

"You're an angel," Abby said.

Iris snorted. "Don't think I've ever been called that before," she replied. "Here, take this pie into your kitchen. I'll be in before you know it."

Abby headed toward the back door, feeling guilty for allowing her sister-in-law to do her work.

"Hello, girls," she heard Iris say soothingly, and she had to grin. She had never thought of chickens as girls before. She had a lot to learn about farming, that was for sure.

James had been pleased that the eggs were gathered, but Abby felt compelled to admit it was Iris who had done it.

"She's a sweet gal," he said. "She reminds me of my mama."

Abby knew his mother had died in childbirth years ago. "Mothers are very special people," she said softly.

He appeared to be very interested in the piece of pie on his fork, but she could see that his eyes had misted over. "You'll be a wonderful mother, Abby," he whispered.

She stared at him for a moment in silence. Why would he bring that up right now? She cleared her throat. "What kind of pie is this that Iris brought? It's very good."

He speared another bite and took her cue to change the subject. "You've never had rhubarb pie before?"

"Rhubarb?" She poked at the tart red and green chunks that swam in the sweet pink juice, the flaky crust crumbling under her fork. "I've never even heard of it. Perhaps rhubarb doesn't grow in New York."

"Come here and I'll show you." James pushed his chair away from the table and led Abby to a garden patch next to the well. He pointed to a leafy plant growing in the moist, black dirt. Abby had noticed it before, vaguely wondering at its enormous leaves.

"This is a rhubarb plant," he said. "You just reach down and twist on the stalk a little bit." He straightened back up with a slender stalk in his hand. "It's best in the spring."

She smiled up at him, conscious of his nearness as his arm brushed hers. "I think I'll do without the reaching down part for now."

He chuckled, reaching out to pat her stomach. Then apparently catching himself, he jerked his hand away. "Forgive me. I didn't mean—"

"It's all right, James," she said, touching his arm. "After all, you are going to be the child's father." *My goodness!* She hadn't really said that aloud, had she? She had thought of it before, of course, but wouldn't he think that she was being rather presumptuous?

The smile that lit his face was enough to reassure her that she hadn't said the wrong thing. He laid his hand gently on her stomach for a brief moment. "You're right, Abby," he said, his voice husky.

She froze, ensnared by the tenderness that glowed in his sea-blue eyes. What was he thinking?

She didn't have long to wonder. Somehow all of a sudden, she was enfolded in his strong arms. And in that moment, she couldn't think of anywhere else she'd rather be. Couldn't think at all, actually. She just knew that she had come home. She sighed, feeling safe and secure. Loved.

"Uhhh!" The baby kicked. Hard.

James backed away, his eyes wide. Abby had to laugh at the expression on his face, though she wished the moment had not ended so abruptly. "Guess this little one is getting impatient," she murmured, smiling up into James's face.

He grinned. "Me, too."

The look he gave her made her pulse pound and she lowered her gaze to the rhubarb plant. Her commitment to keep her vow was becoming increasingly difficult.

Chapter 5

M mm! Something smells good in here!"
"James!" Abby whirled from the stove. "I
didn't hear you come in."

He grinned at her and her heart lurched. *He truly is
a handsome man*, she thought. *What would it be like—?*

"Did you fall in?"

"What?" She blinked up at him, feeling flustered.

He chuckled. "Did you fall into the flour bin?"

"Oh." She brushed at her face with her apron, then
glanced up to find him directly in front of her. His blue
gaze twinkled into hers as his hands gently cupped her
face.

"I don't think you got it all off," he whispered, lowering his face to her.

Surely he wasn't going to. . . Her arms slid around
him of their own accord, it seemed. He kissed her
slowly and tenderly, then pressed her head to his chest.
She stood in the circle of his arms, stunned at the feelings coursing through her mind and heart.

Even in her brief marriage to Charles, she had
never felt such things. This man seemed to bring out

her innate tenderness and vulnerability. Nevertheless, what was she thinking? She would be breaking her promise to God and sinning against Him if she allowed herself to love James Parrish, even if he were her husband.

She pushed her hands against his chest, her heart suddenly leaden. She could not break the vow she had made to God, not even if she wanted to. *And, oh how I want to,* she admitted to herself.

He released her slowly, searching her face as if he sensed the change in her demeanor. "You're precious to me, Abby," he whispered.

She gazed miserably at his beloved face. How could she have possibly thought she could live with such a man and yet not love him?

"Forgive me if I hurt you," he said.

She reached a hand up to his bearded cheek, loving the feel of the soft bristly whiskers—loving him. "No, I'm the one who's sorry, James." She bowed her head then, ashamed that she should be so weak.

"There's nothing to be sorry for," he told her, trying to draw her back into his arms.

However, she had turned away from him, fussing with the food on the stove.

❦

He kicked at a hay bale that stood next to the barn door, watching as a cloud of dust rose and then settled in the still air. Why had she pulled away from him? She had felt so good in his arms. Just like God made her to fit there. He knew he probably shouldn't have kissed her but, after all, she was his wife!

Dear Lord, surely you haven't brought me this woman just to torture me! I love her, Father. I want her to love me. To want me for her husband. He sighed as he lit the lantern in the chill of the rapidly approaching dusk. What had she meant that day when she said she wasn't a free woman? Would her heart always belong to her first husband, Charles?

Would James have to go on loving her, with no love returned, for the rest of his life? His shoulders drooped at the thought. How many times had he longed to lay close beside her at night, sharing secrets and feeling their hearts beat as one? Didn't she know that he loved her?

He trudged through the evening chores at a snail's pace, his mind tormenting him with thoughts of what a true marriage could be.

❧

Each passing day brought the birth of Abby's baby ever closer. Since the afternoon that he had kissed her, Abby had withdrawn even more from James. *She is holding up well,* he thought, yet he despaired every time he saw that wounded look in her lovely eyes.

"You look tired," he said one evening, watching as she sank into the rocking chair.

She sent him a weary smile. "It's been a busy day."

Indeed, it had been a busy week. Summer was in full swing, and it seemed every day when he came in for supper, there was another row of canned carrots or tomatoes in the pantry.

"You've been working too hard."

She shrugged. "I want to get as much done as I can before the birth."

She looked more than tired, he observed as he studied her. Almost haggard. His conscience pricked him. How could he have let her work so hard, especially with the birthing so close? She was probably used to having someone wait on her, he suddenly realized. "Tell me about your life in New York," he said. Maybe if she would at least talk to him, he could understand more of what she was thinking. After all, he really didn't know her.

She looked slightly startled. "What do you want to know?"

I want to know you, his heart cried. "Anything you want to tell me, love," he replied, moving his chair closer.

She stared into the fire. "I grew up there," she began, her voice soft, as if coming from a great distance. "Mama and Papa were so happy together. . . ." She stopped then, as if that was the end of the story.

"Were you happy?" he prompted.

She twisted her hands together, then apparently noticed what she was doing, and held them quietly in her lap. "Yes," she said. "I was happy I had a wonderful family. I loved God. We went to church."

James nodded, feeling the "but" that must come next.

"Then I met Charles."

The statement dropped into the room like a cold, unexpected shower.

"He convinced me that we should get married." Here she stopped and almost smiled. "So we did. He was a master of persuasion." She glanced at James and shrugged. "Looking back on it now, I'm not sure I ever really loved him. But he convinced me into believing that I did."

James waited, alternating between fear and rejoicing. Fear at what she might say next, yet rejoicing that her heart was not bound to another man.

She shrugged again. "We had only known each other a month before we wed. Papa was livid." She gave James a sad smile. "I was with child soon afterwards. Then. . .a widow."

He grasped her cold hands in his. "What happened, Abby?"

"No one is exactly sure." She grimaced. "I had been over visiting Mama and Aunt Caroline, while Papa went over to our house to talk with Charles about a business matter."

For long minutes the only sound in the room was the crackling of the fire and the squeak of the rocker blades on the smooth floor.

"There was a terrible fire, and Papa and Charles both died." Her voice was flat, devoid of emotion.

What could he say to her? "I'm s—"

"The constable said that Charles set it on purpose."

"What?" Was she saying what he thought she was?

"Only Charles didn't plan on dying in the blaze, too. He was supposed to live to 'share' in my inheritance."

James felt as if someone had punched him in the gut. No wonder she was reluctant to open her heart to someone again. *But I'm not like that*, he cried silently.

She took a deep breath and gently pulled her hands

from his. "So, now you understand why I vowed to God that I would never love again. It was all my fault." She looked away. "I loved Papa and he died. I thought I loved my husband and he turned on me. Now, even Mama. . .she's dying."

How could she think such things were her fault? His heart felt like it was breaking. That phrase had always seemed like a figure of speech to him, until now. What could he possibly say or do to convince her?

Show her the way back to Me, the still, small voice said again.

He bowed his head, surrendering again to the One who is all-seeing, all-knowing, and never-changing. "Our lives are in Your hands, Father God," he whispered. "Take what we have and who we are, and use us for Your good. We are nothing without You. . . ."

He heard his wife softly weeping and his heart rejoiced to hope that God's spirit was at work in her life.

❦

Hours later, James woke with a start. He could hear Abby thrashing around in the bed, her breaths coming in short gasps. Was it time?

He flew to her side, his own heart pounding. Abby's eyes were squeezed shut, her face contorted with silent terror. A chill traveled down his spine as he felt her fear.

"Jesus!" he prayed aloud, a near frantic urgency in his voice. "Oh, dear Lord, please help my wife. Release her from this consuming fright."

Abby's eyes flew open and James held his breath,

watching as the glazed look in her eyes cleared and her rigid body relaxed. Dropping to his knees, he pressed her limp hand to his face.

"What happened, Abby?" His voice trembled as he spoke.

Abby released a shuddering sigh. "Thank God," she whispered. "It was just another bad dream."

She closed her eyes. "I've had similar nightmares, but. . .but. . ." She opened her eyes to search his face. "This was the worst, by far. Oh, James, I thought I was surely going to die."

He stared at her, his thoughts racing. Apparently she had more to deal with than he had thought. This wasn't simply a woman going through grief. *Father God, please guide my every word*, he prayed. "What was the dream, Abby?"

She shook her head. "I can't. . . ."

"Yes, you can." He tenderly took her chin in his hand. "God doesn't want a child of His to be so tormented by fear."

"Maybe I'm not really God's child."

His heart broke at the bleak words. "Abby, you know God's Word. I've heard you quote the scriptures when I read at night." He smoothed a wispy dark tendril from her forehead. "The Bible says that if you believe in your heart and confess with your mouth that Jesus is Lord, that you are saved."

She nodded. "I've done that. But I don't feel His love, James!" Her voice was pleading. "Why would He make all those terrible things happen to me?"

He took her hand in his. "Abby—"

"I'm so afraid, James! I'm so afraid." Her hand tightened on his. "I just know that something is wrong with my baby. I just know—"

"Hush, now. You mustn't talk like that."

Pursing her lips together tightly, Abby turned her face toward the wall, but not before he caught the glint of betrayal in her eyes.

"Abby, please look at me," he pleaded gently. Minutes ticked by. The darkness in the large room slowly lightened by the break of dawn, yet she remained motionless.

James prayed silently, waiting.

Finally, she turned her eyes to meet his.

"Abby, as God's child, He says to you in Jeremiah 29:11 that He thinks thoughts of peace and not evil toward you. God does not do terrible things to us. Our enemy, Satan, is the one who does that."

She stared at him stonily. "Then why doesn't God stop him?"

"There will come a day when Satan will be bound and rendered helpless. You can be assured of that." He pressed her hand. "But in the meantime, despite life's most dire circumstances, if we saturate ourselves in the God's Word, we can experience His peace. Still, a part of the responsibility is ours, too, sweetheart."

She shook her head questioningly. "How is that?"

He smiled, patting Abby's bulging middle lightly. "When our baby is born, he will be hungry. And you will have milk to feed him, right?"

She raised her eyebrows.

"What if this little one chooses not to open his mouth? Will you be able to give him any milk?"

"Of course not. But—"

"You've been doing that to God, Abby. He's waiting for you to accept His peace and His mercy."

She turned her head away again, her long braid sliding over their joined hands. After a long time, her muffled words drew James' attention. "I think He's angry with me."

James gently drew her face toward his. "God is love, Abby. He *is* love."

"But I don't—"

"I know. You've thought and felt and said for so long that God is angry with you and that He doesn't love you—you don't feel or know the truth anymore." He smiled into her eyes, letting all of his love for her show in his face. "You need to start speaking truth and life instead of lies and death. The Word of God says in Proverbs that the power of life and death is in the tongue."

"Oomph!" Abby put a hand over her stomach, her eyes wide. "That was hard!"

James chuckled. "Nothing wrong with that little one."

Abby's dark eyes grew wistful. "I wish I could feel as sure as you do about it."

James ached to kiss away the cares of this woman the Lord had given him, but she needed more than his human love right now. He caressed her face with his eyes. Couldn't she see how much he had grown to love her? He picked up her small hands and placed them on her stomach, chuckling as the child within moved in response.

"My dear," he said, placing his hands on top of hers, "our Heavenly Father is the Creator of all life—including the life of this little one whom we are so anxious to meet. Don't you think that the God who breathes His life in us can be trusted to watch over us all?

"Listen, Abby. The next time you are tempted to allow fear to crowd your thoughts, why don't you pray and ask God to remind you of a Scripture that will replace your fear with His peace."

As the sun rose and the light seeped into the dim room, peace filled Abby's heart for the first time in a very long while.

Chapter 6

"The love of God has been shed abroad in my heart by the Holy Ghost and His love abides in me richly." Abby hummed softly, the words of the scripture from Romans going over and over in her mind like the phonograph records that Mama played. Since James had taught her to use the Scriptures to pray, a whole new spiritual world had unfolded for her.

Abby finished rolling out the piecrust to her satisfaction, then she carefully transferred it to the pie tin. Wouldn't James be surprised to see that she had made him a rhubarb pie? She had gotten the recipe from Iris the last time they had gone to town.

Sinking into a kitchen chair to rest for a minute before cleaning up the floury mess, she patted the warm lump that rolled underneath her apron. Surely this child would come soon!

A familiar twinge of fear prickled in her heart. "Oh God, don't let—" she started, then stopped, shaking her head. "For God has not given me a spirit of fear, but of power, and love, and a sound mind," she said aloud. "Thank You God. I praise You for Your Word that gives me strength. Your word is a lamp unto my feet and a light unto my path."

She smiled as the child moved again. "I know, little one. I feel His peace, too." Funny how she had known all these Scriptures since she was a small child and yet never realized the power that she possessed as a child of God. It was amazing, really.

She picked up the letters from Mama and Aunt Caroline. James had brought them home from town yesterday, presenting them to her with a smile. "You must be missed," he had said.

Her cheeks grew warm now as she recalled the tender way he had taken her into his arms. It seemed that he had begun to do that more and more often, she mused. Not that she minded, really, but he made it awfully hard to say aloof. Especially when he looked at her with such tender expression in his eyes. She dared not call this feeling "love," but then what else?

She turned back to the letters with a sigh, rereading each one. Apparently, that rascal Aunt Caroline wasn't the least bit repentant of her shenanigans. Abby thought of the elderly woman and smiled. It was so good to hear from her family. Yet, she didn't yearn for home as she expected she would. Had she truly found a home of her own with James?

Her heart warmed as her gaze fell on the cradle. James had brought it home in the back of the wagon, covered carefully with an old quilt.

"I thought we might be needing this soon," he had

said, presenting the gift to her almost shyly.

Abby ran her fingertips over the glossy oak. "It's beautiful," she whispered. There were even little heart cutouts in the headboard and a lovely white satin blanket. "You shouldn't have spent so much money," she said, fingering the coverlet.

He chuckled, the sound making her heart sing. "I'm not very good at working with wood, Abby. If I made the cradle, the poor child would probably have fallen through the bottom the first time you laid him in it!"

She laughed, then succumbed to the impulse to run her fingers through his light hair. "I never heard of a farmer who wasn't handy with a hammer," she teased gently.

He smiled down at her, the merriment in his eyes fading into a different emotion. Pulling her to him, he wrapped his arms around her carefully. She leaned against him, reveling in his closeness.

"You must know that I love you, Abby," he whispered into her hair.

She stood still. Did she know that? She thought of him. Thought of all the little things that made up James Parrish. His attentiveness. His gentleness. The way he prayed for her and the baby, his handsome head bowed.

Yes, she knew that he loved her. Even more, she knew that she loved him. And yet, there was the problem. She couldn't love him, or anyone. She had promised.

She sighed now as she dumped the chopped rhubarb into the pastry-lined tin. *It won't help to keep going over and over it,* she told herself sternly. She had made a vow to God, and she intended to keep it.

Abby gathered up the large leaves she had cut off the tops of the rhubarb stalks. If she chopped them and fried them with a little bacon grease, she could serve the greens with the salt pork and boiled potatoes she was planning for supper. Feeling rather pleased with herself, she got out her sharpest knife.

"I'm as hungry as a bear," James said from outside the back door.

She could hear him scraping the mud off his boots, and smiled. She would have liked to have met his mama, and thanked her for raising such a thoughtful son.

"I'm glad you're hungry, because supper is on the table." She couldn't help smiling at him as he clumped through the door and rewarded her with a kiss on the tip of her nose.

"You're a sight for sore eyes," he said, grinning at her. "When's that baby ever going to come? He should have been here two weeks ago!"

She blew out a good-natured sigh. "You weren't supposed to ask me again, remember?"

He poured water into the basin and plunged his hands into it, scrubbing vigorously. "A man can't help wondering, you know."

Abby smiled behind his back. "I heard my Aunt Caroline tell many an anxious woman, 'The pear will fall when it's ripe.' "

He laughed aloud. "Sounds like your Aunt Caroline's a pretty wise gal."

"She sent me to you, didn't she?" Abby could have bitten her tongue the minute the words were out of her mouth. Now he would think that she. . .oh dear. There he was looking at her like that again and. . .

The kiss was slow and sweet. Abby thought maybe she had gone to heaven. . .except that there wasn't any smoke in heaven, was there? Smoke? "Oh no! My pie!" She pulled out of his arms and rushed to yank open the oven door.

As she thumped the pie onto the sideboard, relieved to see it still intact, James peered over her shoulder.

"Some of the juice ran over," she mumbled, waving the smoke away with her apron.

James grinned at her sheepishly. "Seems I ought to be praising God for Aunt Caroline."

"What? Oh." She felt her face get red. Was he trying to torment her? She shouldn't have let him kiss her, and he knew it. "Supper's getting cold," she said tartly. She pulled out her own chair without waiting for him and sank into it.

James leaned back in his chair, trying in vain to hold back a snicker. He shouldn't tease Abby so much, he knew, but he couldn't help it. He loved the way she got all flustered and pink-cheeked.

She sent him a mock glare over the table, and he obediently closed his eyes to offer the blessing. He had scarcely said "amen," before she was up and bustling around again.

"Come sit down with me, woman!" he ordered playfully.

She ignored him, busily dipping lemonade into their stoneware mugs. James sighed and turned his attention to the meal. Everything smelled so good. He took an enormous helping of greens, wondering where she had gotten them this time of year. He thought that she had already harvested all the turnips and collard greens.

She dropped heavily into the chair across from him, wiping her forehead with her apron. "Sure is hot for September, isn't it?"

"Mm hmm," he said, his mouth full of potatoes. He took a sip of lemonade. "Fine supper you cooked, Mrs. Parrish."

She grinned at him, the weariness momentarily lifting from her brow. "My mama taught me right, I guess." She watched as he savored a mouthful of greens, her eyes widening when he grimaced.

Good grief! Where did she get these nasty things? It was all he could do not to spit them out on his plate.

"Is something wrong?" Her face was troubled.

He coughed into his napkin, then hastily gulped some lemonade. "Just took a bite of something bitter," he said mildly.

She frowned, tasting a bit from her own plate. Her eyes watered. "You needn't have been so polite, James. They're downright inedible."

He tried not to laugh at the misery on her face. "It's not the end of the world, love. Where did you find these, anyway?"

She made a face. "Well, I wanted to surprise you, so I made a rhubarb pie and—what?"

He closed his eyes briefly, then glanced at her. "Abby, rhubarb leaves are poisonous."

"What? Oh, no, James! I didn't know—"

He reached across the table to capture her shaking hands in his own. "It's all right. Neither one of us ate enough to have any effect."

"How could I have been so stupid?"

His thumbs stroked the backs of her hands soothingly. "I won't tell anyone if you won't."

She sniffed. "I hope you don't think I was trying to k–kill you." A giggle slipped out with the last word, as the humor of the situation struck her. "I can just see the *Denver Post* headlines now: 'New Bride Kills Husband with Mess of Greens.' "

James let loose with the guffaw he had been suppressing. Soon they were howling together, tears streaming down Abby's face. James took a drink, trying to regain a modicum of control, but nearly choked on the liquid when Abby started giggling again.

Finally, they turned their attentions to the cold potatoes and pork, trying not to look at each other, lest they start again. Abby reached for the salt cellar, accidentally bumping James's hand. Their eyes met, which only started James off again with a snort. Abby got tickled all over again, her breath coming in short gasps.

"Stop laughing, James," she said between giggles. "I can't breathe!"

He raised his eyebrows. "Maybe you should take some of these greens to the next church social. Sure would liven things up a bit."

She made a face at him. "You said you wouldn't tell anyone about them."

"Who said I would tell anyone? We could just put them out on the table and let them speak for them—what's wrong?"

She giggled again. "Nothing. I just thought I felt—" Her eyes widened, and she grasped her middle.

James felt his mouth go dry. "Is it time?"

She nodded. "I think so. It must have been those greens."

How could she joke at a time like this? He scraped his chair back and rushed around the table to her. "Shouldn't you lie down?"

She smiled up at him, and his heart turned over. "I think it will be awhile yet, sweet—James." Her face flushed as she caught herself, yet she didn't break eye contact with him.

He stroked her smooth cheek with the back of his fingers. Had she really started to say what he thought she did? Could it be that she was beginning to feel for him even a small bit of what he felt for her? *God, please let it be so!*

"What can I do for you, love?" he whispered. He would never admit this to her, but he was scared stiff at the thought of losing her in childbirth. *God, please help me. . . .*

She leaned her head into his hand. "Just to know that you're here is enough, James."

❦

Abby's predictions proved true. Hours had passed since

she felt her first labor pains. James had been almost frantic at first, but he regained his composure as he realized that the birth was not imminent. He had sat next to her throughout the long evening, marveling at the way her stomach would become rock-hard with each contraction. Easy and relatively pain-free at first, they were now becoming harder. More painful. Much more frequent.

"I think it's time to get Ada," Abby murmured.

James stirred from his dozing in the chair next to hers. "What, love?"

"I think you'd better get Ada now," she said, grimacing. *Whew. That one was the hardest yet.*

James clapped his hat on his head, then bent to kiss her tenderly. "Shall I help you into the bed before I go?"

She nodded, fighting back the urge to pant. She didn't want to alarm James, but she was beginning to think that the baby would be here sooner than she had anticipated.

"Hurry, please," she whispered as the door slammed behind him. Why, oh why hadn't she let him fetch the midwife when he wanted to an hour ago? Weeks before, Abby had decided that she'd rather have their neighbor, Ada McReady, as a midwife than a doctor from Denver City. Ada had assured Abby that she had delivered plenty of babies in her fifty years. And it was nice that she lived so close. Abby had met her a time or two in town, and Ada's husband Andy had dropped by with a loaf of her friendship bread when Abby and James had first wed. She was a sweet woman, and at this moment, Abby hoped she was also a speedy woman.

She lay back against the pillow, fighting back the tears. She hadn't realized it would hurt so badly. She tried to pray, but it seemed no words would form in her mind.

She felt like her insides were ripping; the pain and pressure increasing with each contraction. Where were James and Ada?

She felt the familiar blackness of fear beginning to creep at the edges of her mind. What if something was wrong? What if the baby was stuck? What if something happened to her child? All the fear that had been held at bay during the last few weeks of peace came flooding over her.

The pain tore at her, making her cry out. She squeezed her eyes shut tight, trying to think. She should pray. . .she should quote some Scriptures. . . "Jesus!" She screamed the name in prayer, unable to think of anything else.

Immediately the darkness vanished from her mind and calmness descended on her spirit. "Jesus," she whispered. He was there. She could feel the presence of God with her, as strongly as if another human being stood next to her holding her hand. He was God and He loved her. He would not abandon her.

Another wave of pain pulled downward on her body. She gritted her teeth. " 'The Lord is my light and my salvation. Whom. . .shall. . .I. . .fear. . .?'

" 'He that dwelleth in the secret place of the most High shall. . .abide. . .under the shadow. . .of the Almighty.'

" 'The Lord is. . .my. . .strength. . .' "

She opened her eyes to see James beside her, his strong voice repeating the words with her. He took her hands and held them tightly between his own. "I'm so proud of you," he whispered.

She smiled at him as Ada moved the quilts to check her. "He heard me, James," she whispered. "Jesus. . .He heard me."

James smiled at her through his tears. "I told you He would," he whispered.

"Well, Mrs. Parrish, I hardly think you needed me," Ada boomed. "You done almost had this babe without me."

Abby squeezed her eyes shut as the searing pain swept through again. "How much. . .longer?" she panted.

"Two or three more good pushes, honey. I can see 'is head already."

James gripped her hands tightly, his eyes never leaving her face. "You can do it, sweetheart," he whispered.

"The Lord. . .is. . .my strength. . .aaagh!" She gave one final push, and it was over.

Seconds later, she felt the hot, wet body of her daughter, lying on her abdomen.

"Hello, little one," she said softly, reaching down to touch her with her fingertips. Her eyes filled with tears when she heard the baby's first quavering wail. "Is she all right, James? Is she truly all right?"

He watched while Ada severed the cord. Then he tenderly wrapped the baby in the soft blanket that awaited. He laid the baby in Abby's waiting arms. "See for yourself, love," he whispered.

And she did see. A beautiful, perfect baby girl. "Thank You, God," she breathed. "Thank You, thank You, thank You!"

She tore her eyes from the child to find James. He had moved across the room and was staring into the fire, his back to her. She frowned. Whatever was he doing way over there? She kissed the baby's soft forehead, and then she knew.

"James, come here please," she called softly. She watched him hesitate, then turn to face her.

She studied his dear face as he came near. Oh, how she loved this man. He had married her, taken her in, provided for her, loved her. . .and what had she given in return? Was he so unsure of her feelings? Did he not know that she wanted him to be a father to her baby—their baby? Could she make him understand?

How she longed to tell him that she loved him—but that was not to be. She choked back the lump that arose in her throat. *God, why did I make such a vow?*

But if she wasn't allowed to give him her heart, at least she could give him this gift. She caressed his face with her eyes as he knelt down by the bed. "James, we need to choose a name for our daughter."

She watched as his eyes, focused on her face, filled with tears. He leaned over to place a tender kiss on her cheek, then bent to kiss the baby's face as well.

"Isn't she beautiful?" Abby murmured.

James nodded, finally finding his voice. "Just like her mama," he whispered.

"Well, it don't look like you folks'll be needin' me anymore." Ada's loud voice made Abby jump. "I'll come check up on y'all tomorrow."

James jumped up to show the midwife out, and Abby turned her attention back to the baby. "Happy birthday, little one," she whispered. She smiled up at James as he neared her side again. "She wants her papa to hold her."

Chapter 7

O h, Abby. What a beautiful baby!" Iris held the baby close, her face radiant. "God has truly blessed you!"

Abby smiled. "It's hard to believe she's two weeks old already."

"And I love her name! Anna Joy." Iris kissed the baby's cheek gently. "I'm sorry I couldn't come earlier. I just wanted to make sure. . ."

"Oh, I'm glad you waited," Abby assured her. She would never admit to Iris that every day she had feared a visit from her sister-in-law. Of course, she loved Iris dearly. But, since James had informed her of a small-pox outbreak in town, Abby had feared that little Anna would come down with the dreaded disease.

Even now she cringed inwardly as Iris bent her face near the baby's. What if she was carrying the disease? After all, people were in and out of her boardinghouse every day. She heaved an inward sigh of relief as Iris handed little Anna back to her. The baby gazed into her face, her blue eyes wide and innocent. Abby's arms tightened around her little daughter, her heart overflowing.

She was still almost brought to tears each time she considered that this little human being had been entrusted to her care—hers and James's, that is. She glanced over to where he sat at the table, nursing a cup of tea. "Did you tell Iris that I have a new recipe for her to serve at the boardinghouse?"

James grinned at his sister. "Have any guests you'd like to see leave early, Sis?"

"What are you talking about, James?" Iris demanded. "Abby is a wonderful cook!"

"Oh, I agree, Iris." He darted an amused glance at Abby. "She's very frugal, too. After she made a rhubarb pie, she cooked up the leaves for greens."

"Oh no!" Iris gasped. "You didn't!"

Abby laughed. "I'm afraid so. I'm a city girl, remember?"

"Things are never dull around here anymore, that's for sure." James sauntered over to Abby, putting an arm around her shoulders. "God knew what he was doing when He sent me this lady."

Iris chuckled. "I can see that. So—do I get a nephew next time?"

Abby gulped, heat rising to the surface of her cheeks. Iris couldn't possibly know their situation. Undoubtedly James would be too embarrassed to tell his sister. "Well, I—"

"All in good time, Sis. We don't want to rush things when we've only just started to get to know little Anna."

"Well, just don't wait too long." Iris jumped to her feet and smoothed down her skirt in one fluid motion.

"Now, I'd best be gettin' get back to town. A family's coming in from the Springs tonight." With a quick hug for Abby and a peck on the cheek for James, she was gone.

Abby sank down into the chair with a sigh. "Sometimes just watching Iris makes me tired."

James laughed aloud. "I know what you mean. She's always been a fireball." He crossed over to the cradle, and leaned over to hear Anna's soft breathing. "Think we'll ever take her up on her suggestion?"

Abby wrinkled her forehead. *What was he talking...? Oh! How could he so casually mention that subject when he knows that I'm bound by my vow to God?* "I don't—"

He lifted his head to look at her then, and the look in his eyes took her breath away. "I want us to be a real family, Abby," he whispered.

"We are a real—"

"No, we aren't." He crossed over to her then, standing close enough that she could feel the heat radiating from his skin. "I want you for my wife—in every sense of the word."

She shivered as he ran his hands down her bare arms. Didn't he know how badly she wanted that, too? She closed her eyes against the pleading in his. "Don't you understand, James? I can't!"

He pulled her into his arms almost roughly. "Abby, you're my wife. I asked God for a wife and He sent you."

She pushed her face into the strength of his chest. Confusion flowed through her. If God had truly sent her to James, then He expected her to be the best wife she could be. Certainly God expected one's best. But then. . . She knew God also required obedience. And if she had made a vow to Him, she must not break it. Something terrible would surely happen to James or the baby.

The hopelessness of the dilemma swept over her. She was trapped. Trapped with a loving, desirable man who was her husband—and yet he wasn't. "I don't know what to do," she admitted finally.

His arms tightened around her, and he held her close for a long minute. Then he pulled away enough to look in her eyes. "I promised you that I would always love you and care for you, Abby."

She met his gaze miserably. "I know. And I'm thankful."

His grip tightened slightly. "But that's not enough for me."

She felt a burning shame well up. Was she taking advantage of him? Or was he saying that he now regretted marrying her since she couldn't—or wouldn't—meet his needs?

James watched the emotions play across her face and wondered at her thoughts. He was pretty sure by now that she felt at least a bit of love for him. Why couldn't she take that final step and admit it? Oh, he knew full-well of her vow. But he had assumed that, by now, she would have realized her flawed logic. He had thought that, perhaps after the baby was born. . . He heaved a great sigh and dropped his hands from her shoulders. "Guess I'll tend to the chores."

The evenings were turning chilly now, he thought vaguely as he trudged toward the barn. He glanced back at the house, watching through the lighted window as Abby knelt to pick up little Anna. A lump rose in his throat, and he turned his eyes back to the well-worn path. "God, surely You don't require her to honor a vow that she made in ignorance," he cried aloud.

Only the lonely cooing of the doves answered him in the still night air.

After several days of strained conversation between them, James longed to return to their easy camaraderie. Perhaps he had been too impatient. Maybe he had just pushed her too hard when she wasn't ready. They could use a good laugh together, he decided. He pushed open the back door, surprised to find the house dark and cold. Why hadn't she lit the lamps?

"Boy, I'm hungry for some greens tonight," he joked as he removed his hat.

Abby barely spared him a glance, her face anguished as she rocked Anna in the dim light.

James felt his heart contract. "What's wrong, Abby?" he whispered, coming to stand in front of her.

"I knew it. I just knew this would happen," she moaned.

He wasn't sure she was even aware of his presence. He stopped the monotonous motion of the rocker with his foot. "Abby!" he said, concern ringing in his voice. "What is it?"

She lifted her eyes to his, and his heart went cold.

Father God, please help me, he prayed silently. He knelt down in front of her. "Abby. Tell me what's wrong."

She shook her head. "I knew it would happen. He doesn't love me, James. You said He did, but He doesn't."

"Abby." James took a deep breath. "Please stop talking nonsense. And tell me what has upset you."

Her body hunched over the baby. Her shoulders heaved with wrenching sobs. "Oh, James. She's sick, James. Our little Anna is sick. I just know she's going to die!"

He wrapped his arms around her. *God, help us,* he pleaded silently.

Tenderly, James lifted the infant from Abby's lap and into his arms. "Oh, dear God." The unchecked prayer slipped from his lips when he saw the blister-like spots that covered the soft, pale skin. "Dear God."

Hugging the baby to his chest, he let the tears fall. Yet, even as he held the child in his arms, his heart was filled with a sense of peace. He pressed a kiss onto the small forehead and drew a deep breath. "I can't put my feelings into words, Abby. But I feel confident that our baby won't die."

Abby shrugged her shoulders. "God allowed her to get sick. Why wouldn't He let her die?"

"I can't promise you that He won't, Abby, but I trust Him to do what is best for Anna and for us. He clutched the baby's feverish body closer to him. "We must trust Him with Anna. He loves her even more than you do."

"Don't you see? Tragedy just seems to follow me—"

"No," he said gently. "I don't see. Trials and tests

and tribulations come to us all, Abby. Not just to you." He laid a comforting hand on her cheek. "God will give us the strength to face even this."

He handed the baby back to Abby, then strode over toward the fireplace. He stirred up the fire and threw another log on. After lighting the lamps, he shrugged into his coat and jammed his hat on his head. "I'm going to fetch Ada. She's as good as any doctor in these parts. Besides, she's a woman of deep faith and she can help us pray." James paused at the door, his hand gripping the knob. He turned to watch his wife. She sat in silence, blinking at the light. "I'll hurry back as quickly as I can, but don't just sit there and cry while I'm gone. Pray."

The door slammed behind him. Abby leaned her head back in the rocker and closed her eyes. *Pray? My prayers won't help. I've prayed and prayed in the past. Has God ever answered my prayers?*

Anna whimpered, and Abby automatically held her closer, adjusting her blankets. It had been hours since the babe had nursed. Abby's breasts felt achingly full, yet the baby refused to eat. "Come on, little one," she coaxed. "You need to eat." The child sucked weakly for a moment, then turned her head away. Her little mouth clamped closed.

Abby sighed and her tears threatened to overflow. The child wouldn't have enough strength to get well if she didn't eat soon. Abby slowly buttoned her bodice, suddenly recalling James' words of a few months ago. "Part of the responsibility is ours, love," he had said. "Just as you can't feed a baby who refuses to open its mouth, you limit God by refusing to accept His ways and His comfort."

Was she really doing that, she wondered? Could it be that God had really been there through her whole life, and she had refused to accept Him, the very One who would strengthen her?

It seemed that she had begun to learn His ways just before Anna was born, but somehow, she had fallen and slipped back. She could see that clearly now as she looked back on the last few weeks.

She had slipped out of the habit of reading God's Word daily and had stopped praying so much when Anna arrived healthy and happy. How could she have done that? How could she have forgotten the way His presence comforted her during the birthing? "Oh God, forgive me," she cried inwardly. Was He angry with her? Was that why her baby was sick?

A few months ago she would have assumed this to be true, but now. . .she wrinkled her brow as she struggled to recall the verses James had shown her. Wasn't there one that said something about there being no condemnation for those who were in Christ Jesus? Yes, she was sure of it. James had explained that that verse meant that once she had confessed her sin and asked God to forgive her, He would. He wouldn't be angry with her. She sighed in relief.

" 'Why so downcast, oh my soul? Put your hope in God!' " The verse from Psalms popped into her mind with such clarity that she was startled. Could she really put her hope in God at a time like this?

She sat up straighter, feeling determination flood through her. "I will." She said the words aloud. "I choose to trust God this time."

Hoisting herself out of the rocking chair, she carried the whimpering baby over to the window. Gazing out into the star-filled night, she felt her heart stir within her. If God, who created all things, could love her, then she surely could trust Him.

Abby tenderly placed Anna into her cradle in hopes that the baby would rest. As she eased back into her rocking chair beside the cradle the door flew open. James strode inside, followed by Ada. The neighbor scurried to the baby's cradle and began examining her with a physician's skill. James came up beside Abby and put his arm around her. "Don't be afraid," he whispered in her ear. She laid her head against his shoulder.

"I'm not," she whispered, marveling at the thought. "I'm not afraid."

As Ada worked over the child, rubbing a concoction of Croton Oil and Tartaremetic Ointment into the tiny chest, James began to sing a familiar hymn. Abby closed her eyes, joining her voice with his. The presence of God filled the room in a way that Abby had never experienced before. She opened her eyes, almost expecting to see Him standing beside her. When their song ended and Ada finished her nursing tasks, an expectant hush filled the room. James gently lifted the baby from the cradle, his hands trembling. The trio of adults huddled around the child, and Abby sensed God's presence encircling them as James began to pray.

"Father God, we bring little Anna to You." His voice broke. "God, we dedicated her to You when she was born. She belongs to You, not us. But God, we love her, and we know that You have the power to heal her." He dipped his finger into a jar of oil that Ada had retrieved from her bag of medicines and doctoring supplies.

"Father God, in Your Word, You teach us, if there are any sick among us, that we are to anoint them with oil and they will be healed."

Ada placed a gentle hand on the baby's chest and added her voice to James's prayer. "Dear Lord, on behalf of this precious little child, Anna, we pray that You will touch her body and spare her life."

Abby wanted to join James and Ada in their spoken prayers, but she was too choked with emotion to vocalize her petition. The words refused to leave her lips. She silently pleaded with the Lord, adding an emotional "Amen" to the others' prayers.

She felt her heart constrict as James rubbed a drop of oil onto Anna's forehead. Something gave way inside Abby at that moment. She couldn't hold back the tears as she realized, clearly and finally, that God loved Anna—and God loved her. He wanted them both to be well and whole. Although she couldn't fully fathom the thought, she suddenly understood that God loved her much more than she loved her own baby. She, Abby Parrish, was His child, just as Anna was her child. It was as if she had never understood that before.

She reached over and took the baby from James, her heart rejoicing in fresh revelation. God Almighty loved her!

Anna's sudden loud cry took Abby by surprise, and she smiled up at James when he chuckled. "I think she's hungry," she said in amazement.

He nodded, placing a large hand on the child's head. "I believe the fever's gone."

Abby pressed her cheek to Anna's face. It was smooth and cool. She felt fresh, happy tears streaming down her cheeks once more, but she let them fall freely. "Thank You, God," she whispered.

The next few weeks were filled with wonder and joy, as Abby marveled constantly over God's love for her and His healing of Anna. Finally she felt as if her heart was beginning to understand what God's Word said.

"It's like I see things so much clearer now," she said to Iris one day.

The older woman bounced Anna on her lap. "That's what happens when we open ourselves up to the Holy Spirit and let God teach us through His Word."

"For the first time, I feel like I really know God loves me."

"And your husband does, too."

Abby jumped. "James, I didn't hear you come in." Her face burning, she refused to look at Iris. Was he trying to embarrass her?

Iris handed the baby to him. "This little girl wants her daddy, and Aunt Iris needs to get back to town."

She bent to hug Abby and whispered in her ear. "Don't deny yourself your husband's love, Abby."

Abby clenched her jaw. How could Iris know anything of her feelings? How could she know the many nights Abby had lain in bed, exhausted, yet sleep would not come? How could she know the anguish of love that could never be fulfilled?

Iris straightened up and patted her shoulder. "Bring that little one for a visit soon," she said, her bright tone belying the meaningful look in her eyes as Abby finally met her gaze.

Abby nodded shortly, then blew out a sigh as the door swung shut behind her sister-in-law.

"What was that all about?" James's handsome face wore a frown.

Abby shrugged. What could she tell him? That she was ashamed because his sister had guessed the truth about their marriage? Or that even though she was now assured of God's love for her, she could never give her husband that same assurance of her love? Perhaps she should just go ahead and tell him of her love and disregard her vow to God. Yet, the very thought made her shudder. Surely she owed God even more, now that He had healed little Anna.

"Abby?" *What is going on in her mind?*

"I. . .I'm sorry, James." She gave him a wan smile. "Guess I lost my train of thought."

He fought against a twinge of rising irritation. For days now, he had watched as she fluctuated between joy and despair. "Abby, if you're worried that I'm going to force myself on you now that you're no longer with child—"

"Oh no!" She looked shocked. "I never thought that."

Well, that's good, at least, he thought grimly. *Or is it?* Didn't she know how much he desired her as his wife? He had tried to be kind and very patient. But things didn't appear to be changing any time soon. He had prayed the best he knew how. Quite frankly, his hope was waning. How long must his heart wait to hear her utter sweet words of love? His frustrated thoughts found their way into words before he had time to consider the consequences.

"Abby, I don't know what more I can do to win your love. Won't you ever love me—like I love you? Must you cling to that absurd vow of yours forever?"

Her face flushed, and he could have kicked himself for airing his regrets and disappointments so. Why had he so frankly exposed his feelings? Surely such bluntness would only hinder his cause, not help.

"I'm sorry," she said again. Her voice was quiet, filled with resignation.

So this was the way it was going to be. He placed the infant in her cradle, then turned abruptly toward the door. "I'm sorry, too, Abby. More that you could know."

The door banged shut, punctuating his words with finality. Abby stared after him, despair threatening to overwhelm her. "God, what else can I do? I promised You. And I have to keep my vow, don't I? I promised that I would never give another man my heart. And now that I know how much You love me, how could I even about breaking my vow?"

She buried her face in her hands. What had she done? *I never should have married you, James*, she thought in agony. *You're too good of a man to be stuck with me.*

The baby whimpered, and Abby tended to her automatically. "Mama loves you," she whispered through her tears. "Mama won't ever leave you, little one," she crooned.

God had saved her baby's life, and she owed Him a great debt, of that she was sure. Now she felt it was even more imperative that she keep her vow. Maybe she should do James a favor and leave. Then he would be free to find someone who could be the true wife he deserved.

❦

The following days were agony as a heavy silence settled between them. James spoke to her only when necessary, his mouth held in a grim line the rest of the time. He had moved out to the barn, for all practical purposes, even sleeping in one of the empty stalls.

Does he despise me so much that he can't even sleep in the same house? Abby wondered. She felt at an impasse, unable to find a solution. They couldn't go on like this much longer—and surely not for the rest of their lives.

"I should never have married you, James," she said softly one night.

He whirled around, his blue eyes filled with pain. "Please, don't utter such words ever again. I love you dearly, Abby. God answered my heart's prayer when

He brought you into my life. No matter how you feel about me, I love you. You are my wife and I am totally committed to you." His voice broke on the last words, and he turned away from her again.

She was powerless to resist the urge to wrap her arms around him. It was the first time she had dared touch him in days. With the gesture of affection, the floodgates of her soul opened. She laid her head against his strong back, feeling him stiffen at her touch. Then turning in her arms, he gathered her against him. He buried his face in her neck, and she felt his hot tears mingling with her own.

"I don't know what to do, James," she sobbed. "I don't know what to do."

He held her as if he would never let go. "Hush, now. We'll figure out the rest later." His arm tightened around her, protecting her, shielding her, giving her hope. Could there possibly be a way to have her husband's love and God's approval at the same time? She felt almost traitorous in thinking it.

She pulled away from him, searching his face as if she could will him to know how much she loved him.

He took a deep breath. "I'm sorry for my behavior of late, Abby." He cupped her cheek in his large, work-roughened hand. "I just love you so much, and I don't understand why we—"

"But you know why, James," she burst out in frustration. Why did he have to make it worse?

"No, I don't know why. If it's because you made some sort of promise to God out of ignorance—"

"It doesn't matter." She stepped back from him, as if putting physical distance between them would help her get ahold of her thoughts. "It doesn't matter. I made the vow, and I have to keep it."

"I don't believe that, Abby."

"What?" She stared at him as if he had lost his senses. "Doesn't God require obedience?"

He ran his fingers through his hair. "Yes. Yes, of course He does. But I don't think that's what we're talking about here."

She frowned. What was he getting at?

"I think that out of your pain and confusion, you tried to make a bargain with God."

She had never looked at it that way before. "But I still promised."

He sighed. "I know." He looked like he wanted to shake her. "But don't you understand? God brought us together, Abby. He has blessed you with a future and a hope."

She shook her head. It couldn't be that easy. She couldn't simply sit back and take what He had handed her, even if it was something good.

"God loves you," James said, as if reading her thoughts. "He sent Jesus to die, to forgive our sins, but also to give us life, and even abundant life, the Bible says."

Could that really be true? She pressed her hand to her forehead. "I'm just so confused."

"God is not a God of confusion, Abby." James reached for his Bible. "It says in here that God does not give us a spirit of fear, but of power and love and a sound mind."

"But—"

"Do you think being fearful and worried about this is what God wants for you?"

She shrugged. "But I don't deserve—"

"Deserve?" James interrupted. "Why, Abby, none of us deserves a single one of God's gracious gifts. We don't deserve them, nor can we earn them." He smiled. "I knew there was something that was keeping you from understanding this." He pulled his Bible from the table and intently flipped through the pages until he came to the verse he had been seeking. "Here, read it for yourself. The second chapter of Ephesians, verse eight. Do you see it?"

She looked where his finger jabbed the page. "For by grace are ye saved through faith; and that not of yourselves: it is the gift of God: Not of works, lest any man should boast." She read it again, aloud this time. Before she could say anything, he was flipping pages again.

"Now, read this one," he pleaded.

"For. . .ye have been called unto liberty; only use not liberty for an occasion to the flesh, but by love serve one another." She squinted up at him. "What does this mean?" she whispered. Surely it didn't mean what she suspected.

James framed her face with his hands. "It means," he said, "that you are free. It means that we obey God out of love and gratefulness, not out of duty, debt. . .or fear."

She was speechless.

James put the Bible down and drew her into him arms gently. "Father God, please reveal Your love to Abby. Open her eyes of understanding. She is not to serve You out of anything but love and gratefulness. Nor for anything she needs to repay, and not because of anything she has done or not done. She is Your child because she accepted Your Son. And she is righteous in Him alone."

❦

Abby lay in bed, her mind racing. Could it really be as simple as James made it sound? That she didn't have to work and strive to pay her debts to God?

She closed her eyes, hearing the chilly fall wind howling past her window. She shivered, pulling the quilt up tighter under her chin. In the faint light of the banked fire, she could see James sleeping in front of the hearth. *Dear James.* She smiled, glad that he had moved back in the house from the barn. She pictured him lying next to her, his arms holding her close.

Her cheeks burned guiltily at the thought. Surely God would be displeased with her if she broke her vow, and something bad would happen. It just couldn't be as easy as James had made it sound.

She heard Frank whimper outside the door, and she groaned. That dog never could stand to be outside when a storm was brewing. And from the sound of that wind, they were in for some snow tonight.

She crawled out of bed, shivering as her bare feet touched the icy wood floor. She must be crazy, getting up to let a dog in the house. Somehow the big creature had grown on her, she supposed. She'd better make sure the baby was warm enough, too. They were over-due for the first snowstorm of the season.

Frank scratched at the door again. "I'm coming," she murmured. Glancing out the window as she made her way to the cradle, her heart stopped.

Surely she was imagining it—no! There was an-other flicker—"James!"

He woke with a start.

"James! The barn is on fire!"

"What?" He pulled his trousers on over his long johns. "Get some water and prime the pump," he yelled over his shoulder as he flew out the door.

Her hands shaking, she grabbed the tin bucket, full of water, from its place beside the door. Closing the door softly behind her so she wouldn't awaken Anna, she stepped into the chill of the night. She ran toward the pump, refusing to think of what would happen if the fire reached the house.

Images of her home in New York, charred beyond recognition, flashed into her mind. She could imagine Papa's anguished cries for help, could smell the burn-ing flesh—"Jesus!" she cried aloud. "Please help us!" She tripped over Frank and went sprawling, but some-how she managed to keep most the water from spilling. She clambered back to her feet, hot tears streaming down her face. *Fear not, for I am with thee.* The bit of Scripture floated into her mind. *Fear not. Fear not.*

She reached the pump, feeling for the handle in the dark. Her breath came in short gasps, whether it was from exertion or fear she wasn't sure. The water began to flow, and as it did, she felt God's presence flow over her once again like the day He had healed Anna.

I will never leave you or forsake you, Abby. The Spirit's gentle voice broke into her consciousness.

James stumbled up with two buckets. "Keep pumping, Abby!" he shouted.

She obeyed, listening as the water gushed out to fill the pails. "I love you, James," she said suddenly.

For a long moment, James stood motionless. "What did you say?"

"I said I love you and I want to be your wife."

"Hallelujah!" He dropped the buckets and swung her into his arms.

"James, the barn!" she murmured against his lips.

He set her down reluctantly and grabbed the buckets. "God will see us through, Abby," he said.

And so He did. The fire somehow stayed contained in the tack room, destroying everything in there, but not moving beyond to the stalls. "It's a miracle," James said the next morning, as they stood gazing at the soot-covered room. Snow had fallen lightly, making the scene seem cold and unreal.

Abby nodded, her heart too full for words. The night had certainly been one to remember. After the fire was finally out, she and James had collapsed onto the rockers in front of the fireplace.

"Thank God you saw the sparks in time, Abby," James had said, his voice hoarse from the smoke.

She nodded. "I got up to let Frank in and glanced out the window."

He ran a hand through his hair, leaving it standing on end. "We didn't lose any of the animals. That's the most important thing." He stared at the fireplace, as if lost in thought.

Abby felt her stomach clench. Was he thinking the same thing she was? How could she have blurted that out, there by the pump? It wasn't as if anything had changed, really. . . .

"Did you mean what you said out there, Abby?"

She felt the blood rise to her face, but she couldn't ignore the look in his eyes as he turned to gaze at her. "I. . ." She saw the uncertainty flicker across his dear face. "Yes."

He slid down to his knees in front of her, laying his head in her lap. "You don't know how I've longed to hear you say those words."

She tangled her fingers in his blond hair. "I've wanted to say them for a long time," she confessed. "I do love you, James."

He raised his head. "What changed, my dear one?" he whispered.

How could she explain it? She shrugged. "I guess I. . . finally figured out that God is on my side. He is not hovering over me, just looking for ways to hurt me."

James nodded. "He is Love."

"Yes." She put a hand to his reddened cheek. "And

so, last night, I felt that God wanted me to make another vow. A vow I am more committed than ever to keeping."

He looked stunned. "What do you mean, Abby?" His voice was strained and his eyes pleaded with her. "What are you saying? I thought you. . ."

"No, wait." She grasped his hands. "Let me tell you what I promised God. I vowed to love the Lord my God with all my strength, my soul, my mind, and my spirit. I intend to keep my vow and to never love another like I should love Him alone."

James gripped her shoulders. "Is there room in there somewhere for me?"

She moved into his embrace, her heart overflowing. "Always," she whispered. "I promise."

Epilogue

I t's a boy!" James's joyful shout was music to Abby's ears. Could it be possible that almost a year had gone by since the night of the barn fire? That night was forever imprinted on Abby's memory. It was a night of endings, as well as sweet beginnings. The ending of fear and bondage. The beginning of life and love.

"I told you I wanted a nephew. Now, here he is," Iris sang out joyfully from beside the bed. "God has blessed you again, Abby."

Abby looked up to find her husband's tender gaze fixed on her face.

"Thank you," he whispered. "You've given us another beautiful child."

Her eyes filled with tears. How had God taken a bitter vow and turned it into an unending promise of joy? She held out her arms for her new little son, then clasped James's hand. She kissed Anna's little forehead as she snuggled up close. "Mama and Papa will love you both forever," she vowed softly. And she smiled, knowing this was a vow that would remain forever unbroken.

AMY ROGNLIE

Amy has drawn on her home in Colorado for scenes in her story that assure readers God is love and He is ever willing to forgive. Amy is a pastor's wife and mother of three young children. She loves reading and writing (of course), gardening, cooking, and crocheting. "I'm just an ordinary person whom God has blessed with some talents," Amy says. "I firmly believe that if I will use what He has given me to the best of my ability, He will bless the results." Amy has had two historical romance novels published by **Heartsong Presents**.

A Letter to Our Readers

Dear Readers:

In order that we might better contribute to your reading enjoyment, we would appreciate your taking a few minutes to respond to the following questions. When completed, please return to the following: Fiction Editor, Barbour Publishing, Inc., P.O. Box 719, Uhrichsville, OH 44683.

1. Did you enjoy reading *Prairie Brides?*
   ❏ Very much. I would like to see more books like this.
   ❏ Moderately—I would have enjoyed it more if _____
   _____
   _____

2. What influenced your decision to purchase this book?
   (Check those that apply.)
   ❏ Cover   ❏ Back cover copy   ❏ Title   ❏ Price
   ❏ Friends   ❏ Publicity   ❏ Other

3. Which story was your favorite?
   ❏ *The Bride's Song*   ❏ *A Homesteader, a Bride, and a Baby*
   ❏ *The Barefoot Bride*   ❏ *A Vow Unbroken*

4. Please check your age range:
   ❏ Under 18   ❏ 18–24   ❏ 25–34
   ❏ 35–45   ❏ 46–55   ❏ Over 55

5. How many hours per week do you read? _____

Name _____

Occupation _____

Address _____

City _____ State _____ Zip _____

If you enjoyed

Prairie
BRIDES

then read:

The Heart of a Child

**Four Historical Stories
of Couples Brought Together
by the Faith of a Child**

One Little Prayer
The Tie That Binds
The Provider
Returning Amanda

If you enjoyed

Prairie
BRIDES
then read:

The Painting

A Timeless Treasure of Four
All-New Novellas

Where the Heart Is

New Beginnings

Turbulent Times

Going Home Again

If you enjoyed

Prairie

BRIDES

then read:

Resolutions

Four Inspiring Novellas Show a Loving Way to Make a Fresh Start

Remaking Meridith

Beginnings

Never Say Never

Letters to Timothy
